ARNALDUR INDRIÐASON (ARD nal dur IN drith uh sson) won the CWA Gold Dagger Award for *Silence of the Grave* and is the only author to win the Glass Key Award for Best Nordic Crime Novel two years in a row, for *Jar City* and *Silence of the Grave*. *Strange Shores* was nominated for the 2014 CWA Gold Dagger Award, and the books in this series have been nominated for numerous writing awards all over the world in other languages. More than seven million copies of his novels have been sold worldwide. Indriðason makes his home in Reykjavík.

D0110579

Additional Praise for Arnaldur Indriðason

"In this riveting prequel set in late-1960s Reykjavík, Indriðason plumbs the backstory of his series lead, somber Inspector Erlendur Sveinsson. . . . The investigation slowly but surely gathers powerful, page-turning momentum. This installment stands on its own, but it's all the more impressive for giving new insight into Erlendur."
—*Publishers Weekly* (starred review)

"*Reykjavík Nights* nicely illustrates the qualities that make his books so deeply pleasurable."
—Marilyn Stasio, *The New York Times Book Review*

"Indriðason's prequel unfolds with the same precision, economically depicted characters, and authenticity as his Inspector Erlendur novels, but a livelier energy replaces the middle-aged Erlendur's noir melancholy."
—*Kirkus Reviews*

"Brilliantly written."
—*Booklist*

"A writer of astonishing gravitas and talent."
—John Lescroart, author of *The Suspect*

"Like the late Stieg Larsson, Indriðason has a knack for Nordic noir."
—Associated Press

"Every one of these writers is good [Håkan Nesser, Kjell Eriksson, Åke Edwardson, Helene Tursten, Karin Fossum], but in my book, Arnaldur Indriðason is even better."
—Joe Queenan, *Los Angeles Times*

Arnaldur Indriðason

INTO OBLIVION

AN ICELANDIC THRILLER

Translated from the Icelandic by
Victoria Cribb

Picador

———

Minotaur Books
A Thomas Dunne Book
New York

*'We're just one big barracks slum to them,
aren't we? One big . . . Camp Knox?'*

Detective Erlendur Sveinsson

INTO OBLIVION. Copyright © 2014 by Arnaldur Indriðason.
English translation copyright © 2015 by Victoria Cribb. All rights reserved. Printed in the United
States of America. For information, address Picador, 175 Fifth Avenue, New York, N.Y. 10010.

picadorusa.com • picadorbookroom.tumblr.com
twitter.com/picadorusa • facebook.com/picadorusa

Picador® is a U.S. registered trademark and is used by Macmillan Publishing Group, LLC,
under license from Pan Books Limited.

For book club information, please visit facebook.com/picadorbookclub or e-mail
marketing@picadorusa.com.

The Library of Congress has cataloged the Minotaur Books edition as follows:

Names: Arnaldur Indriðason, 1961– author. | Cribb, Victoria, translator.
Title: Into oblivion : an Inspector Erlendur novel / Arnaldur Indriðason ; translated from the
 Icelandic by Victoria Cribb.
Other titles: Kamp Knox. English
Description: First U.S. edition. | New York : Minotaur Books, 2016. | Series: Inspector Erlendur ; 11
 | "A Thomas Dunne book."
Identifiers: LCCN 2015039303| ISBN 9781250077349 (hardcover) | ISBN 9781466889293 (e-book)
Subjects: LCSH: Erlendur Sveinsson (Fictitious character)—Fiction. | Reykjavík (Iceland)—
 Fiction. | Mystery fiction. | Suspense fiction. | BISAC: FICTION / Mystery & Detective / Police
 Procedural. | FICTION / Suspense.
Classification: LCC PT7511.A67 K3613 2016 | DDC 839'.6935—dc23
LC record available at http://lccn.loc.gov/2015039303

Picador Paperback ISBN 978-1-250-11143-2

Our books may be purchased for educational, business, or promotional use.
For information on bulk purchases, please contact the Macmillan Corporate and Premium Sales
Department at 1-800-221-7945, extension 5442, or write to specialmarkets@macmillan.com.

Originally published in Iceland under the title *Kamp Knox* by Vaka-Helgafell

Previously published in Great Britain under the title *Oblivion* by Harvill Seeker,
an imprint of Vintage, a Penguin Random House company

First published in the United States by Thomas Dunne Books for Minotaur Books,
an imprint of St. Martin's Press

First Picador Edition: February 2017

10 9 8 7 6 5 4 3 2 1

1

A fierce wind was blowing over Midnesheidi Moor. It had swept south from the highlands, across the choppy expanse of Faxaflói Bay, before ascending again, bitterly cold, onto the moor where it whistled over gravel beds and ridges, whipping a pale etching of snow over the sad, stunted vegetation. Exposed to open sea and northern blast, only the toughest plants survived here, their stalks barely protruding above the level of the stones. The wind raised a shrill screeching as it penetrated the perimeter fence which loomed out of this bleak landscape, then hurled itself against the mighty walls of the aircraft hangar which stood on the highest ground. It raged with renewed force against this intractable obstacle, before hurtling away into the darkness beyond.

The noise of the wind carried into the vast interior of the steel-frame hangar. One of the largest structures in Iceland, covering 17,000 square metres and as tall as an eight-storey building, it had doors opening to the east and west that could accommodate the wingspan of the world's biggest aircraft. This was the operational hub of the US Air Force 57th Fighter Interceptor Squadron on Midnesheidi. Here, repairs were carried out to the fleet of AWACS spy planes, F-16 fighter jets and Hercules transports. Huge pulley systems for manoeuvring aeroplane parts hung from girders running the length of the roof.

At present, however, work in the hangar was suspended for the most part due to the installation of a new fire-extinguisher system. A specially reinforced scaffolding tower reached right up to the ceiling at the northern end of the building. Like everything to do with the hangar, the job was a Herculean task, involving the laying of a network of pipes along the steel roof girders, which connected to a series of powerful sprinklers, spaced at intervals several metres apart.

The scaffolding tower stood on its wheels like a mobile island in the hangar. It was assembled from a number of smaller platforms with a ladder in the middle leading up to the main platform at the top, where the plumbers and their mates had been at work. Stacks of pipes, screws and brackets lay heaped around the base of the structure, together with toolboxes and adjustable spanners of all shapes and sizes, the property of the Icelandic contractors who were installing the sprinkler system. Nearly all the construction and maintenance work at Naval Air Station Keflavík was in the hands of local entrepreneurs.

All was quiet apart from the desolate howling of the wind outside when suddenly a low whine came from the direction of the scaffolding. A section of piping fell to the floor and rolled away with a clatter. Shortly afterwards there was another, more substantial rush of air and a man hit the ground with an oddly muffled thud, as if a heavy sack had been dropped from the roof. Then all was quiet again apart from the keening of the wind.

2

At times the patches on her skin itched so badly she wanted to claw at them with her nails until she drew blood.

She had been a teenager when she started developing these rashes, like eczema but coarser. She didn't know what she had done to deserve such a disfiguring affliction. The doctor had spoken of accelerated cell division in the skin, which resulted in these raised red patches with a scaly white crust that tended to cluster around her elbows and forearms, on her calves and, worst of all, on her scalp. She had received medical treatment in the form of drugs, ointments and creams, but these were only intermittently effective in keeping the rashes and itching at bay.

Then recently her doctor had told her about this place down south on the Reykjanes Peninsula. News had spread among patients suffering from the same or similar skin complaints that the water there alleviated the irritation. Something to do with its silica content. Following the doctor's directions, she had stumbled upon the place in the lava field, close to the power station, where the milky-blue, geothermal waste water spread out amid the mossy rocks. It took her some time to clamber there over the rough terrain but when she lay down in the soft water and began to smear the sediment on her skin she experienced a degree of relief from the itching and even a sense of well-being. She slathered the mud all over her face, hair and limbs, convinced that it was easing her symptoms and sure that she would come here again.

Since then she had visited the lagoon every so often, each time with a feeling of pleasant anticipation. She left her clothes on a clump of moss as there were no changing facilities and was always on her guard as she didn't wish to be seen. She wore a swimsuit under her clothes and brought along a large towel to dry herself with when she got out.

The day she came across the body she had immersed herself full-length in the silky water, letting it lap her in warmth and comfort, and applied the mud to her skin, hoping that the silica, or whatever the doctor had called it, the minerals and algae would work their magic. The water felt warm and soft, the sediment soothing, and the location amid the old lava flow was tranquil and unusually beautiful. She savoured every moment, enjoying this time alone with her thoughts.

She was on her way back to the edge when she saw what looked like a shoe floating in the water. At first she was indignant, thinking some antisocial litterbug must have thrown it in the lagoon, but when she went to remove it, she discovered to her horror that it was still attached to its owner.

*   *   *

interview room in the remand prison at Sídumúli was small
and drab, with uncomfortable chairs. Yet again the brothers were
being uncooperative and their interviews were dragging on.
Erlendur had expected no different. The brothers, whose names
were Ellert and Vignir, had been cooling their heels in jail for
several days now.

It was not the first time they had been in trouble with the law
for smuggling alcohol and drugs. Two years ago they had been
released from Litla-Hraun after serving a three-year sentence for
the same crimes, but their spell inside had done little to improve
their characters. It appeared that they had simply picked up where
they left off and in fact there was ample evidence to suggest they
had continued to run their business from inside. The interviews
were intended to clarify this point.

An anonymous tip-off had led the police to focus on their
activities, and as a result Vignir was seized with twenty-four kilos
of hash in a potato store not far from Korpúlfsstadir, to the
north-east of Reykjavík. The police also found two hundred litres
of American vodka in gallon bottles and several cardboard boxes
of cigarettes. Vignir denied all knowledge of the goods, claiming
that he had been tricked into visiting the shed – someone he
didn't wish to name had lent him the keys and told him he could
lay his hands on some free potatoes there.

The brothers had been under surveillance for several days
before the police took action. A search of their home turned
up a stash of cannabis intended for sale. They had done little
to refine their methods over the years; their last arrest had
taken place in almost identical circumstances. Marion, who
regarded them as brainless, petty thugs, was sick to death of the
pair of them.

'What ship did the goods come in on?' Marion asked wearily. Erlendur had already put the same question twice.

'There was no ship,' retorted Vignir. 'Who told you that? Was it Ellidi? The stupid fucker.'

'Was the resin imported by sea too or did that come by air?' asked Erlendur.

'I don't know who that shit belongs to,' said Vignir. 'I don't know what you're talking about. I've never been near that shed before. I only went there to nick some spuds. Who's been feeding you this crap?'

'There were two padlocks on the shed: you had keys to both. Why are you acting like that's nothing?'

Vignir didn't answer.

'You were caught with your pants down, and you're sore about it, but that's just tough,' said Marion. 'Face facts. And stop pissing about so we can get this over with and go home.'

'I'm not keeping you here,' said Vignir. 'You can bugger off for all I care.'

'True,' said Marion, glancing at Erlendur. 'Shall we call it a day?'

'Why do you think Ellidi's got it in for you?' asked Erlendur. He knew that the Ellidi Vignir was referring to had sometimes worked for the brothers, selling drugs, collecting debts and threatening punters. He was a violent thug with a long record of convictions for assault.

'Was it him?' asked Vignir.

'No. We don't know who it was.'

'Sure you do.'

'I thought Ellidi was your mate?' said Erlendur.

'He's a dickhead.'

7

At that moment a detective stuck his head round the door and asked Marion for a word. Marion accompanied him out into the corridor.

'What's up?'

'A body,' said the detective. 'On the Reykjanes Peninsula. Near Svartsengi.'

3

The woman who had found the body was aged about thirty and immediately volunteered the information that she suffered from psoriasis. To prove it, she showed them the dry patches of skin up one arm and particularly around her elbow. She was about to show them her scalp as well but Marion had seen enough and stopped her. The woman was insistent that her skin disease should be mentioned as it explained why she had chanced on the body in this unlikely, out-of-the-way spot.

'I'm usually alone here,' she said, looking at Marion, 'although I know other people visit the lagoon too, even if I've never seen any of them. There are no facilities or anything. But the water's lovely. It's the perfect temperature and lying in it makes you feel so much better.'

At this point she was sitting in a police car, describing to Marion and Erlendur how she had come across the body. Marion was beside her in the back seat, Erlendur behind the wheel. Around them were other patrol cars, an ambulance, a forensics team and two press photographers – word about the discovery had already reached the news desks. There was no road to the lagoon, which had formed three years earlier as an outflow from the Sudurnes District Heating Utility at Svartsengi. The geothermal power station was visible a little way off, lights ablaze in the winter darkness. The woman had been bathing in the western end of the lagoon, having hiked to it over the lava field from the Grindavík road. The water was shallow there and she had wallowed in it for an hour or so, before deciding to head home. The days were short at this time of year; dusk was falling and she hadn't wanted to stumble through the winter gloom again like last time when she'd had real difficulty finding her car.

'I stood up and . . . it's always struck me as an incredibly beautiful place but a bit creepy too. The steam rising from the water, being all alone out here in the lava, you know . . . So you can imagine what a dreadful shock it was when I saw . . . I waded further out than I've ever been before and suddenly I saw a shoe. The heel was sticking up out of the water. At first I thought it was just a shoe – that someone had lost it or chucked it in the pool. But when I went to pick it up it was stuck and . . . stupidly I tugged harder and then I realised it was . . . it was attached to . . .'

The woman faltered. Marion, aware that she was badly shaken by her grisly discovery, was taking the interview slowly. When they had carried the body up to the road the woman had tried to avoid looking at it. She was close to breaking down as she related what had happened. Erlendur attempted some words of comfort.

'You've coped extremely well in difficult circumstances.'

'God, it was a shock,' she said. 'You ... you can't imagine what a horrible shock it was. All alone out there in the pool.'

Half an hour earlier Erlendur had pulled on a pair of chest waders and splashed out to the body, accompanied by two members of the forensics team. Marion had watched from the shore, smoking. Fortunately, the Grindavík police, who had been first on the scene, had had the sense not to touch anything until the detectives from CID arrived. The technicians took photos of the body and its position, their camera flashes illuminating the surroundings. A diver had been called out to comb the lagoon bed. Erlendur bent over the body, up to his waist in water, trying to work out how it had been transported to this spot. Once forensics had seen enough, they lifted the body out and carried it ashore, discovering something odd about it as they did so. The limbs appeared to have sustained multiple fractures, the ribcage had collapsed into the spine and the spine itself was broken. The corpse hung like a rag doll from their arms.

It was evening by now and pitch dark but floodlights, powered by a diesel generator, had been set up around the site and in their harsh glare the battered state of the corpse became even more evident. The face was crushed and the shattered skull gaped open. From the clothes, they guessed it was male. He had no ID in his pockets and it was difficult to guess how long he'd been lying in the water. Clouds of hot vapour formed continually above the wide surface of the lagoon, enhancing the eeriness of the scene. It was too dark to conduct a proper search for tracks now; that would have to be postponed until first light tomorrow.

The corpse was covered up and carried by stretcher over the lava field to the Grindavík road. From there it would be conveyed

11

to the National Hospital morgue on Barónsstígur in Reykjavík, where they would wash off the mud and conduct a post-mortem.

'And that's when you notified the police?' Marion prompted, as the three of them sat in the car. The heater was on and condensation had formed inside the windows. Outside, beams of light played over them, there was a sound of voices and shadowy figures flitted past.

'I ran across the lava to the car and drove straight to the police station in Grindavík. Then I brought them back here and showed them the place. Then more police cars turned up. And then you two. I won't be able to sleep tonight. I don't suppose I'll be able to sleep for a long time.'

'That's only natural. It's no fun at all experiencing something like this,' said Marion. 'You should ask a friend or relative to keep you company. Talk about what happened.'

'So you didn't notice any other people near the lagoon when you came here today?' asked Erlendur.

'No, no one. Like I said, I've never seen anyone else out here.'

'And you don't know of anyone who comes to bathe in the lagoon like you?' asked Marion.

'No. What can have happened to the man? Did you see the way he . . .? God, I couldn't bear to look.'

'No, that's understandable,' said Marion.

'This skin disease, psoriasis – does it cause a lot of irritation?' asked Erlendur.

Marion shot him a look.

'They keep developing new drugs to suppress it,' said the woman. 'But it's not comfortable. Though the itching's not the worst part. The worst part's the blemishes.'

'And the lagoon helps?'

'I think it does. It hasn't been scientifically proven, but I think so.'

She smiled weakly at Erlendur. Marion asked the woman a few additional questions about the discovery, then let her go. They all got out of the car and the woman hurried off. Erlendur turned his back to the north wind.

'Isn't it obvious why his face and body are mashed up like that?' he asked Marion.

'Are you implying he was beaten up?'

'Wasn't he?'

'All I know is he's a mess. Perhaps that was the intention. So you're thinking he met someone out here, they came to blows and he was supposed to disappear permanently in the lagoon?'

'Something along those lines.'

'It might look like that,' said Marion, who had examined the body before it was taken away, 'but I'm not convinced the man died as the result of a beating. No ordinary beating, anyway.'

'How do you mean?'

'I've seen bodies smashed by a fall from a great height, and I have to say this reminds me of that. Or a serious car crash. But we haven't been informed of any.'

'If it was a fall, it must have been a pretty big one,' said Erlendur, peering around, then up into the blackness overhead. 'Unless he came from up there. Dropped out of the sky.'

'Into the lagoon?'

'Is that so absurd?'

'I wonder,' said Marion.

'It doesn't help that he's clearly been in the water some time.'

'True.'

'So he can't have been beaten to death on the scene,' said Erlendur. 'If it was a fall, as you say. Someone must have brought him out here so he wouldn't be found straight away. His body must have been deliberately sunk in the pool. In this strange white mud.'

'Not a bad hiding place,' said Marion.

'Especially if he'd sunk properly. Nobody comes out here. Except the odd psoriasis sufferer.'

'Did you have to interrogate her about her condition?' asked Marion, watching the woman's car speeding away. 'You've got to stop prying into people's personal lives.'

'She was upset. You saw that. I was trying to distract her.'

'You're a policeman, not a priest.'

'The body would probably never have been found if it weren't for that woman's psoriasis,' said Erlendur. 'Don't you find that . . . a bit . . .?'

'Of a strange coincidence?'

'Yes.'

'I've known stranger. Bloody hell, it's cold,' said Marion, opening the car door.

'What's this place called, by the way? Do you know?' asked Erlendur, surveying the power station with its billows of steam rising to the sky and dispersing into the night. The answer came back instantly.

'Illahraun,' said Marion, the know-all, getting into the car. 'Formed during the eruption of 1226.'

'Evil Lava?' said Erlendur, opening the driver's door. 'That's all we need.'

4

The following day the pathologist confirmed their suspicion that the man's death had not been caused by a beating. He couldn't count all the broken bones and calculated that the victim must have fallen at least twenty metres. The pattern of fractures indicated that he had not landed feet first, nor did the pathologist think he had tried to break his fall with his arms. All the indications were that he had landed face down on a very hard surface. After a preliminary examination, the pathologist expressed doubt that the man could have fallen off a cliff on the Reykjanes Peninsula. For one thing, the surface the man landed on appeared to have been smooth, and, for another, he could find no evidence to suggest the man had been on the seashore or in the mountains. Not from his clothes, at any rate. He was dressed in jeans and a leather jacket, with only a shirt on underneath. On his feet he wore cowboy boots with heels, pointed toes and cut-out decorations.

'What kind of mudbath did you pull the poor guy out of?' asked the pathologist. 'I've never seen anything like it.'

He was a stooped, elderly figure nearing retirement, white-haired and gaunt, with a large pair of horn-rimmed glasses on his nose. He wore a white coat with an apron over the top. The cadaver lay on the table in the cold, unforgiving glare of the lights. There was a tray of scalpels and forceps beside it, and the room stank sickeningly of formalin, disinfectant and open human torsos. Erlendur was ill at ease; he would never get used to the smell of this place and its association with death. He tried not to look at the body more than absolutely necessary. Marion, who had thicker skin, was undisturbed by the sterile environment and the sight that confronted them on the pathologist's slab.

'He was found in the run-off lagoon from the power station at Svartsengi,' said Marion. 'That's where all the mud comes from. It's rumoured to have healing powers.'

'Healing powers?' repeated the pathologist, momentarily diverted.

'It's supposed to be effective against psoriasis,' explained Erlendur.

'You learn something new every day,' said the pathologist.

'Did you notice any sign of skin disease on the body?'

'No, Marion. You can forget the idea that he was there because of psoriasis.'

'Could he have fallen out of a plane?'

'A plane?'

'For example. Judging by the state of him, it must have been a fairly substantial drop.'

'All I can say at this stage is that he must have fallen from a great height onto an extremely hard surface,' said the pathologist. 'I don't know about a plane. Though I wouldn't rule it out.'

'Can you give us an idea how long he was in the water?' asked Marion.

'Not long. Two, maybe three days at the outside. I may need to take another look but that's my provisional estimate.'

'He's not wearing a wedding ring,' remarked Erlendur, darting a glance at the corpse. 'There's no mark left by one, is there?'

'No, nothing like that,' said the pathologist. 'I didn't find anything on him, no keys or wallet. Nothing that could tell you who he is. His clothes have already been passed on to forensics. He doesn't have any major scars resulting from accidents or operations; no tattoos either.'

'What about his age?'

'We're talking about a man in his prime, maybe thirtyish. Height just under one eighty; well proportioned, lean and muscular – or was, poor fellow. No one's asked after him yet, have they?'

'No,' said Erlendur. 'Nobody's missed him. At least, the police haven't been alerted.'

'And no one saw him fall?'

'No. We've nothing to go on at present.'

'How about a traffic accident?' asked Marion. 'Any chance of that?'

'No, out of the question – wrong sort of injuries,' said the pathologist, raising his eyes from the body and pushing his glasses back up his nose. 'I think we have to work on the assumption that he died as the result of a fall. And, as I pointed out, I can't see any signs that he tried to break it in any way. He simply fell and landed in a horizontal, prostrate position. I don't know if

17

that means anything to you. It's conceivable he wouldn't have had time to raise his arms. Or didn't want to. The drop was clearly a very long one and we're talking about a high velocity at the moment of impact.'

'If he didn't stick his arms out, and landed flat on his face, as you say, are you . . . are you implying suicide?' asked Erlendur.

'It's possible,' said the pathologist, pushing his glasses up again. 'I don't know. Perhaps you shouldn't discount it.'

'Bit unlikely, isn't it?' said Marion. 'If that was the case, why would someone have wanted to hide the body?'

'I'm simply trying to interpret the pattern of fractures,' said the pathologist. 'I still have to conduct a more detailed analysis and the sooner you two get out of my hair, the sooner I'll be able to get on with it.'

Forensics had a tricky job identifying the comings and goings over the lava field between the Grindavík road and the lagoon. The night after the body was found snow fell in the area, obscuring any tracks in the moss or beside the pool. The diver had been unable to find anything in the mud on the bottom. Conditions were challenging, the water was cloudy and visibility was virtually nil. The police put out an appeal for witnesses who had travelled along the Grindavík road in the days preceding the discovery of the body, in the hope that someone might have seen a vehicle in the area. No one came forward.

Erlendur was greeted by the head of the forensics team, a man in his early sixties, who was poring over the clothing that had been removed from the corpse: underwear, jeans, checked shirt, socks, leather jacket and the cowboy boots. The forensics lab was located on the top floor of CID headquarters. Following the recent creation of the State Criminal Investigation Department, they had been moved from Borgartún in Reykjavík and found themselves plonked in the middle of a semi-industrial zone in the neighbouring town of Kópavogur.

Erlendur, who had risen from the ranks of the regular police and only been with CID for two years, was still learning the ropes and getting acquainted with the other staff. He worked for the most part with Marion Briem, one of the longest-serving detectives, who had originally been responsible for encouraging him to apply for promotion to CID. Erlendur had dragged his feet for several years but eventually, tiring of interminably circling town in a patrol car, he had decided to go for it and got in touch with Marion.

'About time,' Marion had said. 'You knew you'd end up here one day.'

Erlendur couldn't deny that the role of detective appealed to him. He had already had a brief insight into what it involved when he had taken it upon himself, while still a uniformed officer, to conduct a private investigation into the drowning of a Reykjavík tramp in the old peat diggings on Kringlumýri. The police had dismissed the man's death as an accident, but Erlendur, who had encountered the victim on his beat, eventually established that he had been murdered. Impressed by the way he had solved the case entirely on his own, with no assistance from CID, Marion had invited him to get in touch if he ever felt like doing more of this kind of work. It took Erlendur a while to make the transition, but Marion's reaction when he finally did was quite right: Erlendur had known all along that he would end up a detective.

The sediment from the lagoon had been painstakingly washed off the dead man's clothes and everything adhering to the fabric, such as hairs and dirt, had been subjected to close analysis.

'It's mostly just residue,' said the head technician. 'I'm guessing he was probably dumped in that mud hole to hide something.'

'Something on the body?'

'Yes. We won't find much now. But the clothes can tell us a thing or two. For example, it looks to us as though they all come from the States. The jeans are a famous brand. So's the leather jacket. The shirt doesn't have a label, though, and could just as well have been bought at Men's Clothing on Hverfisgata. The underwear's an American make. We don't know about the socks. Black. Hardly worn. The leather jacket's seen the most wear and tear, as you can tell by the elbows.' The technician held up the garment for Erlendur to inspect.

'Then there are these,' he added, handing Erlendur one of the cowboy boots. 'They might get us somewhere. Genuine leather. Newish. Not widely available here, as far as I know. The staff of the shoe shops in town might recognise them. Might even know who bought them. You don't see many people walking around here in cowboy boots. Not Icelanders, anyway. We're analysing the dirt on the soles to see if that can provide any clue to where he's been, but the mud from the lagoon has more or less obliterated the evidence.'

Erlendur contemplated the boot. It was made of brown leather, the sole showed only light wear, and the decoration on the calf depicted a coiling lasso. He surveyed the rest of the clothing, the jeans, the checked shirt.

'Can you tell where the boots come from? Where they were made?'

'Louisiana. There's a label inside.'

'I'm sensing an American theme here.'

'Maybe he'd visited the States recently,' suggested the technician. 'It's a possibility.'

'Or he was a Yank himself,' said Erlendur.

'Yes, or that.'

'From the base?'

The head of forensics shrugged. 'Not necessarily, but we can't rule it out either.'

'There are five or six thousand Americans out there on Midnesheidi, aren't there? Servicemen and their families?'

'Round about that. The lagoon's not exactly on their doorstep, but it's near enough that you'll need to take the base into account.'

5

Erlendur hadn't been down this street in a long while. But Dagbjört, the girl who once lived here, was seldom far from his thoughts. One winter's morning, more than a quarter of a century ago, she had vanished without trace. The question of what happened to her had never been resolved. Erlendur had come across her files when he first joined the police. She had been on her way to the Women's College from her home in the west of town when she disappeared as if the ground had swallowed her up. Erlendur had followed her route to the school many times, past the former site of Camp Knox, the old barracks slum, onto Hringbraut and down towards the lake, passing Melavellir and the old graveyard on Sudurgata. People did go missing like this in Iceland from time to time, but for some reason this incident in particular had touched a nerve with Erlendur. He had read and reread the police reports and press coverage, and had walked all possible routes between her home and the school. He had sometimes toyed with the idea of talking to people – relatives or friends – who had known her, but he had never actually gone ahead or embarked on any kind of systematic investigation. It had all happened a long time ago and there was every reason to believe that the girl had taken her own life, yet she would not leave Erlendur alone, no matter how hard he tried to push her away and forget the case. She haunted him like a ghost risen from the grave, ensuring that he was subject to constant reminders of her.

This time it was the obituaries. Only this morning he had been reading her father's. Her mother had died some years back. There were two notices, both of which touched on the incident obliquely. One had been written by a former colleague of her father who described him as a loyal and reliable workmate, who had been good company in happy times but had never really recovered from the loss of his daughter. The other was written by the dead man's sister and traced his early years, saying that they came from a large, close-knit family, and that later he and his wife had lost the apple of their eye in a way that defied all comprehension. Erlendur, detecting an old bitterness in her words, guessed that time had not succeeded in softening the pain. But then it rarely did.

It was nearly midnight when Erlendur finally left the street and headed home. He had noticed that Dagbjört's old house was vacant and there was an estate agent's notice in the kitchen window. The wind was still blowing from the north and was forecast to continue for the next few days. Loose snow swirled alongside the pavement and Erlendur hugged his coat tighter around him as he strode away.

He and Marion had stayed late in the office that evening, reviewing the case of the man in the lagoon. More than twenty-four hours had passed since the body had been found but so far no one had come forward to report him missing or say they recognised him by the detailed description that had been released to the press. The man seemed to have neither family nor friends. When Erlendur returned from his meeting with the head of forensics, he had found Marion resting on the battered sofa in the office. Marion had brought the sofa along from CID's old headquarters on Borgartún where they used to be based when they came under the state prosecutor's office.

'An American?' Marion had exclaimed irritably when Erlendur reported his conversation with forensics.

'It's one possibility,' said Erlendur.

'A serviceman, you mean?'

Erlendur shrugged. 'Don't forget the international airport's located in the military zone. Our man could have flown in from anywhere in the world. We can't take it for granted he's an Icelander. And we can't be certain he wasn't thrown out of a plane over the lagoon. A plane from a domestic airport like Reykjavík. Though it could equally have come from the base.'

'Where are you going with this?' asked Marion.

'Maybe we should start by checking all flights over the area in the last few days. We're probably talking light aircraft. The question is, should we submit a request to the base as well and find out if the Defense Force are missing one of their men?'

'On the basis of the cowboy boots?'

'All his clothes – nearly all of them – had American labels. Though of course most of them could have been bought in Reykjavík, so that doesn't tell us much per se.'

'No. What else do we have?'

'The proximity to the base.'

'So you want to link the American clothing to the naval base and conclude from this that we're dealing with a soldier? Isn't it a bit of a long shot?'

'Maybe,' said Erlendur. 'But when you take into account the clothing and the proximity, it hardly seems unreasonable to send an inquiry to the military authorities. If the man had been found on the other side of the country in Raufarhöfn, I wouldn't be considering this angle. But it might just turn out that the army are missing one of their men.'

'They're under no obligation to inform us if so.'

'But at least we'd have checked the possibility.'

'Won't they have heard about the discovery of the body by now?'

'Presumably.'

'Surely they'd have got in touch if they suspected he was one of theirs?'

'Perhaps,' said Erlendur. 'I don't know how their minds work. Seems to me that lot go their own sweet way without taking too much notice of us.'

'*That lot*? Are you opposed to the army?'

'Is that relevant?'

'I'm not sure,' said Marion. 'Are you?'

'I've always been opposed to the army,' said Erlendur.

He was standing in a stiff northerly breeze near the place where Camp Knox used to be during the Second World War, when the country was occupied, first by the British, then by the Americans. The site was now buried beneath the Vesturbær swimming pool and other buildings, mostly residential. Nothing remained of the old army barracks. Named after Frank Knox, the then US Secretary of the Navy, and originally serving as the American naval operating base in Iceland, Camp Knox had been one of the largest of the eighty such camps constructed in and around Reykjavík during the Allied occupation. The camps had all gone now, though they had enjoyed a remarkable afterlife as a solution to the post-war housing shortage. Once the soldiers had departed, Icelanders from the countryside had moved in their droves into the prefab Quonset and Nissen huts with their curving roofs and walls; in their heyday as many as three thousand people had lived in the former camps.

Erlendur remembered the last gasp of these barracks slums. They had been slowly but surely coming to the end of their existence when he first moved to the city. He remembered Múli Camp and another big one on Skólavörduholt near the modern town centre. There he had encountered the worst poverty he had ever seen. The huts, which were constructed from corrugated iron, flimsy fibreboard and even cardboard, had never been intended as civilian housing and offered hopelessly inadequate protection against the Icelandic climate. Drainage and sewage disposal were primitive at best, rat infestations were endemic, and although plenty of decent, respectable people lived there, the camps were notorious for their grim conditions and colourful occupants. The residents were sneeringly referred to as 'Campies' and said to stink of the camp.

If the police report was to be believed, the girl's route to school in the mornings would have passed the old barracks. During the search for her, particular stress had been laid on finding out if she had entered the camp. A number of the huts were searched, along with the ramshackle sheds and lean-tos they had spawned, and the residents were questioned about whether they had seen the girl. Many of them assisted in the search. But this proved no more successful than any of the other efforts to find her.

The reason Camp Knox had been subjected to particular scrutiny was that, shortly before she went missing, the girl had confided in a friend that she had met a boy from the camp, and the friend had interpreted her words as meaning that she had fallen for him.

The boy's identity never came to light.

6

It was past midnight and Marion Briem had fallen asleep on the office sofa when the desk phone suddenly started ringing. All the other staff had gone home and the shrill sound repeatedly shattered the deep silence in the building. Marion awoke, rose from the sofa and snatched up the receiver.

'What the hell? What time is it?'

'Marion?'

'Yes?'

'Sorry . . . is it very late?'

It was the pathologist. Marion sat down at the desk, checking the clock.

'Couldn't it wait till morning?'

'What, oh, yes, of course,' said the pathologist. It was well known that Marion liked to nap on the office sofa and would sometimes spend the night there. 'I didn't mean to disturb you. What time is it anyway?'

'Twelve minutes past midnight.'

'Oh, that late? Sorry, I didn't realise. I'll talk to you tomorrow. I should be off home myself. I am sorry, I had no idea how late it was.'

Marion knew that the pathologist, Herbert, had lost his wife several years ago and now lived alone. They'd had no children, and once she was gone, he had only an empty house to return to. It didn't cross his mind to try and meet another woman. Marion had once raised the possibility with him when they were down at the morgue but his reaction had been lukewarm.

'What's up?' asked Marion, feeling more awake. 'Any news?'

'Hadn't we better leave it till tomorrow?'

'No, come on, out with it. You've woken me up now. The damage is done.'

'He bit his nails.'

'The man from the lagoon?'

'Bit them down to the cuticles. Probably an old habit from childhood. That doesn't help us, unfortunately.'

'What do you mean?'

'Well, we might have been able to find some residual traces under his nails – if he'd been in a fight, for example.'

'Ah, I'm with you.'

'I get the impression he worked with his hands. Did some job involving a workshop. The lagoon cleaned them to some extent but I found traces of dirt, grease and oil around his fingernails, or what's left of them. It's all I can think of. A garage. Machine shop. Something along those lines.'

'Grease?'

'Yes, and it's not just the dirt.'

The pathologist explained to Marion that he'd noticed the

man's hands were covered in small cuts or abrasions, old and new, as well as being calloused from manual labour. He recognised the signs since his own brothers were both mechanics. It was this that had led him to suspect that the body was that of a tradesman or labourer. He was no more than thirty-five years old and enough of his teeth were still intact for them to be compared to dental records if he couldn't be identified by other means.

'Do you think the lagoon was supposed to conceal this?' asked Marion. 'The dirt on his hands? The small cuts?'

'I think the lagoon was intended to conceal his body, that's all. But of course it's not my place to express an opinion.'

'Can you see anything to suggest that he might have been American? An American from the base? A foreigner?'

'A serviceman, you mean?'

'Yes, maybe.'

'He was wearing cowboy boots and –'

'That's not enough. Did you find anything that could link him to the base? Anything that could place him at Keflavík? Erlendur was talking about the possibility.'

'Not that I noticed. But there's another detail I should mention,' said the pathologist. His voice suddenly sounded threadbare, as if the late hour was catching up with him.

'Yes?'

'All the evidence is that the man died as the result of falling from a great height, as we've discussed. From what I can deduce, he landed on a smooth surface, a pavement or tarmac, maybe even a concrete floor.'

'Yes, you've already told us that.'

'Well, perhaps I am repeating myself, but there are so many strange aspects to this death. Like, for example, the fact that he landed flat on his face without raising his arms to protect himself. I don't believe he fell directly into the lagoon from a plane, as you two were suggesting. If that were the case the impact would have mainly come from hitting water. No, the surface he landed on was much harder.'

'In other words he fell from a great height,' said Marion, yawning. 'Everything points to that. So there are only three possibilities: accident, suicide or murder. If it was an accident or suicide, it's very puzzling that anyone would have wanted to hide his body in a mudbath. But if it was murder, it's much easier to understand why the perpetrator would have wanted to cover his tracks. I believe we can rule out suicide, in any case. Involuntary manslaughter or an accident aren't inconceivable, but then we have to ask ourselves why it wasn't reported. Murder is by far the most plausible conclusion.'

'Yes, that's why I wanted to talk to you straight away,' said the pathologist. 'I just didn't realise it was so late. You see, I found something on the back of the man's head where it's relatively undamaged.'

'What was it?'

'An ugly contusion that I missed initially because it's under his hair. It looks as if he received a heavy blow to the head.'

'Really?'

'There's no doubt.'

'Isn't that just the result of his fall?'

'No. He landed on his face. This is on the back of his head.'

'Are you positive?'

'I don't know if I'll be able to prove it conclusively by further examination,' said the pathologist, 'but the odds are that the man was dead before he fell.'

7

Marion and Erlendur were gazing out over the lagoon, watching the diver lowering himself into the water. It was his second attempt. On his first he had found nothing in the area where the body had been lying, but he had wanted another chance to make a more thorough search. Marion was sceptical, seeing it as nothing more than a ploy to squeeze more money out of the police, but didn't say so out loud. The police had called on the diver's services before when they needed to drag harbours or lakes. He was in his forties, a carpenter by trade, a volunteer member of the rescue team and one of the most capable divers in the country. He had a powerful lamp attached to his head which lit up the water as he submerged, and Marion and Erlendur watched it moving slowly to and fro under the milky-blue surface.

According to the diver, the lagoon bed was covered in a thick layer of sediment which hampered his efforts. Even if there was some clue sunk in the mud, the cloudiness of the water would make it almost impossible to spot. The lagoon had the detectives stumped. They had never encountered conditions quite like this before and were unsure how to proceed. They had discussed emptying it by pumping out the water but this had been dismissed as impractical. Then Erlendur had suggested dragging the bottom and, as no one had come up with a better solution, preparations were under way.

Combing the shores of the lagoon for clues had as yet produced no results. The snow had obliterated any tracks that might have been left by the person or people responsible for transporting the body there. And the conjecture that the man had been thrown out of a plane had to be taken as seriously as any other, despite indications that he had already been dead before he landed. Reykjavík air traffic control were unaware of any flights over the area in the past week but there were a number of privately owned light aircraft based at the domestic airport and the police were in the process of contacting their owners. The police had also put out a request for information about traffic through smaller airstrips in the south of Iceland, such as those at Selfoss and in the Westman Islands. And they were still awaiting a response from air traffic control at Keflavík about the movements of private planes from the international airport.

Even before the snow fell no tyre marks had been visible in the environs of the lagoon the evening the body was found. And anyway it was inaccessible to vehicles except perhaps for large, specially equipped four-wheel drives. The most likely scenario was that the body had been carried over the shortest route from the Grindavík road to the pool, then floated some way out into the water before being sunk. The diver could see no sign that it had been weighted down.

Marion had relayed to Erlendur the gist of the pathologist's phone call the night before, particularly the detail about the bruising on the back of the man's head. The pathologist had rung again at lunchtime and repeated his conviction that the man had either been dead before he fell or at least unconscious from a heavy blow to the head.

'That explains why he landed flat on his face,' said Erlendur, watching the diver's progress.

'That's what Herbert thought,' said Marion. 'He reckoned it was the most plausible explanation. That he'd been struck.'

'Could he deduce anything about the implement – about what he'd been struck with?'

'We're maybe talking about a wheel brace, a length of piping or some other blunt instrument. He said it was hard to tell. Though he didn't think it was a hammer. No sign of sharp edges. The skin wasn't broken but it must have been a pretty heavy blow.'

The diver surfaced briefly, then went under again, his head-lamp glowing in the water. Heat radiated constantly from the lagoon, condensing into vapour which was swept across the surface by the breeze before dispersing. Erlendur was entranced by the sight: the subterranean fires and bleak terrain of the Reykjanes Peninsula had brought about this convergence of hot water, steam and moss-green lava, and endowed it with an unearthly beauty.

'So the man's hit on the head, then pushed off a tall building,' he said.

'Yes. Possibly.'

'So it would look like suicide?'

'We have to consider that.'

Marion and Erlendur had spoken to a manager at the power station who said it was out of the question that the man was a member of his staff. Nobody was missing; everyone had reported for work as usual. He was astonished that a body should have turned up in the run-off lagoon. Few had any reason to go there, though he had heard of people bathing there because of the supposedly beneficial minerals.

The man, a tall, overweight, ruddy individual, with a red beard covering half his face, had walked back to the lagoon with them and was now watching the diver. It occurred to Erlendur to ask him about flights over the area and the man replied that there was quite a bit of activity thanks to the presence of the international airport and the American naval base on Midnesheidi. The roar of the military jets could be deafening at times. There were a few light aircraft too but the people working at the power station were less aware of them.

'Why do you ask – was he thrown out of a plane or something?'

The man said it half jokingly. So far no details had leaked out about the state of the body or police speculation that the multiple fractures and unrecognisable face were the result of a fall from a great height. When Erlendur merely shrugged and gave no answer, the man stared at them both in disbelief.

'Was he seriously thrown out of a plane?' he exclaimed.

'We have no evidence of that,' said Marion.

'But you're considering the possibility?'

'No, we're not,' said Erlendur firmly.

'What made you think he might have worked for us?'

'We may be talking about a manual worker of some kind, and given that he was found on your doorstep, it was only natural to enquire about your staff. You say you're not missing anyone, but what about men who used to work for you? Have you had any trouble over the last few months or year? Anyone been given the sack? Anyone issued threats? Any tensions you can recall?'

'No, I can't remember any problems of that sort,' said the man.

The diver reared up out of the water. Steam poured off him and he resembled some creature of the swamp as he waded towards them, his shape distorted by the oxygen tank and mask. He took out his mouthpiece when he reached the shore where they were standing.

'I quit,' he said. 'I can't find a thing in that bloody muck.'

'Difficult to see?' said Marion.

'Difficult? It's like diving in soup'

'What's the matter with him?' interrupted Erlendur, his attention distracted by the sight of a uniformed officer hastening over the lava field towards them.

The officer and his partner had been sitting in a patrol car on the Grindavík road, guarding the crime scene, when they received an urgent alert over the radio, and had tossed a coin to decide who should abandon the warm interior and dash over to the lagoon with the message. He had lost.

Marion and Erlendur watched him scrambling over the jumbled rocks, and wondered what was up. The diver, who had started peeling off his wetsuit, stopped to follow what was going on.

'What now?' he said.

'They want to talk to you!' shouted the officer breathlessly when he was finally within earshot, gesturing to the patrol car up by the road.

'What's he bawling about?' asked Marion.

'Sounds like someone wants to talk to us,' said Erlendur.

'A woman rang in,' called the officer, panting. 'Her . . . brother's missing and she thinks he might be . . . might be your man.'

8

The woman who stepped hesitantly into the morgue on Barónsstígur looked somewhat younger than her brother, in her late twenties perhaps. Observing her dismay, Erlendur reassured her that it was all right; she need do nothing that would distress or be too much for her. They could leave whenever she wanted to and she needn't identify her brother unless she felt up to it. Others could do that now that the police had such a solid lead. She said she had never been here before and Erlendur replied that it was hardly surprising since most people only entered a morgue once and by then they were past caring. She was very grave but smiled faintly at this and he was relieved that his attempt to lighten her mood had not backfired. She had never seen a dead body before either. Erlendur did his best to warn her, since identifying her brother in his present state was bound to be a harrowing experience. But she was resolute, keen to know as soon as possible whether her fears had any basis in fact, desperately hoping they hadn't. Marion, who was with them, stayed in the background.

They had already had a conversation at her flat. Nanna had phoned the police that lunchtime after failing to get hold of her brother for the past three days. She had seen the news about the body at Svartsengi but had not connected it to her brother until suddenly she started awake in the middle of the night with the thought: what if it's him? She hadn't slept a wink after that and had spent all morning plucking up courage to speak to the police. She had assumed she would have to come down to the station but was asked to wait in for the officers who would be round to see her shortly. A note was taken of her name, address and phone number. The police took her call very seriously: it was their first serious lead.

Nanna turned out to live in a comfortable basement flat in the Melar district in the west of town. She told them she had moved in after splitting up with the man she'd been living with, and that she was very happy here. She was petite and pretty, with short black hair. She wouldn't have mentioned her recent break-up only she wanted to explain how kind her brother had been to her throughout the wretched business. He had helped her find a new place and make a fresh start.

'There's nothing he wouldn't do for me,' she said, her gaze swinging from Marion to Erlendur as they sat facing her in the small sitting room. She had shown them a recent photograph of her brother. They could see at once that it was the man from the lagoon but kept the knowledge to themselves.

Her brother's name, she told them, was Kristvin, and in a low, hesitant voice she began to go over the salient facts about him. He lived in Reykjavík but worked out at Keflavík. He was an air mechanic and two years ago, after completing his training in America, he had been taken on by Icelandair. He was unmarried, had no children and not many friends either; he had become a bit of a loner since returning home from abroad. He told her he had lost touch with most of his old mates while he was away. They didn't have much family either: their mother was dead and their father had had little contact with them since he remarried and moved to Denmark.

'When did you last hear from your brother?' asked Marion.

'About four days ago,' answered Nanna. 'He came over and we had a meal together.'

'And was he his usual self?'

'Yes, he was. He didn't act any differently from normal.'

'Do you see much of each other?' asked Erlendur.

'Yes, that's the thing. We talk pretty much every day. He rings me or I ring him and we meet at his place or mine, or go to the cinema, that kind of thing. I tried to get hold of him – er – the day after he came round. Just rang him at home as usual but he didn't answer. So I tried him again next day and then the next – rang several times – but he never answered. We'd arranged to meet up yesterday. The idea was that I'd go to his, then we'd maybe see a film. But when I went round he didn't answer the bell. I have a spare key in case he locks himself out and I took it with me because I hadn't heard from him and was worried he might be ill or something. So I went inside but there was nobody there. The flat smelt musty as if he hadn't been home for a while. His bed wasn't made, but that was nothing new. I opened the windows to air the place, then went home, feeling worried. Really worried, to be honest.'

'Did you try him at work?' asked Erlendur.

'Yes, yesterday, before I went round to his flat. I phoned and they told me he hadn't shown up at work for two days and they hadn't heard from him. They said they'd called him at home but got no answer. They wanted me to tell him to get in touch if I heard from him.'

She drew a deep breath.

'Then I saw the news about the body on Reykjanes but it didn't cross my mind to connect it with him. They were treating it as murder and it didn't occur to me that Kristvin could have . . . could have died like that. It was just too surreal. Perhaps I was subconsciously afraid, though, because I slept badly last night, then woke up suddenly, thinking it must be him. It had to be my brother, Kristvin.'

She was fighting back the tears now.

'Was he in any kind of trouble?' asked Erlendur.

'How do you mean?'

'Had he fallen out with anyone? Do you think someone might have wanted to harm him?'

'No, I can't imagine it. I just can't. He's never mentioned anything like that to me.'

'The man we found was wearing cowboy boots,' put in Marion.

Nanna nodded. 'Kristvin has boots like that. He wears them all the time. He's got three pairs he bought in America.'

'He was wearing clothes with American labels,' said Erlendur. 'We thought he might be a soldier from the base.'

'I suppose he was wearing his leather jacket?' Nanna said. 'He always wears the same jacket.'

'That fits with the man we found,' said Erlendur. 'Could you let us have the key to his flat?'

Nanna nodded again. They decided it was time for her to

41

accompany them to the morgue and Marion said she should prepare herself for the worst. They rose to their feet and Nanna fetched her coat and put on a woolly hat and gloves. They had sent advance warning to the pathologist who was standing ready beside the body when they arrived at Barónsstígur. It lay under a powerful lamp, covered in a white sheet. The pathologist greeted Nanna and also warned her about the state of the body. She listened in silence. Marion and Erlendur stood at her side.

One of the corpse's arms was exposed. She didn't touch it, as if unable to bring herself to, but stared down for a long while at the cold, lifeless hand; the unfamiliar blue pallor of the skin. She had received her confirmation.

'It's him,' she whispered.

'Are you sure?' said Erlendur.

'I recognise his hands. There's no doubt, it's him,' she said, tentatively taking hold of the hand.

'All right.'

'He never listened to my nagging,' she said.

'About what?'

'I was always going on at him not to bite his nails.'

9

He wasn't surprised that the woman should be momentarily lost for words when he said he was calling to see if he could have a word about her niece, Dagbjört, who had vanished one morning many years ago on her way to school. After a stunned silence, she asked him to say again who he was. He explained that his name was Erlendur, he was a detective, and he had come across her niece's case in the police archives. As he was interested in missing persons, he wondered if he might visit her. He made it absolutely clear, to prevent any misunderstanding, that there had been no new developments and that the inquiry had not been reopened. His interest was purely personal. He omitted to say that he had in fact come across the girl's case long before, shortly after joining the police, had read up on the background and often visited the relevant sites, consumed by curiosity. Nor did he tell her why, after all this time, he had finally, hesitantly, taken the step of contacting one of the girl's relatives. He hardly knew.

Some time ago he had promised himself not to pursue it, unwilling to expose himself to the pain associated with the disappearance of a loved one, yet in spite of that he had gone ahead. The obituaries for the girl's father had made him think. In the end there would be no one left to tell what had happened. No one to provide answers to the questions about her disappearance that had so often plagued him. And perhaps worst of all: no one left waiting for those answers.

After a quarter of a century, the case had long faded from the public consciousness, but when he rang the girl's aunt to explain his business, he realised that it was far from forgotten in that household. The woman was instantly on the ball. After bombarding him with questions about the case and his interest in it, she finally seemed satisfied that he was in earnest and invited him round to see her. Before she rang off, she thanked him for the call and his concern.

'I'm sorry for your loss,' said Erlendur once he had taken a seat in her living room. 'I saw the obituary you wrote for your brother.'

She thanked him again, pushing back a lock of hair that had fallen over her forehead as she poured them both coffee. Her name was Svava, she was around seventy, and had prepared for his visit by baking *kleinur* and brewing strong coffee. She said she needed a pick-me-up too and offered him a glass of chartreuse which he accepted. She knocked hers straight back and refilled it immediately. The bottle was almost empty and he wondered if she often had recourse to pick-me-ups. He sipped his slowly. She had come across in their phone conversation as forceful and assertive; not someone who suffered fools gladly. She demanded straight answers and would not tolerate any beating about the bush. He did his best to satisfy her. He didn't know much about her situation but got the impression she lived alone. A prominently placed photograph showed her beaming at the camera, flanked by three boys and a husband. He assumed her sons had long since flown the nest. He didn't ask about the husband. Perhaps they were divorced. Or he was dead. She soon supplied the answer.

'Thank you,' she said. 'Yes, I felt I had to put a few words down on paper. Felt it would do me good. To write about my brother. It was his heart, you know. My husband went the same way four years ago. So, you've been interested in our Dagbjört for quite a while?'

'Ever since I first read her files, about seven years ago,' said Erlendur. 'I don't remember the actual events – I'm too young – but there was a good deal written about her disappearance at the time and I've read all of it, along with the police reports. About her route to school. The boyfriend she's supposed to have had in Camp Knox.'

'And what . . . do you think you can find out what happened?'

'No, I'm not getting my hopes up,' said Erlendur. 'And neither should you.'

'Then what's the point of this meeting?'

'I wanted to see you, to hear the family's version of the story, if you'd be willing to share it with me,' said Erlendur. 'You mustn't expect me to come up with any magic solution. I'm just . . .'

'What?'

'I'm just trying to get a handle on what happened,' said Erlendur.

'Out of curiosity?'

'Yes, I'll be frank with you – out of curiosity. I have a particular interest in this kind of case. I want to look into her story in more detail. In my own time. If I discover any new evidence, anything that might shed light on the mystery, naturally I'll inform you and my colleagues in CID. I want to gather information about her disappearance and see if I can find a fresh angle. A quarter of a century has passed and soon it'll be too late to . . . do anything.'

'You mean there'll be no one left for you to talk to?'

Erlendur nodded. 'Both her parents are dead. When I read about your brother I thought to myself that if I was going to act, I couldn't wait any longer. It was now or never.'

'I see. You're in a race against time.'

'But as I said, you shouldn't get your hopes up about any new leads. I can't stress that strongly enough. Anyway, I think I've got a fairly clear picture of what happened, from the public point of view, but of course that's only a fraction of the whole story.'

Svava studied Erlendur with searching grey eyes, sizing him up, trying to gauge whether she could trust him. She sensed that he had been honest with her, admitting his curiosity, laying his cards on the table. She felt this was important.

'You're a policeman,' she said, 'but you're not here in an official capacity?'

'No, and I'll quite understand if you don't want to talk to me.'

Svava smiled. 'You're very serious,' she said, 'for such a young man. Why are you . . . why are you doing this?'

Erlendur had no answer ready. Why was he doing this? Why couldn't he leave well alone? Why did he have to reopen old wounds and wallow in grief and loss?'

'Is it something to do with those mournful eyes of yours?' she asked. 'Has anyone ever told you? What beautiful eyes you've got?'

Erlendur was embarrassed; he hadn't been prepared for this.

46

'I'm just interested in missing-persons cases.'

'Why?'

'I have been for a long time. I'm fascinated by accounts of accidents and disasters. I come from the East Fjords where there are quite a few stories of that nature. They've always been part of my life.'

Instinct told her that he was no longer being completely honest, no longer telling the whole truth, and had closed off the small chink he had opened into his soul. He didn't meet her eye as he answered her question but lowered his gaze to the table as if afraid she would interrogate him further. She changed the subject.

'Are you married?'

'No . . . no, I'm divorced.'

'Oh, sorry to hear that.'

'Yes. So . . . now you know plenty about me,' Erlendur said, trying to smile. 'Everything, really, so –'

'I don't believe that for a minute,' said Svava, smiling in her turn. 'But enough to be going on with. No one's asked me about poor Dagbjört for years, then you ring up out of the blue. I won't deny it's a shock. You're the first person to show the slightest interest in her for more than twenty years. So, what do you want to know? How can I be of help?'

10

She was just eighteen when she vanished one dark winter's day in '53. Not long before, she had invited some school friends round to celebrate her birthday. The girls played records on the family's recently acquired gramophone. She had helped her father carry it indoors. It came in an imposing piece of furniture – a large walnut box supported on four legs, with a lid on top and a built-in wireless – and this was given pride of place in the sitting room. They played records that had been released that spring – Alfred Clausen's 'Gling gló', Sigfús Halldórsson's 'Dagný'. One of the girls brought round some of the new singles from America that she had managed to procure from the US airbase at Keflavík, including one by Kay Starr, and Doris Day singing 'Be My Little Baby Bumble Bee'. The girls danced and giggled and, once Dagbjört's parents were safely out of the way, two of them produced some alcohol they had pinched from home. They shared it round and someone took out a packet of cigarettes and started smoking. The cigarettes were passed round too, a few of the girls puffing and making faces, others inhaling with an air of sophistication. They chatted about the school camping trip to Thórsmörk earlier that autumn and the proposed skiing trip to Hveradalir in the highlands after New Year, and exchanged gossip about who was dating who and the latest exploits of various Hollywood stars. A Dean Martin film was currently showing in the cinemas. They preferred him to Frank Sinatra. As the evening wore on they sang their school song with its lyrics about a bright, happy future, and played Sigfús's hit single over and over again: '. . . *the glorious stars will shine / on our love, our joy and delight, / though the song of the breeze has fallen quiet.*'

The girls were close friends and when one morning Dagbjört didn't turn up to school or for the meeting a group of them had arranged for later that day, they rang her house to ask if she was ill. Dagbjört's mother said no, she had gone to school as usual, at least as far as she knew. She called out to her daughter, went upstairs to her room, opened the front door and peered down the street, then stepped out into the garden, repeatedly calling her name. After this she phoned her husband at work and asked if he had heard from her or knew where she was. He was nonplussed. As far as he was aware, Dagbjört had gone to school that morning.

When they still hadn't heard from her by evening, her parents grew seriously alarmed and went out looking for her. They phoned round all their friends and relatives, but no one had any news of their daughter. A number of people came to their house, among them several of Dagbjört's classmates, neighbours and close relatives, and together they retraced her customary route to school. Perhaps something had happened to her on the way. They looked everywhere, walked the streets, climbed into gardens, conducted a thorough search of Camp Knox, combed the park and area around Lake Tjörnin and the streets at the lower end of Thingholt, near the school. By then the police had got their act together, though opinion at the station was that it was a little premature to call out the search parties. They asked if she had ever done anything like this before but the response was a firm negative: she had never disappeared without trace before. No need to worry too much, the parents were told; their daughter hadn't even been missing twenty-four hours and there was every likelihood that she would turn up safe and sound before long.

But Dagbjört didn't turn up. Twenty-four hours passed, then forty-eight, then seventy-two, and still there was no sign of her. Nothing she had said or done in the preceding days had given any clue to her possible movements that morning. She had been her usual self, bright and breezy, bursting with plans as always. She had informed her parents of her wish to continue her education, preferably in medicine, though there were few female doctors in the country at the time. She had told her mother that in the past decade only seven women had completed their medical training in Iceland.

'So, as I'm sure you can imagine, it was an unspeakably awful time,' Svava told Erlendur. 'They said – my brother and his wife Helga – that it was out of the question that she could have taken her own life.'

'What did they think had happened?' asked Erlendur.

'They couldn't begin to understand it. They thought she must have been injured in some way. Maybe she'd walked along the shore, fallen in the sea and couldn't save herself. Got swept out by the current. It was so bloody dark, of course – it was the end of November – and for reasons we don't know she either decided not to go to school and went somewhere else instead or was intercepted on the way. Accepted a lift perhaps. Had some sort of run-in with somebody. We pictured all kinds of situations she could have got into but of course we hadn't really the faintest idea what happened.'

'If she had gone somewhere other than school, where might it have been?'

'I suppose it's just possible she walked out to Nauthólsvík cove. Went for a swim in the hot water. But that's clutching at straws. She was young, she loved life and had never shown any hint of depression or anxiety – quite the reverse – she had a very positive outlook, was doing well at school, had a good gang of friends. Her parents said she looked forward to school every day.'

'There was nothing wrong with the weather that morning, was there?' asked Erlendur. 'No chance she'd have had to urgently seek shelter?'

'No, it was frosty and still,' said Svava. 'They combed all the shores here, all the way south to the Reykjanes Peninsula. Never found a thing.'

Svava poured them both more coffee. Erlendur still hadn't touched his freshly baked doughnut.

'There was talk of a diary,' said Erlendur, remembering this detail from the police files. It had not helped the inquiry as it had turned out to contain nothing but the musings and dreams of a growing girl, incidents from school life, books she was reading for her studies and her opinions of the various subjects. The occasional comment about her teachers and fellow pupils, all very innocent. She had also stuck in cuttings from the papers, pictures of actors and so on.

'Yes, that's right. I saw it among my brother's papers. It didn't help us at all, as you probably know.'

'You didn't notice if there were any pages missing, any she'd torn out?'

'There could well have been. The diary's a sort of file with loose pages, so it's impossible to say. You can take them out or add them in as you like. If she removed any, they must have been lost long ago.'

'Yes, I suppose so.'

'Of course, the biggest puzzle was that boy from Camp Knox,' Svava added after a brief pause.

'The one her friend mentioned?'

'Yes. Dagbjört was in the habit of taking a detour, to avoid the old army barracks – she wasn't the only one. There was often bad feeling between the kids from the camp and the ones living in the houses nearby. As far as her parents were aware, she didn't know any boys from Camp Knox. So it would've had to have been a recent development. Naturally they tried to track the boy down and asked around about him, but he never came forward. So I don't know if there was any truth to the story. They questioned the residents of the camp and searched some of the huts – there were a lot of lowlifes living there, as you'd expect. But nothing came out of it.'

'Was she seeing any other boys?' asked Erlendur.

'No – if you mean boyfriends, we didn't know of any and neither did her friends. We thought this girl had probably misunderstood or misheard something Dagbjört said about a boy from Camp Knox. But maybe you should talk to her yourself.'

Erlendur nodded. 'I was planning to. Was Dagbjört actively scared of walking through the camp then?'

'Well, she wasn't keen on it and I know Helga warned her not to go there – she'd heard tales about drunkenness and so on. There were single mothers with three or four kids, some of the poorest people in Reykjavík, and men in all kinds of states trying to crawl into their huts at night. I remember her telling us – one of the mothers we met when we were looking for Dagbjört. She was complaining about it to the policemen with us. Asked why it was that louts and thugs were allowed to run riot in the camp and nothing was done about it. Those poor women and their children had a very raw deal. The kids were bullied at school too. One of the other mothers told us her two daughters had been driven out of school by a gang of boys and said they were never going back. I seem to recall one of them was actually beaten up. That sort of thing was bound to make the camp children stick together.'

Svava looked Erlendur in the eye and spoke firmly.

'I'm aware I might be prejudiced,' she said, 'and it can't be helped, but I don't believe Dagbjört had met a boy from the camp. I think it's quite out of the question. I just can't picture it. Can't picture it at all.'

'Because . . .?'

'Because she had her head screwed on,' said Svava. 'That's why. I know I shouldn't talk like this but it's a fact. It's what I feel and I should be allowed to speak my mind. I don't believe she was seeing a boy from the camp, and anyway it was never proved. No one in the huts was aware of any relationship or recognised Dagbjört.'

'Couldn't she have been seeing this boy anyway, in spite of the fact no one saw them together?'

'We went over it endlessly day in, day out,' said Svava. 'Did he exist? If so, who was he? Did he know what happened? Did she meet him that morning?'

'But you don't think he existed?'

'No, I don't. Though my brother disagreed. All I can say is that if there was a boy, he never gave himself up. He knew we were looking for Dagbjört. He'd have heard about our search and would have told us if he knew anything.'

'Unless he was involved?' said Erlendur. 'Since he didn't come forward, doesn't that point to a guilty conscience?'

'Of course, if you look at it that way,' said Svava. 'My brother talked a lot along those lines; Helga too. They were sure this mystery boy must have played some part in her disappearance. Convinced of it.'

'The police put out an appeal in the camp for him or any witnesses who might know something about Dagbjört's movements or their relationship to come forward.'

'Yes.'

'But nothing came of it.'

'No. Nothing. Apart from two or three false leads the police followed up that turned out to have nothing to do with her disappearance. That was all.'

11

Kristvin's flat was a typical bachelor pad, located on the top floor
of a four-storey block in the Upper Breidholt district, with a fine
view north to Mount Esja. The small kitchen had a table with
two chairs, a large fridge, a few plates and glasses in the cupboards.
There was little to eat apart from bread that was going mouldy
and a few bumper packs of chocolate that looked to Marion as
if they came from the base, and some Rio Coffee in its signature
blue-striped packets. There was a fixture for a bin bag on the
door of the cupboard under the sink but no bag, and Marion
guessed Kristvin must have taken the rubbish with him the last
time he left home and chucked it in the chute on the landing.
An automatic coffee machine on the worktop next to the cooker,
a box of American breakfast cereal beside it. A plate and spoon
in the sink. Kristvin's last breakfast, Marion thought.

The bedroom was furnished with a single bed and a small
bedside table on which lay two thick American paperbacks.

Science fiction, judging by the covers. The bed was unmade and the sheets had not been changed in a while. The half-empty wardrobe contained a couple of pairs of jeans and checked shirts, a leather jacket, a dark suit, and a wide assortment of T-shirts. At the bottom of the wardrobe were two pairs of cowboy boots, one as good as new, the other scuffed from heavy wear.

There were more sci-fi novels on the bookshelves in the sitting room, a few pieces of shabby furniture – sofa, table and an old chest of drawers on which stood a newish stereo, and two large speakers in the corners. Beside the stereo was a stack of records, mostly American rock. Marion pictured Kristvin listening to music the evening before he went to work for the last time. There were a couple of posters on the sitting-room walls – the Rolling Stones and Neil Young. The drawers in the chest turned out to contain bills, tax returns and some letters his sister had sent him in America.

Marion was struck by how austere it was; how little it gave away about the occupant, apart from his taste for science fiction and American rock. Nothing unusual in that. His years spent studying in the States had left their mark. There was no sign that he had received any guests during the last days of his life, nor any evidence to suggest he had been involved with a woman.

The only surprise was the contents of the fridge. The forensics team had subjected the flat to a meticulous examination, taking photographs and samples, searching for any clues as to how Kristvin had died. They found some dog ends in an ashtray in the sitting room, then told Marion to look in the fridge. It was at this point that Erlendur turned up.

'Where have you been?' said Marion, holding the fridge door open and peering inside.

'I got held up,' said Erlendur, hoping he would get away without elaborating. No such luck.

'How come?' asked Marion. 'What were you up to?'

'I had a meeting in connection with a matter I'm looking into.'

'What are you looking into?'

'A case you're aware of – I've told you about it.'

'Which one?'

'The Camp Knox case.'

Marion regarded him in surprise. 'You mean the girl from the Women's College?'

'Yes.'

'You're finally doing something about it?'

'I'm not sure. I spoke to her aunt. It went all right.'

'Was she helpful?'

'Yes, she was, as a matter of fact. What have you got there?'

'This,' said Marion, opening the fridge door wide to show Erlendur the cache within.

The interior was jam-packed with well-known American brands of beer and vodka, as well as eight cartons of cigarettes. Forensics had left the freezer compartment open too so they could see an old cigar box containing more than twenty roll-ups which, they were informed, contained marijuana.

'Seems to have slipped his mind that beer's illegal in Iceland,' commented Erlendur. 'You won't find gallon bottles like those in the state off-licence either.'

'And certainly not cigarettes like these,' said Marion, sniffing a roll-up. 'Probably smoked them himself. We found dog ends in an ashtray in the sitting room.'

'All from the base, I'd guess,' said Erlendur, picking up one of the cigarette cartons.

'The question is how big a scale was he operating on? Was this just the tip of the iceberg?'

'Aren't these the same brands as the stash we found in the brothers' shed? The vodka and cigarettes, I mean?'

'Looks like it.'

'Reckon they've got contacts on the base too?'

'We'd better ask them. What did the aunt say?'

'Aunt?'

'The girl's paternal aunt,' said Marion, closing the fridge. 'Haven't you just come from seeing her?'

'She doesn't believe the girl had a boyfriend,' said Erlendur. 'Or he'd have come forward during the search.'

'Unless he bumped her off himself.'

'She reckons there was too big a class difference. That the girl would never have got mixed up with a boy from Camp Knox.'

'What would she know about it?'

'She claims she knew her niece well.'

'Bit of a snob, is she?'

'She said she was trying not to be prejudiced but that's the way it looked to her. Her niece would never have associated with a boy from the slum.'

Marion had long been aware of Erlendur's fascination with Dagbjört's story; had discovered it during a quiet period at work. Erlendur had been talking about his hobby of collecting accounts of people getting lost in violent storms and barely making it home alive or never being found; about accidents at sea, avalanches and other natural disasters. Marion was intrigued by this unusual pastime and found that Erlendur was especially interested in missing-persons cases and had read up exhaustively on Dagbjört's disappearance. Was obsessed by it, in fact. Marion only knew about the case by hearsay but immediately recognised that Erlendur was in earnest, and got the impression that he felt the police could have done a better job at the time. Marion didn't necessarily agree and argued the point with Erlendur, before eventually encouraging him to take action instead of endlessly shilly-shallying. Erlendur implied it was too late. Marion dismissed this as nothing but a pretext: the longer he delayed, the more time would pass, and it was never too late to reopen a cold case. So it was in large part due to Marion that Erlendur had finally taken the plunge and contacted Dagbjört's family.

'So, what now? What's your next step?' asked Marion, sniffing at one of the dog ends.

'Maybe talk to the girl who heard Dagbjört refer to a boyfriend,' said Erlendur and followed Marion out onto the balcony. 'Could Kristvin have been operating a smuggling racket from the base and got into a spot of bother as a result?'

'I'm wondering what his sister knows,' said Marion. 'Whether she's told us everything.'

Marion leaned over the balcony railing and peered down at the car park belonging to the block. The balcony faced north and Erlendur lifted his eyes to the icy slopes of Mount Esja.

'Could he have fallen from here?' Marion wondered aloud.

'Wouldn't people have noticed?'

'I don't know. If it happened at night, no one about, a silent fall. Bearing in mind he could have been dead already. Or unconscious.'

'There are no signs of a struggle in the flat,' Erlendur pointed out.

'No, true.'

'And why was his body taken all the way out to Svartsengi?'

'Search me,' said Marion. 'We should have another word with his sister.'

'Did you notice her hair?'

'Yes.'

'Didn't it look like a wig to you?'

'That was obvious,' said Marion.

That evening it was reported on the news that two men had gone missing on the Eyvindarstadir Moors in the north of the country. They were hunters from Akureyri, who had failed to return home at the expected time. Conditions in the area had deteriorated since they set out and the north Iceland rescue teams were preparing to launch search parties. According to the report the two men were friends, in their twenties.

Erlendur and Marion were listening to the radio in the office. Otherwise the local news was dominated by the coming elections. The Conservatives' slogan was: 'War on Inflation'. The Commies had twisted this into 'War on Living Standards'. The announcer gave the latest on the hostage crisis in Teheran: Ayatollah Khomeini was refusing to receive Jimmy Carter's negotiators. A British art historian in the royal household had admitted to spying for the Russians. Polish dissidents had been sentenced to prison.

'Same old,' said Marion, switching off the radio.

They had not yet managed to get hold of Kristvin's sister to question her about the goods in his flat, but Erlendur had spoken to his boss and arranged to meet him at the Icelandair premises at Keflavík airport the following day.

'I just hope to God they're well equipped and know the area. No one should go on a trip like that without the proper gear,' muttered Erlendur after the announcement about the two missing men.

'It wouldn't be the first time,' said Marion.

'People should take proper precautions,' said Erlendur. 'It's madness to go charging up into the mountains at this time of year, trusting in luck. You never know what might happen.'

He said this with such a chill in his voice that Marion turned to look at him.

'Are you talking from experience? Is that why you're so obsessed with all those stories?'

'People should just take care,' said Erlendur, dodging the question. 'Or things can go badly wrong.'

Marion said goodnight and headed home, stopping off on the way at a popular Danish-style *smørrebrød* place to buy a prawn sandwich. Once home, Marion sat in the quiet house, eating this takeaway accompanied by a glass of port, and thought about Kristvin and the milky-blue lagoon, his sister's wig and the stash in the fridge. As so often, once the day's hectic business had receded, memories of Katrín began to intrude, of their intermittent relationship that had ended so abruptly. Marion had met her at a TB sanatorium in the 1930s and they had shared painful recollections of their time there and the lasting impact of the disease.

She had stayed on in Denmark but travelled a great deal, and over the years she had sent Marion an assortment of little souvenirs from all over the world. But now those days were over and their correspondence had dwindled until in the end she had stopped writing altogether.

Towards midnight Marion finished the port and went to bed feeling a faint sense of misgiving, without knowing why.

12

Kristvin's sister Nanna could not hide her surprise when Marion Briem and Erlendur turned up early next morning at the nursery school where she worked, asking to speak to her. She was busy dressing the children in their outdoor clothes and after a bit of a tussle she beckoned the two detectives to come out into the playground with her as they were short-staffed due to illness and she had to supervise. Marion asked if she shouldn't be taking time off; it must be tough coping with her brother's death, all the more so given the circumstances and the news coverage. Nanna replied that she preferred being at work to moping around at home with nothing to do: she had to keep herself busy. This seemed sensible to Erlendur.

Nanna was Kristvin's next of kin. The day before, she had asked Erlendur when the post-mortem would be completed so she could start planning the funeral, but he hadn't been able to inform her. She repeated her question as the three of them stood by a large sandpit, watching the children play, but again received a vague reply. She also wanted to know how the investigation was progressing and was told that naturally it would take time and no results could be expected just yet.

The bitter north wind had dropped, giving way to milder weather. It was still early and the city was dark under an overcast sky. A two-year-old boy started howling, turning a pained gaze on Nanna as a little girl hit him over the head with a pink plastic spade, then shovelled sand over him. Nanna moved the toddler out of harm's way and comforted him, before putting him down in another, more peaceful sandpit.

'She's a little terror, that one,' Nanna said apologetically as she came back, nodding towards the girl who appeared to Erlendur to be already casting around for a new victim.

'Yes, she's quite something,' said Marion. 'We've talked to your brother's neighbours. They speak well of him. Say he was quiet. They weren't aware of many visitors. There was an elderly man living opposite him on the third floor –'

'Yes, Jóhann,' said Nanna.

'You know him?'

'I've seen him about. Kristvin had a lot of time for him.'

'Jóhann obviously felt the same. He told us your brother was very kind; used to carry his groceries upstairs for him and would always ask if he needed anything when he was going out to the shops himself. He mended the old man's kitchen sink for him.'

'They got on well. Kristvin told me Jóhann found it tough at times, living on the third floor.'

'I take it your brother moved there when he came home from America?'

Nanna nodded. 'He stayed with me for a while to begin with,

but then he found this flat on the top floor of a block without a lift, in the back of beyond. The cheapest place he could find. He took out a mortgage. Owed a lot on his student loan as well.'

'But he had a good job,' Erlendur chipped in.

'Yes, he was on a decent wage once he started work at the airport.'

'Was he involved in smuggling?'

'Smuggling?'

Nanna was momentarily flustered, but quickly realised that this was the intention.

'We found various items in his flat that we have reason to believe came from the naval base,' said Erlendur. 'Cigarettes, beer and vodka.'

'Oh, that. I don't know if any of it was smuggled – yes, probably. It was mostly for his own use but he sometimes gave me some. I asked him to buy me stuff from time to time – gave him the money. You can get it dirt cheap down there compared to the prices at the state off-licence, and of course you can't get beer here.'

'And the dope?' said Marion.

'Dope?'

'We found cannabis in his flat. Marijuana.'

'Oh, the grass,' said Nanna. 'Was it in the freezer?'

'Was he dealing in drugs from his flat?'

'No, he wasn't. Not drugs. Occasionally beer and vodka. Jóhann bought some, for example. And one or two other people he knew.'

'Any idea who they were?' asked Marion.

'Is it important?'

'Could be.'

'Were you aware he used drugs?' asked Erlendur.

64

'Yes, of course. We both did. Mostly me, though.'

'You?'

'Yes.'

'What . . .?'

'It helps with the pain.'

'What pain?' asked Erlendur.

Nanna looked at them searchingly.

'You must have noticed the wig.'

They didn't react.

'This here.' She pointed to her head. 'Do you think I wear it for fun?'

They still didn't say anything.

'I have cancer,' said Nanna. 'It's not long since I finished the second lot of chemotherapy and they say it went well but they can't promise anything. Just like the first time. Kristvin's grass helped – it made me feel less sick during the treatment. When he was in America he'd read that marijuana can help cancer patients, so he thought it was worth giving it a try.'

'Did he get it from the base?' asked Marion.

'Yes.'

'Shouldn't you have told us this yesterday?'

'I was going to but then we . . . we went to the morgue . . . I thought I'd die before him, you know. Because of the cancer. Then . . . then I didn't hear from him and suddenly . . . suddenly he's dead. In this horrible way.'

'You shouldn't be at work,' said Marion, taking Nanna's hand. 'Can't we drive you home? You really shouldn't be here. Isn't there anyone who can come and keep you company?'

The little girl was still wreaking havoc. This time she destroyed a sandcastle that two other children had taken great pains over, and they burst into tears. Another helper ran over and grabbed the girl by the scruff of her neck when she tried to make off. Nanna went to comfort the castle-builders and help them start again.

'The little pest,' she said when she came back, and heaved a deep breath. 'She'll be a handful one day.'

'Are you all right?' asked Marion.

'I'm fine,' said Nanna. 'I'd rather look after the kids than hang around at home. It's nothing. I'm all right.'

'Who sold him the drugs?' asked Erlendur.

'I don't know. All I know is he got them from the base. He had contacts but he didn't tell me who they were and I didn't ask too many questions. He said he was careful. I kept asking him about that and telling him to watch himself, and I know he did. My brother was no fool. He knew what he was doing.'

But look how he ended up, Erlendur wanted to say, but stopped himself. He had no desire to increase her suffering; she had enough to cope with. He believed Nanna was telling the truth and that she was desperate to find out what had happened to her brother. He didn't believe for a moment that she could have played any part in his death, though Marion had hinted as much on their way to the nursery school. Marion wanted to pursue this angle because she hadn't come clean to them about the booze or drugs, but Erlendur thought she'd simply had too much else on her mind at the time. Marion took the view that she was hiding something from the police about the goods. But Erlendur dis-agreed, especially now that Nanna had admitted to using the drugs for medicinal purposes and apparently didn't regard the fact as a big deal.

'How did he travel to and fro?' asked Erlendur.

'To and fro?'

'Between Reykjavík and Keflavík.'

'Oh, he had a car,' said Nanna. 'Haven't you found it?'

'What sort of car?' asked Marion. 'We didn't find any car registered in his name.'

'That's because it was mine – it's still in my name. A Toyota Corolla. I sold it to him. We just hadn't got round to transferring ownership. And as Kristvin had only paid me half, I still use it quite a bit too, so . . .'

'You took turns using it?' finished Erlendur, and wrote down the details: two-door, grey, six years old, constantly breaking down.

'Yes, but he's been using it for the last few weeks.'

13

A spell in custody had done nothing to soften up Ellert and Vignir, or make them any more amenable. They were as insolent and insufferable as the day they had been locked up in Sídumúli Prison, and still stubbornly denied any wrongdoing. They had much in common, although it wasn't obvious from their appearance that they were brothers. One was stocky and ungainly, with a thick head of hair; the other tall, lanky and almost totally bald. They lived together – always had – and were described as very close. Vignir, the ungainly one, was the elder, and acted as spokesman for them both, as far as the police could gather. Ellert was a more shadowy figure who kept a low profile and stayed in the background. Perhaps that was why he was known as 'the Old Lady'. But, according to police informants, he was the real mastermind behind the brothers' business and on the rare occasions he showed his hand you would go far to find another thug as vicious as him. He was aware of his nickname and thin-skinned about it. There was a story doing the rounds that a man who used it to his face had spent the next two months in intensive care; he claimed to have been hit by a car, never fully recovered and left the country after a spell in rehabilitation. Whether it was true or not, nobody could say.

Towards midday Ellert was conducted to the interview room and took a seat across from Marion and Erlendur, wearing the same sullen expression that hadn't left his face since he was apprehended. He had made no attempt to resist arrest, any more than his brother, but insisted he hadn't committed any criminal offence and wished to register a protest about the unlawful way in which he was being treated. The fine phrases had been picked up from the TV cop shows he and Vignir spent their lives glued to.

'When are you going to let us go?' asked Ellert, lounging in his chair. 'It's ridiculous banging us up like this. We haven't done anything.'

It was the same refrain his brother opened his interviews with, intended to demonstrate that neither was going to betray the slightest hint of weakness or help the police in any way with their inquiries. Ignoring this, Erlendur and Marion began instead to grill him about the goods he and his brother imported, about their associates, smuggling routes, expenses and profit margin, and what they did with the profits. And further, about the identity of their customers and how the deals were organised. Ellert either didn't answer at all or gave deliberately fatuous replies, repeatedly protesting his innocence and claiming he didn't even understand half the questions. The interrogation ground on like this for three-quarters of an hour until Marion began to nudge the conversation round towards the naval base at Keflavík. The gallon bottles of vodka and cigarette cartons in Kristvin's fridge had been American, from the same producers and in the same kind of packaging as those the police had confiscated during the raid on the brothers' premises, and although there was nothing to indicate any link between the brothers and Kristvin, Marion didn't want to dismiss the possibility out of hand.

'Have you got contacts on the base?' asked Marion.

'On the base?' echoed Ellert.

'At Keflavík? On the naval base? Do you have any business out there?'

Ellert sat up in his chair, looking at them both in turn.

'What kind of business?'

'Do any of your goods come from there?'

'From the base?'

'You heard me.'

'In the first place I'm not aware of any goods,' said Ellert, 'and in the second place I don't know what you're on about. Why are you asking about the bloody naval base?'

'Who do you buy from down there?' asked Marion.

'We don't buy anything there,' said Ellert. 'Weren't you listening? We don't buy anything full stop. The stuff you found isn't ours. None of it belongs to us!'

'Is it the quartermasters who supply you?' Marion persisted doggedly. 'Or the guys who run the clubs? Or the stores? The air crews? Marines?'

Ellert didn't answer.

'How's it smuggled off base?' asked Erlendur. 'By the soldiers? Or is it the contractors? Do you use Icelandic workers as go-betweens?'

'Does the name Kristvin mean anything to you?' asked Marion when Ellert remained obstinately mute.

'Who's he?' asked Ellert. He received little news of the outside world in his cell.

'A customer of yours,' said Marion.

'Never heard of him,' said Ellert. 'And we don't have any customers. Why are you asking me about this bloke? Who is he?'

'We found the same kind of goods at his place as you two deal in. It occurred to us that he might have bought them from you.'

'Unless he was smuggling for you and your brother?' suggested Erlendur. 'Is that it? Was he working for you?'

'Why don't you cut the crap? I don't know the guy.'

During the drive to the prison Marion had been reflecting on the fact that it was only a decade since the police first started arresting people in Iceland for drugs-related offences. The incidents frequently had some connection to the military installation and international airport at Keflavík. Passengers were caught carrying cannabis or LSD, and the proximity of the naval base made it easy for Icelanders to get hold of narcotics imported by members of the Defense Force. The Americans were also a good source of hard currency for purchasing drugs abroad, which was otherwise difficult to come by in Iceland due to the currency restrictions. It had all begun on a small scale, mostly for recreational use at parties, but over time the number of users had grown and some people had spotted an opening for making money by importing drugs themselves. People like Ellert and Vignir.

Vignir was as intransigent as his brother. He denied everything and professed himself as surprised as Ellert when the questions

71

began to touch on the Defense Force and naval base. He tried to fish for more information from the detectives, with little success.

'Who is this guy?' he asked. 'What did he do?'

'It occurred to us that he might have been a rival of yours,' said Erlendur. 'If he was selling the same kind of goods maybe you and your brother didn't like the competition.'

'What . . . why . . . did something happen to him?'

'Or that he was a customer of yours,' continued Marion, 'and was planning to snitch on you.'

'Then there's a third possibility – that he was smuggling stuff on your behalf and helped himself to some of it,' said Erlendur.

'Who the fuck is this guy? What's his name?'

'Kristvin,' said Erlendur.

'Kristvin? I've never heard of any Kristvin. Who is he? Why are you asking about this bloke? Are you implying we did something to him?'

'Tell me about the cannabis you and Ellert deal in: does any of that come from the base?' asked Erlendur, leaving Vignir's question unanswered.

'Now you've lost me.'

'Where do you get the currency to import your goods?' asked Erlendur.

Vignir shook his head.

'From the Yanks?' asked Marion. 'We know you've been dealing in currency on the base.'

'I have no idea what you're talking about,' said Vignir. 'Not a clue. As usual.'

A little later, as Marion and Erlendur were leaving, a prison officer came running after them.

'They've found some car you're trying to trace . . . a Corolla,' he said, reading from a scrap of paper on which he had taken down the message. 'It's out at Keflavík. Parked by one of the barracks on the base and . . .' The prison officer tried to decipher his own scribble. '. . . and, oh yes, the tyres have been slashed.'

14

The two police officers who came across the grey Toyota Corolla had been summoned to the military zone when a fight broke out at one of the dormitory huts belonging to the Icelandic contractors. The men had clashed over a card game during their break. The three huts, in which the workers were put up two to a room, stood in a row not far from the contractors' large canteen. The culprits lived on the same corridor and had been spoiling for a fight for some time. They were both keen poker players and had been betting money on the game. The atmosphere had soured when, not for the first time, the loser refused to pay up. A row broke out, threats were exchanged, and in the end they flew at one another and rolled around the corridor of the hut, before falling, still grappling, out of the door onto the ground outside. At that point two other men became drawn in and it was thought advisable to call the police, who duly arrived to break it up. By then the men were exhausted; one was lying on the ground covered in blood, the other was leaning against the wall, panting and bleeding from the nose and one ear where he had been bitten. The police saw no reason to take anyone to hospital as they all denied they needed to see a doctor, but they were separated and moved to different huts.

The officers' attention was distracted by a grey Toyota Corolla with flat tyres, parked by the end of one of the barracks, not far from the contractors' huts. A description of the missing car had been circulated to police stations around the country and, as far as they could tell, this was it. They had the sense not to touch it and reported their discovery immediately. The military police, notified at the same time, sent a car to the scene. Naval Air Station Keflavík came under the jurisdiction of the US Navy. Whenever the military police were required to deal with Icelandic nationals, they would summon the local police from Keflavík to handle the matter. Similarly, the Icelandic police gave notice if they needed to operate on the base, as in the affair of the brawling poker players.

The Corolla was not much to look at, especially with all the air let out of the tyres. One wing was crumpled from a collision and there was an old dent in the passenger door. The back seat was littered with rubbish, newspapers, fast-food containers and empty beer and soft-drink cans which could only be obtained from the base. The boot contained two Icelandic wool blankets, a half-empty gallon bottle of American vodka and three packets of cigarettes. The spare tyre was lying untouched in its place. The registration papers were in the glove compartment. It appeared the car hadn't been for an MOT for two years.

It was impossible to guess how long or indeed why it had been parked there. The simplest explanation was that Kristvin had stopped off for a snack since many of the barracks had vending machines that sold items like cigarettes, canned drinks and chocolate. While he was inside, someone must have slashed his tyres and left him stranded. An alternative, less straightforward, explanation was that Kristvin had been visiting someone in this or a neighbouring barracks, in other words that he had an acquaintance here or had some business with a resident that involved not chocolate but vodka and cannabis.

After leaving the prison, Marion and Erlendur had headed straight out to Keflavík, discussing the various scenarios as they drove and complaining about how utterly fed up they were of interrogating the brothers.

'I suppose it's hardly surprising the car should turn up here,' said Erlendur, surveying the barracks. 'It's where Kristvin worked, after all.'

Marion walked round the car and bent down to examine the gash in one of the front tyres. It was two centimetres long, made by the blade of a knife, possibly a penknife.

'It all fits, more or less,' said Marion. 'Why do you think his tyres were slashed?'

'I suppose there's a faint chance someone did it for a laugh, but . . . given what we know happened to Kristvin, maybe it's a bit more complicated than that. I think it's much more likely he landed in some kind of trouble here.'

'Which led to him turning up in the lagoon?' said Marion, poking a finger into the slit in the rubber.

'Why didn't he fetch help?' asked Erlendur. 'Change the tyres? Drive away?'

'He needed more than one tyre. He must have been planning to come back later and sort it out.'

'Or he couldn't do anything about it just then.'

'Why not?'

'Because he was in a hurry and didn't have time,' said Erlendur.

'Why was he in a hurry?'

'Because . . . he needed to get away? Somebody was after him?'

'Because somebody was after him,' repeated Marion. 'He had to make an urgent getaway and didn't have time to worry about the car.'

'Who let down the tyres? The man or men who were after him?'

Marion straightened up: '. . . who thought Kristvin might escape by car and wanted to prevent him.'

'So Kristvin made a run for it? Are you implying he was killed here on the base?' asked Erlendur.

'I'm beginning to wonder. Though perhaps the tyres were slashed because the car was left here unattended and some vandals just happened to be passing. We can't rule that out.'

'But you don't think it's likely?'

'No,' said Marion, 'I don't. Kristvin worked on the base. And was involved in shady business here that could have got him into hot water. Doesn't it all point to the same thing?'

'Maybe,' said Erlendur.

'You're not convinced.'

'We're not just talking about Icelanders any more, are we?' said Erlendur. 'His assailants, I mean?'

'No, I think that's clear.'

The military police stood a little way off, watching Marion and Erlendur examine the car and listening to their conversation without understanding a word. Forensics had arrived to collect the Corolla for inspection at their workshop in Kópavogur and were waiting for a lorry. Marion strolled over to the two American policemen, exchanged introductions and explained that members of the Icelandic CID would need to interview the residents of the neighbouring barracks.

'Is that strictly necessary?' asked one of the men.

'The owner of this car was murdered,' Marion informed him in competent English. 'I thought you were aware of that. We need to find out why his car's here, what business he had visiting the barracks.'

'Was he murdered in one of the barracks?'

'We don't know.'

'Was he murdered on the base?'

From the stripes on his shoulder the policeman appeared to be an officer, maybe a sergeant. He was young, in his twenties, and spoke with a noticeable Southern drawl. His companion, who was around the same age, contributed nothing to the conversation.

'We don't know,' repeated Marion. 'That's why we need to –'

'Why don't you find out first?' interrupted the young sergeant, making no effort to appear accommodating. 'I don't believe the folks round here would care to be questioned by you people.'

His arrogance, the way he said 'you people' and cut Marion off short, angered Erlendur and made him want to step in and give the guy a piece of his mind. But he bit his lip.

'Maybe it would be better if we spoke to your superior officer,' said Marion.

'I doubt that would make any difference,' said the young man. He adjusted his cap which had tipped forward on his brow.

'All the same,' said Marion and turned to Erlendur. 'We need to find someone with a grain of sense around here.'

The Americans conferred, then announced they would contact

headquarters. The one who spoke for both repeated, defiantly, that the Icelandic police shouldn't assume they would be granted permission to interrogate American nationals on US territory, unless the circumstances were exceptional. On the other hand, he made no objection to the Corolla being removed from the scene. The lorry, which had arrived in the interim, reversed up to the car and the driver attached a hook under the bumper, then winched the car into the trailer and secured it. Then he got behind the wheel again and the lorry moved off, under police escort.

15

While they were awaiting a green light from the base authorities for the Icelandic police to question Defense Force personnel, Marion and Erlendur drove over to the Icelandair premises where Kristvin had worked as a mechanic. These were located inside the military zone, like everything relating to international civil aviation in Iceland. Plans had long been afoot to move the international airport, by constructing a smart new passenger terminal outside the perimeter to the west of the base, but little progress had been made so far. The old terminal building was no longer fit for purpose and it was hardly appropriate that every time Icelanders wanted to travel abroad they had to pass through a US military checkpoint. It was yet another bone of contention in the bitter controversy over the American presence in the country that had been raging ever since the Defence Agreement was signed with the United States after the Second World War. Opposition came principally from those on the Left, who wanted not only to throw out the Defense Force but for Iceland to leave NATO as well and declare itself neutral. Support for the military presence tended to come from the Right, who believed that cooperation on defence was essential in these uncertain times and that neutrality in the war between East and West was unthinkable. Others were motivated by profit. They wanted to charge the Americans for the lease of the site on Midnesheidi, but this was countered with the argument that the army was already pumping a vast amount of cash into the Icelandic economy in the form of contracts. Then there were those who took a more moderate line, not necessarily in favour of the army's presence but regarding it as a necessary evil in light of the Cold War, and feeling that, after the horrors of the last war, the Icelanders ought to do their bit for the Western defensive alliance by remaining a member of NATO. If, at some point in the future, the situation changed, the army would no longer be required. But that time did not appear to be close.

Erlendur reflected on the long-standing dispute about the army that was still simmering in the country as he drove with Marion through the military zone, past the Andrews Movie Theater and the Post Exchange store. Andrews showed the latest Hollywood films long before they reached the cinemas in Reykjavík. The PX store sold everything from stereos to household appliances at a far better price than could be had outside the wire. The car crawled past a large supermarket selling exclusively American goods, various fast-food outlets and clubs like Top of the Rock and Midnight Sun. Erlendur had the odd impression that he was driving through a small American town, sleepy and unprepossessing; the only discordant elements were the dreary weather and the strong-looking fences criss-crossing the area, with conspicuous warning notices banning entry to non-military personnel. Large barracks were under construction in preparation for the arrival of yet more consignments of troops. And new hangars were rising to house the air force's F-16 fighter jets. On a stretch of open ground a group of armed, camouflage-clad marines were taking part in an exercise. The traffic in the streets, which had names like Air Force Avenue and West Lane, consisted of yellow school buses, grey army trucks, coaches with passengers on their way to the civilian air terminal and utility vehicles belonging to the Icelandic contractors. In the midst of all the asphalt and concrete there were glimpses of the inhospitable Icelandic landscape – windswept gravel plains and hardy vegetation – reminders of what Midnesheidi Moor had looked like before it was occupied by the superpower.

To Erlendur's mind, everything that passed before his eyes was simultaneously Icelandic yet bizarrely alien. Marion apparently read his thoughts.

'Weird place.'

'Yes,' said Erlendur. 'Very weird.'

'Why are you opposed to the army?'

'How can you be anything else?' said Erlendur, looking north to where a control tower loomed against the sky. Beyond, in the distance, he could see the mountains, Esja and Skardsheidi, which only enhanced the air of unreality.

'You didn't answer my question,' said Marion.

'Because it doesn't belong here.'

'I didn't think you were political.'

'Political?'

'Yes.'

'I'm not.'

'You're against the army.'

'That has nothing to do with politics,' said Erlendur.

'Really? Isn't it all a question of Right versus Left, Yanks versus Russians, the Cold War? The Keflavík protest marches? Isn't that political?'

'I loathe politics.'

Icelandair handled all the international civilian air traffic that passed through Keflavík and had facilities for their planes in a large hangar that stood just to the north of the terminal building. Here, checks and maintenance were carried out on the fleet, and the company also serviced any planes belonging to overseas operators that landed in Keflavík and required inspection or other assistance.

Kristvin's boss, who had been expecting a visit from the police, invited Marion and Erlendur into his office which was overflowing with all kinds of books and instruction manuals on the most obscure details of aircraft engineering. The two phones on his desk were practically buried. The walls were lined with grey filing cabinets, covered with yet more piles of papers. A window faced the hangar, where an Icelandair Boeing 727 passenger plane was parked. One of its engines had been opened up and men were swarming around the fuselage.

The boss's name was Engilbert. His rather short, muscular body was clad in blue overalls and he had a bush of black hair combed back off his forehead. He offered them coffee that had been sitting in the jug all morning. They declined. Marion lit a cigarette. Engilbert poured himself a coffee, took a half-smoked cigar from an ashtray, lit it and blew out a stream of smoke.

'It's a shocker about poor old Kristvin,' he said. 'Do you have any idea what it's all about or what actually happened to him?'

'No, not as yet,' said Marion. 'Are you aware of any problems he'd been having lately? Did he fall out with anyone at work? Get into a fight?'

'No, nothing like that. Far as I know everything was fine,' said Engilbert.

'He hadn't missed work or anything like that?' asked Erlendur.

'No, he was always very punctual, a good worker. Was a bit of a loner but got on fine with the rest of the crew here. Studied in the States. They're the best, the guys who train over there.'

'No problems with drink or drugs then?' asked Erlendur.

'Nope, none that I know of.'

'He drove back to Reykjavík after work, didn't he?' said Erlendur. 'Your men don't stay on site?'

'No, that's right, he commuted every day. All the men do.'

'Did he work in this hangar?'

'Yes, mostly. Maybe you should talk to Venni – I reckon he knew him best out of all the mechanics. Full name's Vernhardur – a good kid. I think they were mates.'

'Do you know if Kristvin had any friends here on the base? Among the American servicemen, I mean?'

'No, I wouldn't know, but Venni might. I don't think he had much contact with them, but it's possible. After all, he lived in the States for a while. I didn't get to know him that well.'

'He'd parked his car by one of the barracks,' said Marion. 'Any idea what business he might have had with the residents?'

'No, none.'

'Know if he used to take cigarettes or vodka back to town with him?'

'I wouldn't be surprised,' said Engilbert.

'Oh?'

'No, lots of them do it, but it's not like they're involved in large-scale smuggling,' said Engilbert awkwardly. 'They just buy for their own use, you know.'

'Is that what you do?' asked Erlendur, noticing Engilbert's discomfort.

'Well, I have done, yes, I'm prepared to admit that. I hope I'm not confessing to a major crime here. I use the cigarette vending machines and so on, like you do; maybe take home a few cans of beer for my mates.'

'What did you mean when you said Kristvin mostly worked in here?' asked Erlendur. 'Do you have facilities on another site?'

Engilbert stubbed out his cigar and nodded, relieved by the change of subject.

'When we've got a rush on, we're allowed to use the air-force facilities,' he said.

'Oh?'

'When the planes are piling up, we're given a bay in . . . Come on, I'll show you.'

Engilbert stood up and went out into the hangar, with Erlendur and Marion on his heels. He walked through the massive doors that opened to the south, rounded a corner and pointed across the broad expanse of the runway to a colossal, box-like building plonked down in the middle of the featureless landscape.

'What's that?' asked Marion.

'Only one of the biggest buildings in the country,' said Engilbert grandly. 'Hangar 885, the pride of NAS Keflavík. You could fit two or three football pitches in there, apparently.'

'Hangar 885,' repeated Erlendur.

'And Kristvin worked in there?' said Marion.

'Yes, now and then,' said Engilbert. 'We need extra space at peak times when the jobs are stacking up, and Kristvin would work there along with the rest of the crew. Part of the hangar's closed for building work at the moment, but it's due to finish soon, so –'

'I meant, had he been working there recently?' asked Marion. 'Before he died?'

'Yes, actually,' said Engilbert, scratching his head. 'We had a bit of a problem with an inbound plane from America. Didn't have room for it ourselves so they let us service it in the big hangar.'

'What was wrong with it?' asked Erlendur.

'Faulty landing gear. Kristvin worked on that. In fact, it was probably the last job he did for us before he died.'

'What plane was this?' asked Marion.

'A transport. C-130 Hercules. The biggest there is.'

'Isn't it fairly standard for planes like that to land here?' said Erlendur. 'Hercules, I mean.'

'Sure, yeah,' said Engilbert. 'Except . . .'

'What?' prompted Marion.

'Oh, it's just that some guys from Reykjavík air traffic control were out here the other day about another matter and happened to mention the operator,' said Engilbert. 'Its status was a bit of a mystery.'

'Which operator?'

'NCT.'

'NCT?'

'The aircraft's registered under a civilian operator, a commercial airline calling itself Northern Cargo Transport. They stop over in Keflavík quite regularly but air traffic control has no information about their movements – you follow? They found it a bit odd. The guys at air traffic control.'

'No, I don't follow. What do you mean?' asked Marion. 'Why doesn't air traffic control have any information about their movements?'

'There can only be one explanation,' said Engilbert. 'They come in under the air-force call sign. Like the military aircraft from the base. The military aircraft aren't differentiated but all come in under the same call sign.'

'I still don't quite follow. You're saying Northern Cargo Transport's a commercial outfit?'

'That's right.'

'But lands here under cover of the air force?'

'You could put it like that,' said Engilbert. 'They're a civilian operator but use the same call sign as the US air force when they enter Icelandic airspace.'

'Are they operating on behalf of the American air force then?' asked Erlendur.

'Don't know. Looks like it.'

'Why do you suppose they do that?' asked Marion.

'Search me, mate.'

'And Kristvin was working on this plane?'

'Yep.'

'That's a socking great building,' commented Erlendur, his eyes on the hangar.

'I imagine the ceiling must be very high inside?' said Marion.

'Yeah, unbelievably,' said Engilbert. 'You could fit a block of flats in there. And they're working up in the rafters, the plumbers, installing a fire-extinguisher system. Not a job for the faint-hearted.'

'Are these Icelandic contractors?'

'Yes. They have massive work platforms that reach up to the ceiling. I wouldn't want to take a tumble off one of those, I can tell you.'

16

Later that afternoon CID received authorisation from the US commander's office to question base personnel and their families about Kristvin and the car that had been found by the barracks. This was only granted on condition that Marion and Erlendur were accompanied by a special military police liaison officer. Marion objected, assuming the liaison officer was being foisted on them purely in order to spy and report back to the army about what they uncovered. Not only that but the presence of a military representative might make people reluctant to speak to the Icelandic police. But the authorities wouldn't back down: if the Icelandic police wanted to interview American nationals on US territory, it would have to be done in consultation with the Defense Force and in the presence of its representative. Furthermore, it was pointed out that this was an exceptional case and should not be taken as a guarantee of further cooperation.

While they were awaiting approval, Erlendur and Marion had made a quick trip into the neighbouring town of Keflavík to talk to the men installing the sprinkler system in Hangar 885. They were employed by a local plumbing firm and, when asked, said that none of them knew Kristvin. Their boss explained that work on the system had been on hold for the last two weeks because they had been busy with other projects, but that it was more or less finished and all that remained was to tidy up and dismantle the scaffolding, which was not their job anyway.

When Erlendur and Marion returned to the base, the liaison officer was waiting for them by the barracks where the Corolla had been found. Like Marion, Erlendur had been expecting the obstructive young sergeant they had already encountered. But the officer turned out to be a slim black woman of around thirty, with short, jet-black hair under her cap, and a decisive manner. She was in uniform with an MP armband and had a pistol in a holster on her belt. She introduced herself as Sergeant Caroline Murphy and explained that she would be present during the interviews. She came straight to the point.

'I hear you object to this arrangement,' she said as she shook hands, 'but I can't do anything about that. The sooner we get it over with the better, so I suggest we make a start.'

'Fine by us,' said Marion.

'What grounds do you have for believing that this Kris . . . this man was killed on the base?' she asked.

'His car was found here,' said Erlendur. His English was self-taught but serviceable. 'That's all we know.'

'We'd like to establish if that's what happened,' said Marion. 'Have you been here long? In Iceland, I mean.'

'Two years.'

'There aren't many women in the army, are there?' asked Marion.

'Our numbers are growing,' said Caroline, 'though we're not allowed to take part in combat. Yet. Do you have many female detectives in Iceland?'

'No, sadly not,' said Marion. 'Not enough. Did you know that the Icelandic government used to ban black soldiers from being stationed here?'

'Yes, I heard about that,' said Caroline. 'Real nice of them.'

'Ignorant bigots,' said Marion.

'Times have changed, I guess,' said Caroline, displaying rather more tolerance than Marion.

'Ignorant bigots all the same.'

'Shall we start here?' asked Caroline, indicating the nearest block. 'I assume you have a photograph of the man?'

'Yes, let's get down to business,' said Marion.

They went from flat to flat, asking the residents if they knew Kristvin, showing them the photograph and enquiring whether they had seen the grey Corolla or knew what it was doing there. People were mostly very helpful, if surprised by their visit, and inquisitive about the incident. Apparently no one recognised Kristvin from the photo or had noticed the Corolla parked outside, let alone witnessed the tyres being slashed.

The same went for the occupants of the other barracks. Some had noticed the grey car because the tyres were flat, but no one had seen it arrive or knew who owned it or who had vandalised it. No one recalled seeing it in the area before. Occasionally they were invited inside, but mostly they were left standing out in the corridor. Erlendur and Marion kept steering the questions round to cigarettes, vodka and marijuana, and some people took offence while others laughed and said they were well aware of the Icelanders' interest in these items but denied any personal involvement in dealing. Few of the personnel had any contact with the locals. A couple of them said they had seen Icelanders down by the vending machines in the lobby, stocking up on cigarettes and beer. Sometimes they emptied the machines, much to the disgust of the residents.

They only encountered three instances of unpleasantness, with people refusing to answer any questions put to them by the Icelandic police. At this point Caroline intervened and politely requested that they cooperate. When they didn't, she told them that they were welcome to refuse but they would be hauled in for questioning at military police headquarters instead. If that's what they would prefer, it could easily be arranged, she informed them crisply. It never came to that. The individuals in question backed down and answered with curt resentment.

Two hours later they were back where they had started.

'Too bad you didn't get anywhere,' said Caroline, shaking their hands in parting. 'If there's nothing else, I have to get going.'

'Thanks very much,' said Marion.

'By the way,' said Erlendur, 'have you by any chance heard of an airline called Northern Cargo Transport or NCT?'

He approved of Caroline's methods; the way she had observed, quietly and unobtrusively, only stepping in when necessary, and then firmly, without throwing her weight around. He'd had his doubts about her at first, but now regretted this and felt she could be trusted. Far from being obstructive, as he had feared, she had been useful, and he wanted to know if they could trespass on her helpfulness a little further.

'Northern Cargo Transport?' she said. 'I don't think so. What company's that?'

'We don't know,' said Erlendur. 'We were told they have some connection to the air force. And we believe they're American.'

'What sort of connection?'

'That's what we'd like to know,' said Marion. 'They operate Hercules transports which stop over here, and Kristvin, who was a mechanic, serviced one of them.'

'What do you want – you're not asking me to spy on some airline for you?' asked Caroline, smiling.

'We need information about this company,' said Erlendur. 'But it'll probably take us forever if we go through the official channels with all the applications and paperwork and delays. If you . . . I wouldn't call it spying exactly . . . but if you could speed things up . . .'

'I . . . Sorry, but I think you'll just have to go down the regular, time-consuming route,' said Caroline. 'I wouldn't even know where to start.'

'All right,' said Erlendur. 'It doesn't matter. We just thought you might be able to check for us, but we understand your position. Thanks again for your help.'

'You're welcome,' said Caroline. 'It was nice meeting you. I haven't met many Icelandics – you're the first, to tell the truth. Sorry I can't be of any further assistance.'

She was on her way back to her vehicle when Erlendur remembered something that had occurred to him as they were interviewing the residents.

'Just one more thing,' he called. 'Has anything out of the ordinary happened on the base recently?'

Caroline turned back. 'Out of the ordinary? Like what?'

'I don't know,' said Erlendur. 'An accident? Any deaths?'

'No, I don't believe so.'

'Have you had problems with any known troublemakers?'

'No.'

'All right. Thank you again.'

17

She had told Erlendur, when he rang to explain what he wanted, that she would rather they met at a cafe than at her home, and she was already there when he finally arrived, a little late, after being held up at work. They exchanged greetings and he apologised, explaining that things were very busy right now. It was true. The state prosecutor's office and police commissioner had issued a letter rogatory for permission to carry out an examination of Hangar 885, Kristvin's last known place of work. The letter had also contained a request to interview members of the Defense Force in cooperation with the military authorities. The request had been submitted and re-submitted, but no response had as yet been received from Fleet Air Command. Marion thought their lack of enthusiasm might be related to the fact that the hangar housed not only fighter jets and Hercules transports but also powerful AWACS spy planes, early-warning aircraft involved in the surveillance of Icelandic airspace. Presumably the authorities were reluctant to let the Icelandic police, forensics team and photographer loose on the premises. The matter CID had spent so long debating – and the reason for Erlendur's late arrival – was whether to apply to the Icelandic Ministry of Foreign Affairs to put pressure on the base command.

The woman responded coolly when Erlendur said he had not meant to keep her waiting, but asked no questions. She knew he was a detective but was meeting her today in an unofficial capacity; his interest in Dagbjört's case was a private affair. They ordered coffee. He was hungry, having eaten next to nothing all day, so he bought a sandwich and asked if she would like something. She thought for a moment, then accepted a slice of cake. Apart from that she sat and smoked in silence. Her name was Silja and she was forty-four years old, the same age as her friend Dagbjört would have been. Erlendur found himself inadvertently tracing the signs of ageing, the lines etched deeper into her face, the harder expression round her mouth, and tried to picture how Dagbjört might have looked today. He had seen the grainy black-and-white photo printed in the papers at the time of her disappearance, which had been taken a couple of years earlier, when she was sixteen. When he met her aunt, Svava, she had lent him a copy of the same photo, which was much clearer than the published version. As he studied the picture of Dagbjört, who beamed at him, eternally young, through the grey mists of time, he had experienced an odd sensation in his chest and his thoughts had slipped back to his brother who had been lost on the moors of their childhood home in the east. He found himself wondering how Bergur would have aged and whether he would have been able to recognise him as an adult. Bergur had been only eight years old when he disappeared in a blizzard and was never found.

The incident had set an indelible mark on Erlendur's soul. He had been out there with Bergur but lost hold of his hand, and later had been rescued, more dead than alive, from a snowdrift. Ever since then he had been wrestling with the question of why Bergur should have suffered such a cruel fate while he himself was spared. But he had never found any answers or discovered what had become of his brother.

'Strange business about that man they found at Svartsengi,' Silja remarked as they waited for their order. 'Are you on that case, by any chance?'

'I'm part of the inquiry, yes.'

'Do you know what happened yet? Or who he was?'

'I'm afraid I can't comment,' Erlendur replied. 'The matter's under investigation.'

'But it was murder, wasn't it? That's what I read in the papers.'

'As I said –'

'You can't comment.'

'No, sorry.'

'I know I already asked you on the phone but why are you reopening Dagbjört's case now? You said there was no new evidence and it sounds like you have enough on your plate already.'

'No, there's no new evidence,' said Erlendur. 'But her father died the other day and –'

'Yes, I saw. I read the obituaries.'

'I spoke to his sister, and we agreed that I should make one final effort to get to the bottom of what happened to Dagbjört. Time's passing and there are fewer and fewer people left who remember.'

'Fewer left who remember,' repeated Silja, as if the words held a peculiar significance for her. 'Two other girls from our class are gone now, as well as Dagbjört,' she explained after a brief pause. 'And it wasn't that big a class.'

'Your testimony was pretty significant,' said Erlendur. 'No one else knew Dagbjört had a boyfriend, let alone that he lived in Camp Knox.'

Silja had not touched the cake but sipped her coffee and lit another cigarette. She smoked each one only halfway down before stubbing it out.

'I often think of her,' she said. 'We were . . . we were born only three weeks apart and we . . . were so alike, shared the same interests, used to spend a lot of time together. Listened to Doris Day. Giggled about boys. One day she told me she was interested in a boy who lived near her and who she sometimes saw on her way to school, in Camp Knox. They'd met up a couple of times without telling anyone, and she thought she was falling for him.'

'That's all she told you?'

'Yes. She wouldn't tell me his name. Or where he lived, at first.'

'Did she seem ashamed of him?'

'Dagbjört wasn't like that. She didn't have a snobbish bone in her body. But the relationship was still at a delicate stage, I suppose – had only just got off the ground – and she didn't want to say too much about it. Certainly not to her parents. Of course, that's the last thing you . . . kids want to do – you know how it is. So I wasn't surprised they didn't know what she was up to – or what I was talking about when I told them. They were completely floored – to hear there was a boy.'

'Yes, I can imagine.'

'Her mother . . . she was so disappointed,' continued Silja.

'Not that Dagbjört had fallen for a boy from Camp Knox, you understand, but that she hadn't confided in her. They were very close and her mother was great, a really nice woman – always so kind to the rest of us. When she heard about this boy she refused to believe it, said I must have made a mistake.'

'But you hadn't?'

'No,' said Silja. 'I didn't make any mistake.'

'But –'

'Don't be like everyone else and start casting doubt on what I said. I didn't make it up.'

'No, I'm sure, but the boy never contacted the police.'

'No, he didn't.'

'Why do you think that was?'

'How should I know? I can't answer that.'

'No, of c—'

'I have absolutely no idea,' said Silja, lighting yet another cigarette and inhaling deeply. Her voice sounded weary. 'I was just repeating what she told me. Sometimes I wished she'd never told me about him. You've no idea what I went through at the time, and her poor parents hung on my every word because they had nothing else to go on.'

She glanced down blankly at the untouched cake.

'I don't know why it had to be me,' she said. 'I didn't ask for it. It was a really hard time for me too, you know. Really hard. I lost one of my best friends and as if that wasn't enough people cast doubt on every word I said. She'd asked me to keep it a secret, you see. I wasn't to tell anyone, she made me promise, and all of a sudden there I was having to blurt it out to all and sundry. At that stage she was still only missing. She could still have come back.'

The cafe was popular; there was a clinking of spoons and cups, a buzz of cheerful conversation. Every table was occupied and the air was thick with cigarette smoke. Trashy music – the latest Icelandic disco hit – was playing in the background.

'So all she told you was that she'd fallen for a boy from Camp Knox?' said Erlendur.

'Yes, that's more or less it. Next to nothing to go on, really. Naturally I was dying to know more but she said she'd tell me later. We'd just finished gym; I had to hurry into town and she was on her way home, and that was the last time I saw her. Next day she didn't turn up to school or to the meeting we'd arranged later that afternoon with the other girls, and then we found out she'd set out that morning and never arrived.'

'What made her tell you about the boy just then?'

'Well, Camp Knox had a bad reputation,' said Silja, 'and I remember I was saying my brother was afraid of the lads from there. According to him they were hooligans – which some of them definitely were. But she said they weren't all like that and when I started interrogating her, she told me about this boy she'd met who was no hooligan.'

'They were a similar age, then?'

'Yes, I assume so.'

'Could she have been making it up?'

'She had no reason to,' said Silja. 'Why would you think that?'

'Because the boy doesn't seem to have existed,' said Erlendur. 'He can hardly have failed to notice that the girl he was seeing had gone missing. They searched for her for weeks – in the camp as well. You'd have thought it would've been simplest for him to come forward and admit he'd known her, that he was the boy she'd been seeing, and try to help her family.'

'Unless he knew what'd happened to her?' said Silja.

'Exactly.'

'I've thought about it so often, wondering if he played some part in what happened to her. If she met him that morning and they quarrelled. Perhaps she was having second thoughts and tried to call it off – if there was anything to call off. How might he have reacted?'

Silja wasn't the only person who had thought along those lines. The police had always considered it likely that the young man might have been involved in her disappearance, and Erlendur had come to the same conclusion after reading up on the case. The man could still be alive today, in possession of the solution to the mystery. He would be in his mid-forties by now, if he was around Dagbjört's age. Silja seemed to anticipate what he was going to say next.

'Yes, I'm sure the man existed,' she murmured, so quietly Erlendur could hardly hear her. 'Dagbjört wasn't lying. And I know I'm not either.'

'No, of course not.'

'I believe he's still alive,' she whispered. 'In fact I'm sure he's still alive and knows exactly what happened to her.'

18

Vernhardur lived in the town of Hafnarfjördur, a few miles south of Reykjavík, and was happy to come to the CID offices in Kópavogur. He turned up punctually and asked for Erlendur, who had spoken to him on the phone. They took a seat in the office with Marion. Dusk was already falling, and it didn't help that the weather was dull and overcast. The sun hadn't shown its face for days. It didn't bother Erlendur but Marion would have given anything to see a break in the clouds.

Like Kristvin, Vernhardur was a flight mechanic. He was a tall, imposing man with an air of self-confidence that went well with his stately name. He didn't bite his nails but kept them short and neat. His face was clean-shaven apart from a fine pair of sideburns, and he had wavy fair hair, thinning on top.

He told them he had known Kristvin since he'd joined Icelandair. It had been Venni's job to show him the ropes and he had worked closely with Kristvin for the first few months and got on well with him. They were a similar age, both single and soon became good mates. He couldn't believe his ears when he heard that the man found at Svartsengi was none other than Kristvin, nor could he begin to imagine what had happened to him.

'It just doesn't make sense,' he said. 'Kristvin was a gentle guy who stayed out of trouble and didn't have a bad word to say about anyone. That he should end up like that is just, well, like I said, it doesn't make sense. How's his poor sister? He took really good care of her. Maybe you know she's ill?'

Erlendur nodded. 'We found various items in his possession that we have reason to believe came from the base,' he said. 'Beer, vodka and so on. Do you know where he got hold of them? Who his contacts were?'

'He was so afraid of losing her,' Vernhardur continued, as if he hadn't heard the question. 'I've never met a brother and sister so close, such good friends. He was devastated when he heard about the cancer. She put off telling him until he'd started to suspect something was wrong, and . . . he just refused to believe it, couldn't accept that she was so ill. He was determined to help her in any way he could. Whatever it took.'

'Like buying drugs from the base?'

'She told you? What he got for her?'

'If you mean the marijuana . . .'

Vernhardur nodded.

'Any idea who his dealer was?'

'He was in contact with some soldiers. I don't know their names. He didn't tell me and I didn't ask. Didn't want to know. I don't bring anything home from the base myself. No alcohol or cigarettes or sweets. Nothing. And I don't mix with anyone who works there apart from the other Icelanders.'

'Why not?' asked Marion.

'I'm against the army,' said Vernhardur. 'All that black-market shit associated with it. I'm totally against all that. I hate the fact that every time I go to work I have to pass through a bloody military checkpoint. Hate it.'

'If your friend was scoring drugs for himself and his sister,' said Marion, 'why are you so surprised he got into trouble? It's hardly like popping down to the shop for a can of Coke.'

'Well, of course you never know what sort you'll run up against in that scene,' said Vernhardur, 'what kind of scumbags they have in the army. He said it wasn't risky. The quantities were so small it was no big deal.'

'How did you find out? Did he tell you?'

Vernhardur nodded again. 'You mustn't think I was involved – I wasn't. No way. You may think that but I assure you I wasn't. Just to be clear.'

It was the day Kristvin told Vernhardur about his sister's illness. They used to take turns driving to and from work in Keflavík. One day when Kristvin was in the grey Corolla and they were about to head home, he said he needed to run a quick errand and asked Vernhardur to wait for him by the PX – he would only be ten minutes. Vernhardur protested but Kristvin was insistent and set him down by the store. Vernhardur had never set foot in the PX and had no wish to go inside now. Besides, he knew Icelanders needed a sponsor – a member of the Defense Force to sign them in – if they wanted to use any of the facilities or visit the clubs on the base. Vernhardur had never got to know any of the Americans and wasn't interested in doing so. He hung about outside the PX for almost half an hour, feeling like a bum, and was fuming by the time Kristvin came to pick him up. As they drove down to the gate, Vernhardur gave him an earful and Kristvin apologised profusely and promised to explain. Vernhardur thought Kristvin seemed jittery for some reason. As a rule the guards on the gate were fairly lax and the Icelanders who worked on the base and passed this way regularly were waved through. But occasionally there was an unexpected crackdown, as seemed to be the case now.

It was the end of the working day, a queue had formed at the gate and they noticed that a car had been called out for closer inspection. There were three vehicles ahead of them and the first was also signalled to pull over. The next car was waved through, as was the one in front of them. A US serviceman and an Icelandic police officer were manning the gate while another pair searched the cars. Kristvin drove slowly through the barrier, then was given a sign to stop. 'Shit! They're never going to search me?' Vernhardur heard him mutter in a panic. The policeman scrutinised them both through the windscreen, then waved them on. Kristvin heaved a sigh of relief. When they looked back they saw the car behind them being pulled over.

It was blatantly obvious that Kristvin was smuggling some-thing off base – presumably whatever it was that he had fetched while he made his workmate wait for him outside the PX. Vernhardur demanded to know what he was carrying and Kristvin was evasive, insisting he had only fetched a couple of cigarette cartons from the vending machines in the barracks. Vernhardur didn't believe this for a minute – Kristvin wouldn't have been that stressed out about something so trivial – and said he had a right to know. Kristvin had put him at risk without warning him. He had narrowly escaped being arrested for Kristvin's crime and might even have had to do time in prison as a result. It was unbelievably irresponsible and Vernhardur was furious that Kristvin would be so selfish and such a total fucking dickhead as to mix him up in that sort of crap. In the end, Kristvin pulled over in the Hvassahraun lava field and switched off the engine. He explained to Vernhardur that his sister had cancer and that he was supplying her with marijuana to make her life more bearable. He refused to reveal his source but admitted that the drugs were concealed in the passenger door on Vernhardur's side. He had tampered with the panel on the door so it was easy to prise off, and there was a compartment inside. It couldn't be simpler. 'I'm really sorry, mate,' said Kristvin. 'I don't know what I was thinking of. I didn't stop to consider that you were with me. It just didn't cross my mind. Honest!'

'The poor guy, he was mortified,' Vernhardur said. 'Kristvin wasn't the type to get involved in big-league stuff, quite frankly, but he was prepared to do it for his sister.'

'Were there other times, do you know?' said Marion.

'Not that I'm aware of. After that we drove to work in our own cars. Separately. We never referred to the incident again.'

'But he carried on?'

'I wouldn't know.'

'You must have gone ballistic,' said Erlendur.

'I did. He had no right to risk my neck like that. I told him he was crazy – the door was the first place they'd look.'

'So you had no part in it?' said Marion.

'No way,' said Vernhardur.

'And you don't know if he scored any more drugs, or how he financed them, or who he supplied, other than his sister?'

'No.'

'And we're just supposed to believe you.'

'I knew you'd try and implicate me, I said so at the beginning, didn't I? I'm not lying. I'm telling you exactly how it was. I didn't have to mention it but I did. I thought the information might help you.'

He looked at them both, his face grave. 'The marijuana wasn't only for Nanna. Kristvin had picked up the habit long before. But I don't believe he was dealing or making any money out of it. He wasn't the type. He was only buying for himself and his sister.'

'Did he pay for it in dollars?' asked Erlendur.

'I didn't ask. But he must have done if he bought it on the base.'

'Were you working with him in Hangar 885?' asked Erlendur.

'No, I haven't been there in a while.'

'But you know it, of course?'

'Sure.'

'Are you familiar with an airline whose planes are serviced there – American, called Northern Cargo Transport?'

'Yes, I've . . . I know we serviced a Hercules for them recently. Faulty landing gear. In fact Kristvin was working on that in the big hangar – Hangar 885.'

'He didn't happen to mention anything about it, did he?' asked Marion.

'No. What . . . like what?'

'I don't know, anything. Like, for example, what cargo it was carrying, or what he'd seen in the hold?'

'No, he didn't. Did something happen there? In the hangar?'

'Not as far as we know,' said Marion.

'There was another thing Kristvin told me while we were parked up in Hvassahraun,' added Vernhardur hesitantly.

'Oh?'

'I don't know if it has any bearing.'

'What was it?'

'He was rattled after the near miss at the gate and the bollocking I'd given him. And he'd just told me about his sister's illness. He seemed at the end of his tether and let something slip that you should maybe know about.'

'What was it?' asked Marion again.

'He didn't say it in as many words but he implied that he was seeing a woman and that she lived on the base.'

'Really?'

'And she wasn't Icelandic either.'

'An American?'

Vernhardur nodded.

'What were his exact words?' asked Erlendur. 'Can you remember?'

'He didn't come right out with it. I just read between the lines. He was very embarrassed and only hinted at it, like I said, but I twigged at once. He'd got into some kind of relationship with a woman on the base. We didn't discuss it again and I didn't ask any questions. Besides, we saw a lot less of each other after the smuggling incident. But from what Kristvin said, he was going to have to break it off and I assume he did.'

'But you don't know for sure?'

Vernhardur shook his head. 'Just to complicate things, the woman was married.'

'You mean . . .?'

'Yes.'

'. . . to an American serviceman?'

'Yup.'

19

After Vernhardur had left, Erlendur and Marion drove into Reykjavík and went for a meal at Skúlakaffi. It was nearing supper time and Skúlakaffi offered a range of traditional Icelandic dishes, such as salted lamb and boiled haddock, at affordable prices. It was patronised by labourers and lorry drivers who knew they could be sure of a quick, substantial meal there, followed by coffee and *kleinur*. Though no one would claim that the cafeteria, with its worn lino and grubby canteen atmosphere, represented exactly haute cuisine, you could hardly find a more loyal or satisfied clientele anywhere in Reykjavík.

Erlendur and Marion sat down at a quiet table. One of the dishes of the day was the traditional winter delicacy of fermented skate with melted dripping, and Marion was worried that the fish's uniquely putrid stench – a gross combination of decay and urine – would cling to their clothes. But Erlendur couldn't care less and asked for a generous helping of skate with a good dollop of dripping and thickly buttered rye bread on the side. He set to with such gusto, ravenous after his long day, that it was almost impossible to get a word out of him between mouthfuls. Marion, more fastidious, sedately ate a hamburger with gravy, potatoes and redcurrant jelly, and reflected that it would be necessary later to air one's clothes on the balcony and rinse the stench of skate out of one's hair.

Marion remarked that members of the 57th Fighter Squadron at Keflavík had once been quoted as describing Iceland as a 'hardship post': few servicemen stayed longer than a year, though some stayed two or three, especially if they had their families in tow, and most were only too glad to leave once their tour of duty was over. As a result there was a fairly quick turnover of personnel.

'They complain that most of their time here's spent running for cover from the weather,' Marion added.

'Hardship post?' echoed Erlendur, carving into the congealed fat and shovelling it into his mouth with his knife. 'We're just one big barracks slum to them, aren't we? One big . . . Camp Knox.'

Marion smiled. There was some indefinable quality about Erlendur – defensiveness, perhaps – that made him seem tiresomely pig-headed to many, but which Marion found almost charming. Unlike the weather-battered Americans, Erlendur would never use words like 'hardship' or 'inhospitable' to describe a barely habitable wasteland like Midnesheidi.

Marion watched Erlendur wolf down the fermented skate, carefully scraping up the last of the dripping and eating it with relish. He was in his element. But no one who worked with him could have failed to notice that he had been unusually morose of late. Marion put it down to what people had been gossiping about in the office, though not in Erlendur's hearing: his recent divorce.

'I also discovered,' said Marion, pushing away the plate, 'that Hangar 885 was originally built in the fifties for B-36 Peacemakers, the biggest bombers ever made, with a range halfway round the world. That's why it's so vast.'

'Do you think Kristvin could have fallen from the roof in there?'

'The impact injuries the pathologist described imply as much, but the question is what was he doing climbing about up there?'

'Perhaps he threw himself off. Killed himself.'

'And the blow to the back of his head?'

'Banged it on the rafters.'

'And afterwards some person or persons unknown took his body and disposed of it off base?'

'They didn't want to draw attention to the hangar,' said Erlendur. 'It's a base for spy planes, isn't it?'

'What reason would he have had for killing himself?'

'His sister's got an incurable illness.'

'Yes, but he's helping her. Surely he's not going to abandon her just when she needs him most?'

'All right, you've got a point. So it's not suicide.'

'Perhaps he saw something he shouldn't have in the hangar.'

'In addition to which, he was involved in smuggling and acquired the goods from a party we know nothing about, and to cap it all he's got a woman on the base who's married to a soldier. Presumably one of those airmen of yours, who's found out for himself just what kind of hardship post Iceland can be . . .'

'And attacked Kristvin?'

'Maybe he owed the guy money? He was buying dope regularly

from some soldier and maybe he'd got into debt. Then the guy gets wind of the fact he's on the base that evening and pays him a visit.'

'It's as good a guess as any other,' acknowledged Marion.

'Well, I don't know, I haven't the foggiest about what happened in there,' said Erlendur.

Marion shrugged and took out a packet of cigarettes.

'Any news of Camp Knox?'

'No, not much,' said Erlendur. 'I talked to Dagbjört's friend who was the source for the boyfriend and she's sticking to her story. Insists there was a boy. She's convinced he's still out there and might know something. Might even have been responsible for doing away with Dagbjört.'

'Yes, that's an old theory,' said Marion.

'Quite.'

'Do you think it's too late to visit Kristvin's sister?' asked Marion, looking at the clock on the wall.

'Shall we go and find out?'

'By the way,' said Marion, standing up, 'is it right what I hear, that you've just got divorced? Not that it's any of my business.'

'No, you're right,' said Erlendur, pushing away his plate. 'It's none of your business.'

20

Nanna didn't comment on the lateness of the hour. She was clearing up after supper but invited them in and asked if the police were any closer to finding out how Kristvin had died; if that was the reason for this unexpected visit. Marion said they weren't, but that various facts had emerged that they needed to run by her.

She finished tidying up the kitchen, put on some coffee and they sat down. The odour of Skúlakaffi still hung around Marion and Erlendur.

'Have you been eating skate?' Nanna asked bluntly.

'He has,' said Marion, pointing accusingly at Erlendur. 'The place stank to high heaven. Has it followed us here?'

'We could take our coats off, if you like,' Erlendur offered apologetically.

'No, it doesn't matter,' said Nanna, 'I like skate.'

'Are you sure?'

'Yes.'

Erlendur removed his coat anyway and, taking Marion's too, went and hung them up in the small cloakroom. When he returned, he told her that Vernhardur had been in to the station and had described how her brother had gone about smuggling the marijuana off base. He had quite simply concealed the drugs in a hollowed-out compartment in the car door, then driven through the gate on a wing and a prayer. The panel on the passenger door had clearly been tampered with and forensics had found the compartment which, though empty, still contained traces of the marijuana. This had to some extent corroborated Vernhardur's story. It was clear that Kristvin had taken a major risk every time he carried the drugs off the base in such an amateurish fashion.

'He said he had a good excuse,' said Nanna, when Erlendur had finished. 'Said they'd listen when he told them why he was doing it. I know he was inexperienced – he was a complete amateur, like you said. I was always afraid he'd get into . . . into some kind of trouble, and begged him to stop. It wasn't worth it.'

'Are you positive he didn't tell you where he got the drugs from?' asked Marion.

'He wanted to keep me out of it. Said the less I knew, the better it would be for both of us. Kristvin could be very stubborn like that. I stopped asking and he never told me anything.'

'I'm afraid that doesn't sound very plausible to us,' said Marion. 'I hope you understand that.'

'I'm not lying. It's how he wanted it.'

'One would have thought you'd have been anxious to know what kind of risks your brother was running by scoring drugs for you. You don't seem like the type to let him hide things from you. Even if he was only acting in your interests.'

'I don't know what else to say. It's up to you whether you believe me or not. I . . . I'm trying not to think about the fact that he might have . . . that it might have been my fault he died in such a terrible way.'

'You must understand how vital it is that you tell us the absolute truth.'

'I do. Of course I do.'

'Did your brother ever mention working in one of the American hangars, Hangar 885?' asked Erlendur.

'Yes, he mentioned it from time to time,' said Nanna, thinking back. 'They could use the facilities there when they had a lot on. They had a bay or something, but they had to keep to it. It was a controlled area. The army kept planes in there that they weren't allowed anywhere near. They steered clear of them or it would have jeopardised Icelandair's relations with the military. Nobody wanted that.'

'So he didn't snoop around at all?'

'No . . . that is . . .'

'What?'

'No, I don't suppose it's relevant, it's . . . it must have been about a year ago . . .'

'What?'

'There's a man I used to know, a journalist,' said Nanna, and from her expression it was clear she was reluctant to speak of him. 'He and Kristvin were mates – at least until we split up. He was my boyfriend. A bit of a jerk, really. Rúdólf. He . . .' Nanna shook her head.

'What?' prompted Marion.

'It was my fault for getting into such a rubbish relationship. I didn't see it until too late.'

'What didn't you see?' asked Erlendur.

'What a little shit he was. He made a quick exit when he heard about my cancer. I don't know what I saw in him. We met at a disco and ... anyway ... His name's Rúdólf, did I already mention that?'

Marion nodded.

'He asked Kristvin to look into some business on the base for him. In that hangar, if I'm remembering this right. There was some airline Rúdólf wanted information about.'

'Which airline?'

'I've forgotten.'

'Northern Cargo Transport?' suggested Erlendur.

'Something like that, yes, I'm not sure. Northern Cargo Transport. That sort of name. Rúdólf wanted Kristvin to take pictures for him and do a bit of digging around. But that was, you know, about a year ago, so I don't think ... Is it likely to be relevant at all?'

'I don't know,' said Marion. 'We may need to speak to this Rúdólf.'

'Please don't let on that I gave you his name. There's no need, is there? I'd managed to wipe him from my memory. Completely. Oh God, he might start ringing again.'

'We won't say a word,' promised Erlendur. 'Do you know what he was after – Rúdólf, I mean?'

'No. He was curious about this airline. I think Kristvin had mentioned it. That it was a bit fishy. Rúdólf thought there might be a story in it. Offered to get him a camera and everything.'

'In what way fishy?'

'I don't know. But I don't think Kristvin did anything about it. He was shit-scared of losing his job if he did what Rúdólf wanted, though that didn't stop Rúdólf bugging him about it. Saw himself as some kind of . . . hotshot reporter – what do they call it?'

'Investigative journalist?'

'That's it,' said Nanna. 'The pathetic little creep.'

'Is it possible that your brother was in trouble because he owed money to someone on the base?' asked Erlendur. 'Did he ever drop any hints to that effect?'

'No.'

'There's another matter we wanted to ask you about, regarding your brother's activities on the base,' said Marion.

'Oh?'

'I don't know if you're aware, at least you haven't told us . . .'

'Of what?'

'Vernhardur reckons Kristvin had a woman there.'

'Seriously?'

'Do you know anything about that?'

'A woman? No.'

'Your brother didn't go into any details but that was the impression he gave Vernhardur,' said Erlendur.

'Then it must have been very recent,' said Nanna. 'Or he'd have told me.'

'Not necessarily that recent,' said Marion. 'Vernhardur found out, or at least your brother hinted as much, some time ago, when Kristvin accidentally mixed him up in one of his smuggling trips.'

'Who's the woman?'

'She's married, apparently,' said Marion.

'Married? No . . . no way. Really?'

'So you didn't know?'

'No. Not a thing. This is the first I've heard of it. Married?'

'To a member of the Defense Force,' said Marion. 'An American serviceman.'

'You've got to be kidding.'

'Perhaps it was over straight away,' said Erlendur, seeing how much the news had upset Nanna. 'Just a quick fling he didn't think it worth telling you about.'

Erlendur seemed to be going out of his way to excuse her brother and soften the blow. Marion wondered if it was a good or bad quality in a policeman to let oneself become involved in a case like this.

'Anyway,' intervened Marion, 'it's possible that the husband, this soldier, had a bone to pick with your brother.'

'I just had no idea.'

'No,' said Marion. 'Maybe there was more to your brother than met the eye.'

21

The following morning Marion tried to get hold of Caroline Murphy. She had given them her phone number at military police headquarters and Marion rang it several times without success. Meanwhile Erlendur was on the trail of Rúdólf. Nanna thought he had moved recently but didn't know where. There was no reporter with that name listed in the phone book, so the obvious course was to ring the Association of Journalists. There Erlendur learned that Rúdólf was not at present employed, either by a paper or broadcaster. He had lost his job on an evening paper some time ago. The person who answered the phone was unable to divulge the reason, stating only that it was private, but gave Erlendur Rúdólf's address and telephone number. He rang the number, only to discover that it had been disconnected.

Shortly before lunchtime Erlendur and Marion knocked on the door of a small basement flat. It was on Öldugata, in the west of town, in a rather dilapidated corrugated-iron-clad house that had once in its heyday been painted red. Little remained but flaking patches of colour, and the frames of the single-glazed windows were rotten from battling the elements without any help from the owners. A chimney poked up from the roof with a television aerial attached. The wire ran down to the first floor. From there another ran down to Rúdólf's flat.

Erlendur rapped a second and a third time before finally he heard a noise and a man appeared in the doorway, still bleary-eyed with sleep. He looked as if he had stepped straight out of bed, standing there in nothing but his underpants and a duvet wrapped round his shoulders, below which protruded spindly legs and bare feet, with an ugly case of athlete's foot on both big toes, Erlendur noticed.

'What . . . what's all this noise in aid of?'

'Are you Rúdólf?' asked Erlendur.

'Yes, my name's Rúdólf. Who are you?'

'We're from the police,' said Erlendur. 'We'd like a word, if we can come in.'

'In here?' said Rúdólf, as if he had never heard such a preposterous idea.

'Or you could come with us, if you'd rather,' said Erlendur. 'Makes no odds.'

'You what . . . am I under arrest?'

'No, of course not,' said Erlendur. 'We just need to ask you a few questions about a story you were interested in a while back, to do with the NATO base at Keflavík.'

'Hang on, I'll pull on some clothes,' said Rúdólf and moved out of sight. Before long he appeared in the doorway again, this time wearing a pair of tight green trousers and dragging a T-shirt over his head. He hadn't bothered with socks. 'Maybe you should come in,' he said. 'Sorry about the mess, I . . .'

His words trailed off. Erlendur told him not to worry and entered his lair. Marion followed, closing the door behind them. The flat was nothing but a bedsit with a tiny kitchenette and a desk with an old typewriter on it. The bathroom was out in the entrance hall. The mess Rúdólf had apologised for was unbelievable: a chaos of old newspapers and documents, interspersed with milk cartons and leftovers. A fetid odour of rotting food hung over the place, from rancid meat or sour milk. Rúdólf was apparently conscious of the smell since he hastily opened a couple of windows.

'I'd make coffee but, you know, the machine's kaput,' he said, sitting down on the edge of his bed. There was a chair at the desk which Marion drew out. Erlendur, finding nowhere to sit, took up position by one of the windows in the hope of snatching a breath of fresh air. 'So what's this story you were talking about?'

'We believe you knew Kristvin who was found –'

'Krissi? Yeah. Are you here because of him?'

'We hear you asked him to do you a favour since he worked on the base –'

'Who told you that?' asked Rúdólf. 'Was it his sister? Did Nanna tell you that? Was she talking about me?'

'We found a note among Kristvin's belongings,' improvised Erlendur, honouring his promise not to mention Nanna in her ex-boyfriend's hearing. 'What exactly did you ask him to do for you?'

'A note? What kind of note?'

'About a foreign airline that used the airport and –'

'Is that why he was killed?' asked Rúdólf, waking up slightly. He had obviously been drinking the night before and was struggling not only with the unexpected visit but a crippling hangover as well.

'Just to be clear, Rúdólf,' said Marion, 'anything we discuss here is strictly confidential. We understand you're a journalist, though you're not employed at present, but you can't use any of the information revealed in our conversation. I hope you appreciate that. If you do, it could compromise our investigation.'

'Of course,' said Rúdólf. 'Hey, I used to handle the police news. I'm a pro,' he added airily.

'Good.'

'I've got quite a lot on actually,' Rúdólf continued, as if he felt compelled to justify himself. 'I'm a freelance hack and write for various rags. The fishermen's paper and so on. Besides, I heard they're going to offer me my old job back; it's only a question of time –'

'A hack?' queried Erlendur.

'Yeah, hack.'

'Is that . . .?'

'Hack, man, don't tell me you've never heard of that?' said Rúdólf, waking up properly now.

'You mean you're some kind of pen for hire?'

Rúdólf clearly didn't think this worthy of a reply. He retrieved a pair of socks from under the bed, sniffed them, then put them on. Marion asked if he knew anything about Kristvin's relationships with women but Rúdólf said it was ages since he'd had any contact with him so he couldn't help them on that score. Though did that mean Krissi had finally managed to get his leg over? Marion left this unanswered; the less information they gave this journalist the better. Exercising the same caution, Erlendur enquired about Kristvin's purchase of cigarettes and alcohol from the base. Rúdólf admitted having enjoyed the perks while he was seeing Nanna, but said his friendship with Kristvin had ended as soon as he and Nanna split up. He seemed unaware of the drugs; at least he didn't bring them up.

'She has cancer,' said Marion.

'Yeah, I know,' said Rúdólf. 'Total bummer.'

'And you split up.'

'Not because of that – she didn't say that, did she?'

'No.'

'It was just over between us, you know. Shit happens.'

'I'm sure,' said Marion. 'So you don't know if Kristvin was seeing a woman on the base?'

'No. No idea.'

'Did you know of any friends he had there? Icelandic or American?'

'Nope. None.'

Marion steered the conversation back to the foreign airline. Rúdólf was looking much brighter. He had found a hip flask with some spirits left in the bottom and drained it, then tossed the flask on the bed.

'Krissi told me about the Hercules transports the Icelandic crew serviced at NAS Kef,' he said, wiping his mouth. 'They land here fairly regularly, and if they require maintenance, they call on Krissi and his crew, you follow?'

'Nass Keff?' repeated Erlendur, puzzled.

'Yeah, NAS Kef – Naval Air Station Keflavík. Come on, you must have heard the term? Don't you understand anything? Are you from the countryside or –?'

'Just keep talking,' said Marion, signalling to Erlendur to lay off Rúdólf.

'They claim these aircraft belong to a commercial company, so they're treated as if they're from an ordinary civilian operator,' said Rúdólf, glaring at Erlendur. 'That's why the Yanks don't handle the maintenance if they have to stop over here. Icelandair takes care of them just like all the other civilian aircraft that pass through Kef.'

'And Kristvin thought there was something dubious about that?' said Erlendur.

'We used to debate these kinds of issues,' said Rúdólf loftily. 'I was with his sister at the time . . . You've talked to Nanna – did she ask after me at all?'

'No.'

'I don't get it . . . just don't get why she gave me the boot. I've never understood.'

'It's a mystery,' said Erlendur, his eyes travelling round the squalid flat.

'What did Kristvin "debate" with you?' asked Marion.

'This airline,' said Rúdólf, still frowning at Erlendur, uncertain how to interpret his comment.

'What did he say?'

'He? It was more like what I told him. I ran a few checks, called up some of my contacts – I was still at the paper then, you know.'

'Right.'

'In the first place, commercial companies don't operate Hercules,' said Rúdólf. 'They're military transports built for the army and civilian airlines don't use them. So Krissi and I were wondering what a private outfit was doing flying Hercules. Then one of them stopped in transit here and they had to do repairs on it in the big hangar –'

'Hangar 885?'

'Yeah, right, 885. And because it was the landing gear, they had to unload the cargo and it turned out the hold was jam-packed with weapons and among all the crates there was only a whole bloody tank that they had to roll out onto the ground. Krissi'd never seen anything like it. They covered the lot with tarpaulins. Krissi and his crew repaired the undercarriage, then they were told to beat it.'

'Did Kristvin witness the unloading?'

'Yeah . . . well, no, he saw the cargo after they'd covered it up. He took a peek under the tarpaulins and saw what they were transporting. He was curious. He knew the stuff had come out of the plane.'

'Did anyone see him?'

'No. He didn't think so. After that they hastily reloaded and the plane went on its way.'

'And what did Kristvin intend to do with this information?'

'You mean what did *we* intend to do with it?'

'Yes, of course, what did *you* intend to do?' asked Marion, with a weary roll of the eyes at Erlendur.

'I asked him to snap a few pics next time, lent him a camera and all, but the weeks went by and nothing happened. Then I lost my job.'

'Didn't you tell your editor about this?'

'Sure,' said Rúdólf. 'I wanted to go down to the base, take photos in the hangar and talk to the guys there, but we were refused permission and there wasn't much interest in the story at the paper. The bunch of reactionaries who own it didn't want to piss off the Yanks or something. The big papers here are more about burying news than digging it up.' He paused for effect.

'Did it happen again?'

'No, or at least not that Krissi told me. He gave back the camera. Said he couldn't risk lugging it around at work. We stopped talking after I broke up with Nanna. It was over between us. All of us.'

'Do you remember what the airline was called?'

'Yes, it was . . . hang on . . . it ended in "trans" something, "transfer", or . . .'

'Could it have been Northern Cargo Transport?'

'Hey, that's it,' said Rúdólf. 'Northern Cargo Transport. Krissi found that out. He also found out that the plane was in transit from Europe to South America. He didn't know where exactly but of course there's all kinds of conflicts there.'

'I don't follow,' said Marion. 'What do you mean?'

'They were obviously shipping arms.'

'So?'

'Handled by a civilian operator. Northern Cargo Transport.'

'So?'

'So why? Why aren't the Yanks using their own Hercules transports? Tell me that.'

'Do you think Kristvin might have found out why?' asked Marion.

'Dunno. But it's entirely possible.'

Later that day a dispatch marked 'Confidential' arrived from Fleet Air Command. It was their response to the reiterated letter rogatory that had been issued by the state prosecutor's office and police commissioner to request all necessary access to the military base for an investigation into the death of an Icelandic citizen. The letter had stated that there were grounds for believing that the man had been murdered on the naval air station, and that the Defense

Force's assistance with the investigation of the incident would be not only welcome but essential. The inquiry's findings were briefly outlined to explain how it had come to focus on Kristvin's work on the base, more specifically in Hangar 885.

Fleet Air Command's response stressed that, since no direct connection to Defense Force activities had yet emerged from the investigation, the military authorities saw no reason at the present time to cooperate with the Icelandic police or grant them access to restricted areas. This applied particularly to Hangar 885. It was pointed out that the naval installation was US territory and that, if the Icelandic police wished to question American nationals within the military zone, they would be required to submit a special application to the commander's office in each instance, and that all interviews would have to be conducted in the presence of the Defense Force attorney. However, since the Icelandic police's case was at present based on no more than conjecture, they could not expect further cooperation from the Defense Force at this time.

22

The woman bore all the signs of a tough life. From her hands with their swollen knuckles and fingers twisted into the palms it was evident that she was far gone with osteoarthritis. Her small eyes peered colourless from a face scored with wrinkles. Her skin was dry and withered, her lips sunken, and when she spoke her words were accompanied by a whistling through the gaps in her teeth. Her hair was a straggling grey mess. Erlendur had come across her name in the police reports from 1953. At the time she had been living in Camp Knox, struggling to bring up five children as a single mother. She was about seventy but looked ninety.

She lived on Bræðraborgarstígur in the west of town. Erlendur had rung her doorbell twice before he caught sight of a bent figure shuffling towards him, carrying a green net of groceries from the local shop and a shabby handbag. She was on her way home from work. As she came closer he noticed that she was a

129

little lame and wore a threadbare coat and a headscarf knotted under her chin. On her feet she had brown winter boots with woollen socks sticking over the tops.

'Who are you after?' she asked when she reached the door and began scrabbling in her handbag for her keys. Her voice was hoarse and tetchy, as if she didn't care for men hanging around on her doorstep.

'Baldvina,' said Erlendur. 'This is the right house, isn't it?'

'My name's Baldvina,' said the woman, surprised. 'Is it me you're looking for?'

'Yes, I suppose so.'

'Well, I never. What do you want?'

'I'd like a quick word, if you wouldn't mind.'

'What about?'

'You used to live in Camp Knox, didn't you?'

'Camp Knox? Why do you want to know that?' said the woman. She had her keys in her hand and was about to open the door but changed her mind. 'What's it got to do with you?' she added gruffly.

'I wanted to know if you could help me with something,' Erlendur said, noting how her guard had gone up at the mention of Camp Knox. 'I'm looking into the case of someone who went missing near there a long time ago.'

'What's that to do with me?' asked the woman. 'Who are you?'

'My name's Erlendur. You spoke to the police at the time in connection with the missing girl. Remember?'

'The girl?'

'Yes, she was called Dagbjört.'

'Oh, her, yes. I remember. What about her?'

'Could I possibly have a word with you about the incident? I promise it won't take long.'

'No, I can't help you, I'm afraid,' said the woman, opening the door. 'Just clear off, will you, and leave me alone?'

'People said she had a boyfriend in the camp. Do you remember?'

'They thought he'd killed her, didn't they? Easy to blame the camp people for everything. Buried under the floor of his hut, I expect.'

'I hadn't heard that,' said Erlendur. 'Was . . . is that what you've heard?'

'They built the swimming pool where the camp used to be. Expect she's buried under there now.'

Erlendur couldn't tell if she was making fun of him.

'Do you know who her boyfriend was?' he asked, hastily jamming his foot in the door as she tried to close it on him.

'Leave me alone, mister,' said Baldvina. 'I don't want to talk to you. Bugger off.'

'Her father died the other day,' said Erlendur. 'And her mother passed away some time ago. They never did find out what happened to their daughter. But I don't think they ever really stopped hoping she'd come back one day.'

He pulled out his foot and the door closed. A few seconds passed, then he heard the lock rattling and the woman opened the door again and peered at him.

'What did you say your name was?'

'Erlendur.'

She continued to eye him.

'What business is it of yours?'

'The girl's aunt hasn't quite given up hope of finding out what happened. She asked me to do some digging around for her.'

The woman was still sizing up the stranger, with suspicious, grey eyes.

'All right,' she said at last and began to hobble up the old wooden staircase. Erlendur slipped inside and tried to lighten her load by taking the shopping bag but she wouldn't hear of it. He caught some muttered comment about thieving scum. He followed her upstairs to the landing where she laid down the bag, put her key in the lock and opened the door.

'Well,' she said, 'come in then.'

'Thank you.' Erlendur entered the small flat. The woman turned on the lights and went into the kitchen to put away her shopping. Then she re-emerged, took off her coat and hung it in a cupboard.

'Don't just stand there,' she said. Erlendur had not dared to go into the sitting room without permission and was still hovering by the door. 'Go on, sit down. Excuse the state of the place. I'm not used to visits like this and to tell the truth I don't like 'em.'

'No, I'm sorr—'

'Don't waste time apologising, just get on with it and tell me what you want. Wait a moment, though. I should make us some coffee.'

With that she went back into the kitchen and before long a strong aroma of coffee wafted into the sitting room. As he took in his surroundings, Erlendur reflected that she had no need to be ashamed of her housekeeping. Despite the signs of poverty – the shabby old furniture, the lack of all ornaments apart from a few family photos – everything was spick and span. The photographs appeared for the most part to be of her children, grown up and surrounded by their own families. An impressively large

132

group. One daughter had died, he knew, and one of her sons was well known to the police and often on the streets. He'd been in trouble from a young age and still got on the wrong side of the law from time to time. He had crossed Erlendur's path now and then when he was an officer on the beat. There was an old photo of him with his brothers and sisters, and this made Erlendur feel oddly uncomfortable, as if he had been forced into a closer intimacy with the man than he would have liked.

'They didn't half make a fuss about that girl,' Baldvina remarked as she came in with the coffee.

'Yes, well,' said Erlendur, removing his gaze from the photos. 'It was a terrible business.'

'I don't know how I can help. Hasn't everyone forgotten all about it?'

'I gather you were a single mother at the time. It must have been a hard slog bringing up five children on your own,' said Erlendur, his eyes returning to the pictures.

'I had kids by three men,' said Baldvina. 'A mixed bunch. The first was a boozer, no use to anyone. The second was good to me. We had a decent life, had three kids together but then he went and died and left me on my own, and I had no choice but to move into the camp. He had an accident in Hvalfjördur. He was all right, the poor sod; he couldn't help what happened to him. The last one used to knock me about. Biggest piece of shit I ever met. There weren't any more and I'm bloody glad about it and that's a fact.'

Erlendur wasn't sure how to respond to this.

'Yes, the camp was a rough place,' continued the woman. 'I'm not one to grumble but it wasn't easy.'

'They weren't good places to live in, were they?' said Erlendur. 'The huts, I mean.'

'Good places to live in! Are you joking? Some of them may have been better than others but the ones I knew weren't fit for people. They were damp and cold and leaked and the smell of mould used to get into your clothes – "the smell of the camp", they called it. All you had to heat the place was a small oil stove, and oil cost an arm and a leg, and the hut never got properly warm. But the housing shortage was so dire you just had to put up with it. Families used to be squashed in three or four to a hut, with one small room each. Don't know what people would say to that nowadays. And the men used to get smashed out of their skulls and you'd have a hell of a time trying to see the buggers off.'

Baldvina took a mouthful of coffee, her gnarled fingers crooked around the cup.

'But the worst was the chill from the floor,' she said. 'You couldn't put the children down at all for the cold, and water used to collect under it during the spring thaw and flood up into the hut. Then there were the open sewers, and the rats . . .'

She stared down into her coffee cup.

'It's always the kids who come off worst in dumps like that,' she added, and Erlendur saw her gaze flicker to the photo of her son, the homeless alcoholic.

'You said you remembered Dagbjört walking past on her way to and from school?'

'Yes, though I was never sure. They showed us pictures and I thought it was the girl who walked past sometimes, but that's all I could tell them. I knew nothing about her. Never saw her in the camp. Then I heard she was supposed to have had the hots for a boy there but I didn't know anything about that either. Mind you, my friend Begga reckoned she'd been hanging about there, or a girl who looked like her, anyway. Begga lived in the hut next door. Died years ago. Don't know if the police ever talked to her.'

'Begga?' said Erlendur, unable to recall any reference to her in the files. 'I don't think so.'

'She told me once, when I bumped into her years later and we got talking about it, that one of the lads had moved out of the camp around the same time. Begga reckoned it was Stella's boy and that he left because of some business with a girl. Though it needn't have been that girl, I don't think. But maybe you could talk to my son Vilhelm. He may've known the lad. I have a feeling they were the same sort of age.'

'Stella's son? Who was Stella?'

'Oh, she had it tough, poor thing. I didn't see much of her after we moved out of the camp. Heard a few years ago that she was dead.'

'Do you know which boy it was? What he was called?'

'No, I don't. She had several sons. I expect he went off the rails like some of the other kids from the camp.' Baldvina looked back at the photo.

'Where can I find Vilhelm?'

'God knows. He's on the streets. Never been able to stick at anything. He's well meaning, though. Heart's in the right place. He came out of it worst of all my lot.'

'Out of Camp Knox?'

'Camp Knox was that sort of place.'

Erlendur pictured her son now, a frail homeless man with broken glasses. He had once dossed down in a hot-water pipeline, back when Erlendur was investigating the death of another tramp who had long been living rough and had ended up drowned in the old peat diggings in Kringlumýri.

Baldvina's eyes were lowered to her arthritic hands.

'No one was that bothered just because some girl had done herself in.'

23

It was late afternoon when Caroline finally answered the phone. She remembered Marion straight away. Marion wondered if it would be possible to meet her to ask a favour. Although initially reluctant, Caroline yielded in the face of Marion's polite insistence, said she was free that evening and suggested a time and place. Marion asked if they could meet in private. Caroline took a moment to grasp what was required.

'Somewhere off the beaten track would be best,' said Marion. 'I need to meet you where we can be sure we won't be disturbed.'

'Excuse me?'

'If there's some way you could arrange that, I'd be very grateful.'

'Why?'

'Also it would be better if you didn't mention our meeting to anyone.'

'Why . . . why all the secrecy?'

'We'd like to proceed with caution,' said Marion. 'We trust

you. And we don't know anyone else on the base. We won't try and force you to do anything you don't want to. I promise.'

Eventually, after a lengthy pause for thought, Caroline agreed to these conditions. Evidently she was less than enthusiastic about a clandestine meeting with the Icelandic police in connection with a murder that, in her opinion, had nothing to do with her or the US military. She said as much to Marion, adding that she didn't know what they expected of her. Marion asked her to be patient, to listen first before deciding whether or not to help them.

It had been Erlendur's idea that Marion should go alone to the meeting with Caroline. He believed Marion would get on better with her. Besides, there was no need for them both to go; that would only put her on her guard. Grudgingly Marion conceded to this logic and drove south through the early-winter darkness to Midnesheidi. Caroline had given directions to the bowling alley, and after driving through the gate and taking several wrong turns, Marion finally located the place. According to Caroline, the alley was closed for refurbishment. Marion parked some distance away, as she had suggested, found the unlocked back door and wondered how Caroline came to have access to the building when it was closed. She was there already, in ordinary clothes this time: jeans, a college sweatshirt, a thin leather jacket and sneakers.

'I don't like this one bit,' she said as Marion entered. 'I don't know why I'm doing this. Don't know why I agreed to meet with you here.'

'Thanks for going to all this trouble,' said Marion, surveying the empty lanes, the balls in their racks, the beer adverts on the walls. 'Maybe you wouldn't be doing it unless you were the tiniest bit curious.'

'I don't even know what I'm supposed to be curious about,' said Caroline. 'Perhaps you'd care to enlighten me.'

'Of course. There are two things we thought you might be able to help us with —'

'Why me? You don't even know me. You know nothing about me.'

'It's simple,' said Marion. 'We're just regular police officers, you and I. So we ought to understand what needs doing without making things overcomplicated. What we need is access to the police here on the base, but we don't want it to blow up into some major diplomatic incident involving senior military commanders and politicians from the Right and Left, and all the associated hassle. We don't want the press getting in on the act, or the anti-NATO protesters or . . . You see, we had a good feeling about you right from the start, so we wanted to ask if you would help us.'

'I'm not sure what you're talking about.'

'I'm talking about simplifying matters rather than complicating them. I'm talking about keeping things on a personal level.'

'What are the two things you need to know?'

'The Icelander whose body we found had fallen from a considerable height. Such a great height, in fact, that there aren't many places to choose from around here . . .'

'Did it happen on the base?'

'We believe so.'

'From a great height? Are you talking about one of the hangars?'

'Hangar 885, to be precise,' said Marion. 'The Icelander had a reason to be in the hangar because he was a flight mechanic and used to service aircraft there. His company has permission to use the hangar at busy times. We believe it's possible he may have witnessed something in there that cost him his life. We've no idea what it was but there's a chance it's linked to the airline we asked you about the other day—'

'Northern Cargo Transport.'

'That's right. They seem to be involved in some kind of arms shipments, according to a source in Reykjavík, and we wondered if you could check up on that for us. Find out what this company is. What connection it has to the army. And whether it transports weapons. Because if it's a civilian operator, that would be highly irregular.'

'No, that doesn't sound right,' said Caroline thoughtfully.

'Our guess is that if we start making inquiries about this airline through the usual, official channels, doors will be slammed in our faces. Of course, we'll have to go down that road sooner or later, but we'd like to gather information by other means first, if we possibly can.'

'I don't know how . . . what to believe. I don't know who you are. Don't even know what you do, though you claim to be a detective. This is all kind of . . . What's the other thing you want me to look into?'

'We heard that the Icelander, this Kristvin we were asking the residents about, known as Krissi –'

'Chrissy? Isn't that a girl's name?'

'It's short for Kristvin. Krissi with a "K".'

'It's kind of weird the way you use first names when you talk about strangers. It takes some getting used to.'

'It's an old custom here in Iceland,' said Marion.

'I'm aware of that.'

'Perhaps you're also aware that Icelandic women don't take their husband's name when they marry?'

'Yes,' said Caroline. 'Not such a bad idea.'

'No, not bad at all,' said Marion, smiling. 'I hope you don't mind if I call you Caroline?'

'No, that's fine.'

'The thing is, Kristvin had a girlfriend – or lover – on the base. According to our informant, she's married to a serviceman.'

'An American?' said Caroline in surprise. 'Usually it's the other way around – American men get involved with Icelandic women.'

'Yes. Anyway, we think that's why his car was here. He'd been visiting her.'

'We went round every single dorm in the neighbourhood,' pointed out Caroline.

'Well, we wanted to ask if you could go back. Alone this time. Put your ear to the ground. See what you can pick up. One of the residents might let slip some detail that could come in useful. I don't care how trivial. Everything matters.'

'You're not asking much.'

'I know,' said Marion. 'We've been over and over this, my colleague and I, and our conclusion was to approach you for help at this stage, then see what comes out of it. Kristvin was also smuggling marijuana off base, so his business at the barracks might have been related to that. We just don't know.'

'I don't think I told you,' said Caroline, 'but residents are assigned housing according to rank. The dorms where the car was found are enlisted quarters, for the lowest ranks and the least educated. But that doesn't mean they're all murderers, drug dealers or adulterers.'

'No, of course not,' said Marion.

'Not all the personnel are in a hurry to leave,' said Caroline. 'Lots of Icelandics work here and we're on good terms with them.

141

There are good schools, good stores. Maybe the weather could be a little better at times but, hey, you can't have everything.'

'True.'

'I think I'm going to have to turn you down,' said Caroline after a pause.

'Are you absolutely positive? You might want a bit longer to consider.'

'No, I can't do it.'

'All right,' said Marion. 'I don't mean to –'

'I can't work against the interests of the military. Surely you understand that? Regardless of what you guys claim happened. You'll just have to find some other way. It's . . . I can't believe I'm even discussing this.'

'Fine, no problem. All I was going to say is that if an Icelandic civilian has lost his life because of corruption in the army, it'll be easy for you lot to stonewall us and then we'll never solve the crime. We have no say over what the Defense Force does, and besides there are influential politicians and businessmen in our country who are only too willing to grovel to the US. And on the other side there are factions who are implacably opposed to it. So the only sensible way to investigate the incident is through people like us. Ordinary people like us.'

Caroline stared at Marion, the worry plain on her face.

'I can't help you,' she said decisively. 'I won't report our meeting but that's all I can do for you. Do you understand?'

'Are you quite sure?'

'Yes. I'm afraid so.'

'Well, thank you for at least agreeing to meet me,' said Marion. 'I hope you understand my position – why I'm asking this. I'd be grateful if you could keep it to yourself.'

'I've already promised that. But why the secrecy? Why don't you trust the military?'

'In this instance?'

'In general.'

'I think that question could equally be turned on its head,' said Marion. 'Why doesn't the military trust us?'

'That doesn't answer *my* question,' said Caroline.

'Fleet Air Command has no interest in answering questions about Hangar 885 and we can't put any pressure on them unless we know exactly what to ask. We sent a request for access to the area and cooperation with the inquiry into Kristvin's death. They responded that the matter had nothing to do with them. It looks as if they're going to be deliberately obstructive when it comes to anything involving US nationals on the base.'

'Is that so surprising?'

'No,' said Marion, 'maybe not. But we feel they're being unreasonable. They've reached a decision without being prepared to discuss the matter at all. Which makes it look as if they've got something to hide.'

'Like what?'

'Well, for example, if you could –'

'Oh no, I'm not getting mixed up in any of this,' said Caroline. 'No way.'

'If, for example, you could find out who was in Hangar 885 the evening Kristvin died,' persevered Marion. 'I mean, who does have access to it, in general?'

'As far as I know there's not much work going on in there at the moment because they're installing a fire-extinguisher system. So in the evenings it would be mainly security guards.'

'If you could find out who they were . . .'

'Like I said, you're putting me in an impossible position. I'm afraid you'll have to look elsewhere. Sorry.'

Caroline glanced at her watch and said she had to run. Their meeting was over.

'I've never been bowling,' remarked Marion, looking around the alley one last time before leaving again by the back door.

'You should try it sometime,' said Caroline, smiling in spite of her anxiety. 'It's fun.'

24

The house stood strangely dark and silent in the chilly evening air as Erlendur walked up to the door and unlocked it. The last owners had moved out some time ago and put it on the market, and Erlendur had received permission from the estate agent to view it on his own. The agent had told him he couldn't work out why there was so little interest in the property. Admittedly the house was small by today's standards and required some modernisation, but it was a solidly built pre-war concrete structure with plenty of scope for a family and a good-sized garden, he said, as if Erlendur were a potential buyer. Erlendur explained that he wanted to view the house for purely personal reasons; that it held memories for him – which was not a complete lie. The estate agent nodded, familiar with such requests. With people who saw their childhood home on the market and went to look round to indulge in a little nostalgia. Unfortunately, he didn't have time to take Erlendur there himself as it was late and he had to get off home, but Erlendur was welcome to borrow the keys and return them tomorrow. Erlendur had casually mentioned that he was a policeman.

He felt an odd frisson as he stepped into the narrow entrance hall. There was a rail for coats and a wide shelf above it for hats, scarves and gloves. He detected a faint smell of damp and suspected the roof had once leaked. A frosted-glass door led through to a small passage with a kitchen to the right, a sitting room straight ahead and a staircase up to the attic floor where the bedrooms were. He stood for a while in the quiet house, taking in his surroundings by the dim glow of the street lights: the worn carpet, the walls with the lighter rectangles where pictures had been taken down, the curtainless windows.

The kitchen faced the street and had a 'For Sale' sign with the estate agent's telephone number in the window. The fittings, heavy wooden cupboards with worn handles, appeared to be original. There was a small table under the window. He tried to recapture the smells of the past, the echo of voices from the days when all had been brightness and colour in here. Dagbjört's parents had moved out shortly after her disappearance and the house had undergone two changes of owner since then. Now it stood like a derelict farm in the heart of the city, lifeless and dead. It put Erlendur in mind of his parents' croft in the East Fjords, which stood exposed to the rain and wind. It gave him the same sense of transience, and he lamented that nothing could halt the passing of time.

The sitting room, which faced the back, had two large windows and a door from which three steps led down to the garden. Erlendur went over to one of the windows and looked out at the trees and shrubs in their winter sleep, the frosty lawn, the rose beds and currant bushes. The garden had been well cared for, the grass cut and neatly edged, the branches pruned.

Dagbjört had been learning the piano. When describing the house to him, her aunt had said that her parents had bought her an old upright that used to stand in the sitting room. Erlendur pictured it against one wall, the three-piece suite in the middle by the windows, and the dining table at the far end. He assumed the piece of furniture that housed the gramophone had also been kept in here. In his imagination he heard the excited chatter of the schoolgirls as they gathered for Dagbjört's birthday; the strains of 'Be My Little Baby Bumble Bee'.

He walked slowly up the stairs. They emitted a friendly creaking like a polite reminder to treat the empty house with respect. The landing was carpeted and Erlendur found himself in another narrow passage with three doors leading off it. The one nearest him stood ajar and pushing it open he entered the master bedroom. He didn't want to turn on the light; it felt somehow like trespassing. There was a faint illumination from the street and now that his eyes had adjusted to the gloom he could see quite well. The ceiling was high next to the landing but sloped down under the eaves on the other side of the room. A dormer window looked out over the street. There was a built-in wardrobe which was full height by the door but slanted down with the incline of the roof.

Next to the master bedroom was a small bathroom with a sink and bathtub and a mirror fixed to a medicine cabinet. Opposite this was Dagbjört's room which overlooked the neighbour's garden. After a brief hesitation, Erlendur stepped inside. For years he had been wondering about the girl who used to live here, about her life and fate, and now here he was, standing in her room, and although families had come and gone through the house since then, he felt he had never been closer to her than at this moment.

The first thing he noticed was that the view from the window was partly obscured by a stand of tall fir trees belonging to the next-door garden. Walking over, he looked out and saw that the plot on that side had long been neglected, the trees and shrubs allowed to grow wild and unchecked. The firs would have been considerably smaller a quarter of a century ago, so Dagbjört would have had a good view of her neighbour's house. Erlendur wondered if the same people still lived there. He could just glimpse the upstairs windows but couldn't see any lights.

He imagined that her bed must have been under the window, so she could have gazed out at the moon and stars and confided her secrets to them. He ran his hand over the cold walls, feeling the bumps and small cracks, and before he knew what he was doing he had begun to tap them and listen. The exterior walls were made of whitewashed concrete, the interior ones of wood, clad in some sort of insulating material. In those days insulation had sometimes consisted of no more than old newspapers and other rubbish, and Erlendur thought this might be the case here, judging by the hollow sound the walls gave off. He noticed a small door under the eaves which he assumed led to a storage space. The floor was made of varnished boards and he tapped those here and there as well. He didn't know what he was looking for. He hadn't come here to search for anything in particular, only to breathe in the atmosphere and acquaint himself with the house where she had lived. Well, he had done that now and had no wish to linger; he needed and intended to leave, but before he did so he would just check what was behind the little door under the eaves.

It sat flush with the wall and Erlendur hadn't noticed it until he'd started his tapping. The door was no more than a metre high and had a small keyhole but no frame. It was locked and Erlendur, who had nothing on him but a car key, tried his best to force it open, without success. He cast around for the key, then went downstairs to the kitchen again, turned on the light and started pulling out drawers in search of some implement to open the door with. In one drawer he unearthed three keys of varying sizes and dates, and took these up to the bedroom. The smallest key fitted the door under the eaves.

Erlendur lit a match and shone it into the cavity which was small, narrow and cold. There was nothing inside. He assumed the occupants of the house had used it to store the usual kinds of belongings that weren't required every day. The match burnt out and, lighting another, he shone it over the floor and up under the roof. In his heedlessness, he held the flame too long against the ceiling lining and singed it. Startled, he extinguished the match and ran a hand over the surface, terrified that he had set fire to it. As he fumbled in the dark, his fingers brushed against something that was poking out of the lining; it felt like a piece of paper.

Erlendur lit a third match and shone it up under the ceiling, carefully this time. He saw that he had burnt a small hole in the lining. He thanked his lucky stars that he hadn't been stupid enough to set the house on fire with his tampering. Through the hole, which was no larger than a coin, he glimpsed the roof timbers but when he illuminated the surrounding area better he spotted a split in the lining. That was where his fingertips had brushed against some unevenness; something that had been pushed into the crack for concealment and remained there ever since.

With great difficulty he managed to extract it from behind the lining paper: a few folded notes or sheets of paper. Having made sure there was nothing else in this odd little space under the eaves, he moved over to the dormer window to peer at what he had in his hands. There wasn't enough light, so he went into the bedroom that faced the street. It was slightly less dark in there and he could get a better idea of his discovery.

What he had in his hands turned out to be a few lined pages of diary size. The handwriting was for the most part pretty and neat, but in places it degenerated into a scrawl. On one page the name 'Dagbjört' had been copied out repeatedly in the margins, as if she had been practising her signature. The pages were like a message in a bottle from the past, a message which Dagbjört had not intended anyone to read yet couldn't quite bring herself to throw away. Some of the entries were dated, others not. Erlendur saw how her writing had matured from the first notes to what appeared to be the last. Several years had passed in the interim and they showed a young girl growing up. The oldest contained a declaration of love from when she was in the final year of junior school. She had a crush on a boy called Tommi and had decorated his name with small red hearts. Another page revealed she had been angry that day with an unnamed girl in her class. The last note consisted of only a few sentences, scribbled down the day she celebrated her eighteenth birthday.

It's so horribly creepy. I don't know if I can even tell Daddy and Mummy. He seems so harmless. And he's our neighbour. He thinks I can't see him. He stands in his window in the dark, staring at me while I'm getting ready for bed. When I turn off the lights and peer out, I can see him lurking in the shadows. God, it's so bizarre. What's he doing? Why does he stare in at me like that?

Erlendur read the girl's words again before finally raising his eyes from the pages, his mind filled with the silence of the house, the cruelty of fate, ignorance and oblivion.

25

On the way back to town Marion stopped off at the old sanatorium, having meant to go there for a while but never finding the time or the right occasion. Now that occasion had arrived out of the blue, postmarked Denmark. Over the years, the urge to visit the sanatorium had become more and more infrequent and it was a long time since Marion had last walked up the hill to Gunnhildur's Cairn. If patients made it up here in the old days it was a sign they were on the road to recovery. Marion had been admitted to Vífilsstadir, the TB sanatorium, as a child, with only one working lung, and had watched as other children the same age died.

The pavilion where the patients used to lie and recuperate in the fresh air still stood to the west of the main building but was dilapidated from years of disuse and neglect. After parking near the pavilion, Marion lingered briefly among the broken windows and flaking paint. The lights from the hospital cast a faint glow over the surroundings down as far as the lake. Now that TB had been eradicated, the hospital treated patients for other types of respiratory disorder.

Standing in the run-down pavilion, feeling the cold, Marion recalled the visitors who used to come at weekends and talk to their loved ones through the windows of the hospital because they weren't allowed inside. Many of Marion's most painful memories were associated with this place, and also with a spell at the Kolding Sanatorium in Denmark, arranged by Marion's grandmother, which had eventually led to recovery. There had been another Icelander there, a girl called Katrín, who had survived a severe case of pulmonary tuberculosis thanks to a procedure known as thoracoplasty, which involved sacrificing several ribs on one side so the infected lung could be collapsed and cleaned out. Their friendship had developed over the years into a kind of love affair, though Katrín had lived abroad for the most part, working for charity organisations around the world.

The letter from her mother, which had arrived that morning, was in Marion's pocket, read, reread and read again until the words were etched into the memory. Katrín's mother wrote that her daughter was dead. She had been diagnosed with cancer the year she sailed out to Iceland and ended her relationship with Marion. At the time she had only expected to live another twelve months at most. But in the event she had lasted another seven years. According to her wishes she had been cremated and her ashes scattered in Kolding Fjord.

Marion took the letter out now and read it one more time by the faint illumination from the hospital, and thought about Erlendur and his fascination with people who met sudden deaths in accidents, perished from exposure or were lost in the mountains. Once, finding him immersed in this sort of account, Marion had tried to understand what was going through his mind. The young policeman was a frequent source of curiosity to Marion since he seemed so independent in his thinking, was old-fashioned in his manner, never spoke about himself, disliked city life, and took little interest in the times he lived in except when they got on his nerves. He was single-minded, felt no need whatsoever to wear his heart on his sleeve and was perpetually absorbed by this peculiar fixation with ordeals and disappearances.

'What is it about people's suffering and death that you find so gripping?' Marion had asked.

'You can learn a lot about people from these stories,' Erlendur had replied.

'Who all just happen to have lost their lives in unusual circumstances?'

'You could put it like that.'

'But what's so instructive about that? About people getting lost? Dying? What is it you learn from that?'

Erlendur clearly found this hard to answer.

'Why are you asking?' he said at last.

'Because I'd like to know,' said Marion. 'You're the only person I've ever met who's obsessed with this subject.'

'I wouldn't say I was obsessed.'

'Well, you must admit you have an unusual fascination with these tales of ordeals.'

'What interests me are stories about survivors,' said Erlendur. 'People who escape with their lives from dangerous situations in the Icelandic wilderness. How do they cope? Why do some live while others don't, though the circumstances are similar? Why do some get into trouble and others not? What mistakes do people make? How can you avoid them?'

'I reckon there's more to it.'

'What's that supposed to mean?'

'I get the feeling these stories have a personal significance for you.'

'No, I . . .'

'Am I wrong?'

Erlendur stared at Marion, as if unsure whether to speak his mind.

'I suppose it's not exactly . . . not really about the people who get lost or die, but . . .'

'What?'

'. . . but the people left behind, left to struggle with the questions raised by the events.'

'You mean you're interested in those left behind to cope with the grief and loss?'

'Yes, maybe that's it,' said Erlendur. 'They matter too. "Which am I? The one who lives, or the one who died?" I sometimes wonder.'

'Are you a fan of Steinn Steinarr?'

'I think people who experience profound grief feel as if a part of themselves has died, and in my opinion he captures that very well.'

Marion read the letter again, thinking back to this conversation with Erlendur and the quotation from Steinn Steinarr's poem 'Time and Water'.

Enclosed in the letter had been a small piece of folded paper which, when opened, turned out to contain a pinch of Katrín's ashes. Katrín's mother would not herself have come up with the idea of sending them. She must have done it at Katrín's behest, as a final farewell between them. Marion could think of nowhere better to scatter the ashes than the pavilion, and holding out the paper, watched the dust gradually disperse in the wind.

Marion refolded the letter from Denmark, put it back in the envelope and pocketed it again, then gazed over to where the ashes had become one with the darkness, reflecting on Steinn Steinarr's enigma of life and death until the pale blue eyes blurred over with tears.

26

Two days later Erlendur received an unexpected phone call from Caroline. She asked for Marion first, but to everyone's surprise Marion had taken sick leave, an almost unheard of event. Learning that Marion wasn't available, Caroline asked to speak to Erlendur instead. He was taken aback as he'd heard that their meeting had not gone well. He was sitting in his office, going through the old files on the Dagbjört case yet again. He knew he shouldn't be spending time on this now as the investigation into Kristvin's death was top priority. But Dagbjört wouldn't leave him alone, especially since Erlendur had established that the same man was still living next door.

The reason for Caroline's call was simple. She had managed to track down the woman who had been having an affair with Kristvin.

'Are you sure?' asked Erlendur.

'Of course I'm sure,' said Caroline impatiently, 'or I wouldn't be calling. You two can meet her if you like. She's prepared to tell you all she knows, on condition we don't expose her affair, if possible.'

'That's her problem, isn't it?'

'I didn't make any promises.'

'Marion's not in today,' said Erlendur. 'But I could be with you in an hour.'

'Get moving then,' said Caroline, and gave him brief directions before saying a brusque goodbye.

Later she explained to Erlendur how, following her meeting with Marion at the bowling alley, she had gone about identifying the woman. It turned out she lived in the enlisted quarters they had visited a few days earlier. She had stayed in Caroline's mind because of her manner during the original interviews; the unease she had tried to conceal as she stood at the door of her apartment, fielding questions from the Icelandic police about whether she had known Kristvin. The woman had been alone at home and Caroline had felt instinctively that she was hiding something. So she went down to the PX, where the woman worked, struck up conversation with her and asked her in more detail about the grey Toyota Corolla and Kristvin. The woman stuck to her story, expressed surprise at the questions and repeated that she didn't know the Icelander.

Caroline spoke to her again that evening. The woman insisted she had nothing to say to her, but her nerve went when Caroline threatened to haul her in for questioning on suspicion of being involved in Kristvin's murder. The woman swore blind she'd had nothing to do with it but in the end reluctantly admitted that Kristvin may not have been a complete stranger to her. She admitted further that she was scared of her husband and didn't know what he would do if he ever found out she'd been cheating on him, and with an Icelander too, as he had a low opinion of the locals. Caroline asked if there was any chance he might already have heard about her affair and taken action, but the woman said it was out of the question. She and Kristvin had been incredibly careful. She was sure her husband knew nothing about her infidelity.

Caroline had asked Erlendur to meet them both behind the PX, and when he arrived the two women were standing there waiting for him. They climbed into the car and Caroline told him to drive over to the international passenger terminal. He stopped in the car park as if they were ordinary citizens there to pick up friends or relatives from the airport.

Caroline was sitting in the back seat with the woman, Joan, who was plump and blonde with a good-natured expression. She explained that in the evenings she sometimes filled in for her friend who was a cocktail waitress at the Animal Locker, the enlisted club, also known as the Zoo. That's where she had met Kristvin the first time. He had been in with a couple of friends, also flight mechanics, she thought, and the two of them had got talking at the bar. He had told her he loved the States, he had trained there and wouldn't mind living there one day. With his qualifications he could work anywhere in the world and reckoned he would have no problem finding a job in the Promised Land. He had been offered positions by some major airlines when he'd finished his training and had big plans for the future. It was clear he'd been showing off, flirting with the cocktail waitress at the Animal Locker.

'So did you two start meeting up after that?' asked Caroline.

'You promised this wouldn't go any further,' said Joan with a slightly sing-song drawl that Erlendur associated with the Deep South. She'd been smoking when she got into the car and was already lighting the next cigarette.

'We'll have to see about that.'

'No, you promised.'

'You know I can't promise something like that,' said Caroline. 'I'm not sure you appreciate the extreme seriousness of this –'

'You promised –'

'I didn't promise anything. Let's hear what you have to say, then we'll have a better idea of the situation. I'm sure the Icelandic police are very grateful for your cooperation,' she added, catching Erlendur's eye.

He nodded.

'What happened after you met at the Animal Locker?' he asked.

'He didn't know I was married,' said Joan. 'I didn't tell him. Not right away. We met about three times. Once at the hotel near here, in the town whose name I can never remember.'

'Keflavík?'

'That's the one. Then twice at my apartment when Earl flew to Greenland. Earl's my husband,' she explained to Erlendur.

'This wasn't the first time you'd cheated on your husband, was it?' said Caroline bluntly.

'Why do you say that?' asked Joan, with an expression of aggrieved surprise.

'Just a hunch,' said Caroline.

'I won't be judged by you . . . I don't know what –'

'I'm not judging you. Far from it.'

'Earl's –'

Joan broke off and Erlendur sensed that she was seething with rage.

'You bitch!' she spat. 'Ten years ago your kind wouldn't have been allowed to talk to me like that.'

'What did you say? What did you call me?'

'You heard me.'

'Because I'm black? Is that what you mean?'

'You don't talk to me like that,' said Joan. She stubbed out her cigarette in the ashtray in the car door, fished another out of the packet and lit it. 'No nigger talks to me like that.'

'I'll talk to you how I like. White trash!' snapped Caroline. 'Just be grateful I don't lock you up for disrespecting a police officer.'

'You should hear how Earl talks about you people. He hates you.'

'*You people?*'

'Yes, you people.'

'Earl's what?' asked Erlendur, hastily intervening. 'You were about to say something about your husband.'

Joan shot Caroline a look of loathing before turning to Erlendur.

'Earl won't so much as look at me,' she said, the pain breaking through her voice. 'He never pays me any attention. There's no love in him. No affection. I try my best but he's always so cold, and we never have any time together. He's always shooting off somewhere. Things've been like that for a long time and it sucks. It plays hell with your marriage.'

Erlendur couldn't help feeling a little sorry for her, though he had the impression that she had made this speech before. In Kristvin's ear, perhaps.

'So that makes it OK to play around with other men?' said Caroline.

'You shut your mouth! It's not like that,' said Joan, looking to Erlendur for understanding. 'I'm not playing around.'

'Just a minute,' said Caroline. 'Are you saying you don't want to sleep with your husband's buddies in the marines so you turn to locals like Kristvin instead? Icelandics who come to the Animal Locker for a good time?'

Joan ignored her.

'So your husband, Earl, wasn't in the country the last time you saw Kristvin? Is that right?' asked Erlendur, frowning at Caroline to get her to leave Joan alone.

'No, he wasn't. He's still away. But I'm expecting him home soon.'

'Can we get confirmation of that?' Erlendur asked Caroline.

'Oh, you can be sure I'll remember to check up on that,' said Caroline.

'Kristvin drove round to see you in his car, didn't he?' said Erlendur. 'The last time you met?'

'Yes, he parked outside the next-door dorm and we were together for a couple hours. I guess he left my place around eleven.'

'Was he going home after he left you?'

'I think so, I don't know. He didn't mention any different.'

'Were you aware that his tyres had been slashed?'

'No. I knew nothing about that, so I guess it happened while he was with me,' said Joan. 'Listen, I have to get back to the PX. I nearly had a heart attack when you knocked on my door and started asking about Kris, and I was so upset when I heard –'

'Oh, for Christ's sake, don't start claiming you loved him,' said Caroline.

'Shut your mouth!' said Joan. 'You shouldn't go trampling all over other people's feelings. You don't know what I'm like. You know nothing about me.'

'No, that's for sure.'

'Do you know how Kristvin went about getting hold of marijuana?' said Erlendur.

'No,' said Joan.

'Are you sure?'

'I have no idea how he got it.'

'Were you aware he used drugs?'

'No.'

'And of course you've never seen anything like that,' said Caroline.

'Shut up,' said Joan. 'I'm not talking to you.'

'How did he get into this club, the Animal Locker?' asked Erlendur, starting the car. He was keen to return Joan to work before a fight broke out in the back seat.

'What do you mean?'

'Don't Icelanders need someone from the base to vouch for them when they go to places like that? What's it called . . .?'

'You mean a sponsor?'

'Yes. Who was his sponsor? The first time you met?'

'I didn't know him, I think he'd only just been transferred here,' said Joan, sucking in smoke. '"W", I think Kris said. That's all I know. I think he just called him "W".'

'"W"? That's all?'

'Yeah. I have no idea how they knew each other. No idea. I never saw him. I think he'd left by the time . . . by the time Kris and me got acquainted.'

'Did he tell you anything about this "W"?'

'No,' said Joan. 'I don't know who he is. No idea.'

'Is he a soldier?'

'I don't know. There's no point asking me. I know nothing about the guy.'

'This club or bar, the Animal Locker – what kind of place is it?'

'What kind? Well, the officers' club's the fanciest; that's for the highest ranks. The Animal Locker's about as different from that as you can get. It's the enlisted club and there's a reason why they call it the Zoo. There's a hell of a lot of trouble and fighting goes on there. They serve the liquor in plastic cups nowadays because glass got too dangerous. The Zoo's that kind of club. Ask her,' said Joan, pointing at Caroline. 'She comes in sometimes.'

27

Joan stepped out of the car next to the back entrance of the PX without saying goodbye, leaving Caroline and Erlendur sitting in her stale smoke. As she headed for the store she turned and gave them the finger, then flounced inside, slamming the door behind her. Erlendur assumed the gesture was aimed at Caroline, who now moved up to join him in the front seat. She seemed to think so too.

'Screw you too, bitch,' she said.

'Was she wearing a wig?' asked Erlendur, thinking of Kristvin's sister.

'Yeah, she looks like some kind of Dolly Parton freak.'

'Do you think she could be ill?'

'With that on her head? Must be.'

'You should keep an eye on her,' said Erlendur. 'I doubt you can believe a word she says.'

'Not a word,' agreed Caroline, 'and she's probably the last

person who saw your man alive. Apart from . . . I'll check up on her husband, see if she was lying about him.'

'We're not going to arrest her, then?'

'No, let's leave her to sweat a little,' said Caroline. 'I'll keep an eye on her. You're right – she can't be trusted. Who knows what to believe.'

'So you sometimes go to this place, the Animal Locker, your-self?'

'Now and then,' said Caroline. 'I've seen Joan there a couple times, coming on to the customers. She's a slut.'

'You don't recall seeing Kristvin there?'

Caroline shot Erlendur a look.

'I'd have told you – you showed me a picture of him, remember?'

'What about "W"?'

'No,' said Caroline crossly.

'Marion told me you didn't want to help us,' said Erlendur.

'That's right.'

'What made you change your mind?'

'I don't know. At first I thought Marion was asking me to spy on my friends, but when I stopped to think about it, I realised I was wrong. Anyhow, things are so quiet around here, it makes a nice change. And I had a hunch about that dumbass.'

'Joan?'

'I had an instinct that she was stressed and hiding something that time we visited her in the barracks. After Marion talked to me I remembered her and thought I'd pay her another visit, put the thumbscrews on her, and she just caved in. I don't know if I was helping you exactly. I just wanted to find out if she was lying to us.'

'Are you aware of other cases – of soldiers' wives going after Icelandic men?'

'Usually it's the other way around,' said Caroline. 'Joan's a bit of a surprise, in that respect.'

'But not in other respects?'

'No,' said Caroline, laughing with a flash of white teeth. 'The rest is exactly what you'd expect.'

'If she's telling the truth, Kristvin left her place that evening, found his car with the tyres slashed but didn't go back to her. And then what . . .?'

'I'm guessing he met somebody.'

'By chance? Or was it planned? Where was he going? Was someone lying in wait for him when he left Joan's? The same person who vandalised his tyres?'

Caroline stared out of the window.

'Could you track down this "W" for us?' asked Erlendur. 'Is there any way of finding out who he is?'

'I can try. I never heard of anyone called "W" round here, but that doesn't mean anything. It should be possible to look up the names of base personnel starting with that letter.'

'I hope you won't compromise yourself,' said Erlendur, after a pause.

'No, I should be OK. The guys stationed here are a peace-loving bunch, whatever you may think.'

'I've never said they weren't.'

'Marion told me you were opposed to the army being here.'

'That's quite different. It's nothing personal against the people themselves.'

'Then I must have misunderstood,' said Caroline. 'You see, here I was thinking we were fighting a common enemy.'

'Who's that supposed to be?'

'Oh, right, so you don't regard the Russians as an enemy? And what about the fishing dispute a few years back? Wasn't the sea around here swarming with British warships? Weren't they the enemy? The way I understood it, the American government had to step in and persuade the British to back down. You people don't even have your own army.'

'That's what I mean,' said Erlendur.

'Excuse me?'

'In my opinion it would be better if we dealt with our own problems instead of sucking up to military powers like you Americans. That's what I think.'

'Then you need your own army.'

'No, we don't need an army. We've never needed an army. We'll lose all our wars but at least we'll lose them with honour.'

'You're weird,' said Caroline. 'With all due respect.'

'You're probably right,' said Erlendur.

'You think you're better than us?'

'Better? No – where did you get that idea?'

'You people are no angels, you know,' said Caroline. 'You're just as busy smuggling drugs onto the base as the soldiers are smuggling them off. You swap dope for beer, liquor and cigarettes. Even turkey and ham, for Christ's sake! We've known about that for a long time.'

'Yes, so have we. I'm not judging anybody.'

'Are you sure you want me to help you?'

'Of course. My personal attitude to the base doesn't matter.'

'Well, maybe it matters to me,' said Caroline, and Erlendur realised he had made her angry. 'Maybe I have something to say about that. I'm not sure I want to get in any deeper than I already have, and let me tell you I've totally had it with all this underhand shit. Totally had it! I don't know why I let you talk me into this. I just can't understand it.'

Caroline opened the passenger door, stepped out onto the pavement, slammed the door so the whole car shook, and stormed off.

Erlendur drove back to Reykjavík deep in thought, debating with himself whether it would be better at this stage to alert the base authorities to what the investigation had uncovered and request their assistance again. In retrospect, it was hardly fair to expect Caroline to bear the brunt of an inquiry by the Icelandic police. But then she had already made considerable progress and brought to light information that the Icelanders would no doubt have found it much harder, if not impossible, to obtain. She was a vital intermediary. Erlendur's main concern was that they might put her at risk. He had no conception of what sort of danger she might face since he had no criteria by which to judge. He was completely in the dark about what went on behind the wire on Midnesheidi. All he knew was that most, if not all, of the personnel were armed, whereas Icelandic police officers like him were not even licensed to carry a gun.

Turning on the radio news, he found himself instantly transported to a different, more familiar, world. Volunteers were still waiting to mount a search for the two missing men on the Eyvindarstadir Moors. A ferocious blizzard was raging in the area. There was an interview with an old farmer who knew the moors and he made no attempt to paint an optimistic picture. In severe conditions like these, he explained, the men's only chance lay in seeking refuge in one of the shepherds' huts that dotted the highlands.

Erlendur switched off the radio and a familiar shiver ran down his spine as he thought of the two men fighting for their lives on the moors.

28

The door opened after a long interval and the man stared at Erlendur as if utterly unused to visitors. Erlendur had knocked three times, and was turning away when the door finally opened with a slight creak and the man appeared and regarded his visitor without speaking. The seconds ticked by until Erlendur could bear it no longer and broke the silence.

'Are you Rasmus?'

'Who . . . What do you want?'

'I'm looking for information about an old neighbour of yours, a girl called Dagbjört.'

The man continued to stare at him without saying a word. The house had no number on the door or name plate to say who lived there. There was a garage built onto it but no sign of a car. The small patch of garden at the front was as wild and untended as the section Erlendur had seen from the window of Dagbjört's room. The air of neglect also extended to the two-storey building which clearly hadn't seen any repairs for years. Rust streaked the wall from the iron railing of the upstairs balcony and there were further rust stains under the windows. Weeds sprouted from the blocked gutters. It was impossible to see inside the house because heavy curtains obscured all the grimy windows. Erlendur had discovered that there had once been two registered owners, a Danish woman called Margit Kruse, who had died about a quarter of a century ago, and her son, Rasmus. He was now the sole owner, and lived here alone, unmarried and childless, as far as Erlendur could ascertain.

'Dagbjört?' said the man at last, as if he dimly remembered the name and was trying to call it to mind.

'Used to live next door to you,' said Erlendur. 'She went missing in 1953. You were living here then, weren't you? In '53?'

The man didn't answer and it occurred to Erlendur that he was probably figuring out how to get rid of this stranger with the least effort. Which wasn't necessarily abnormal or suspicious behaviour. It was commonplace for recluses like Rasmus to want to be left alone. Erlendur had some sympathy with them.

'Do you remember her?' he asked.

'What are you . . . Why do you want to know?'

Erlendur explained briefly that Dagbjört's aunt had sent him to try and solve the mystery of her niece's disappearance. While he was talking, he studied Rasmus more closely. He was in his mid-fifties, about ten years older than Dagbjört would have been today. The greying hair was plastered to his skull with grease. There was a white pallor about his narrow face and the lips around his small, feminine mouth were so thin as to be almost invisible. They barely moved when he spoke, though occasionally they parted enough to reveal yellowish-brown teeth. He was dressed in threadbare black trousers, shiny at the knees, held up by braces over a creased brown shirt. On his feet he wore felt slippers. Most conspicuous of all, though, were the large eyes that bulged from his white face, hard and gleaming as two marbles. Erlendur wondered if the shifty eyes weighing him up now were those that had once peered across the back garden into Dagbjört's window.

'Anyway,' Erlendur finished, 'I thought maybe we could talk for a minute. You two were neighbours and –'

'No, I don't think so,' said Rasmus. 'I can't help you, I'm afraid. Goodbye.'

He closed the door and Erlendur remained standing there for a moment, wondering whether to knock again. He decided to leave it. He would have to use other methods if he was going to induce this man to talk to him. Instead of returning to the street, Erlendur went into the garden and positioned himself where he could glimpse Dagbjört's window through the fir trees. From the ground little of the room was visible except the ceiling. Erlendur turned and looked at Rasmus's house. It had two large windows upstairs on the side facing Dagbjört's house. From there it would naturally have been easy to see into her bedroom when the firs were smaller. Erlendur noticed the curtains twitching downstairs. Rasmus was watching him, apparently prepared to allow this rude act of trespass to take place without objection. Erlendur took out the diary pages. Read again the bewilderment in the girl's comments about the bizarre behaviour of the man next door who lurked in the gloom, spying on her. Hid there in the shadows while she was getting ready for bed. He read again the question she had written down and concealed in the secret place in her room: *What's he doing?*

'Would you mind getting out of my garden?' He looked up

and saw that Rasmus had opened the back door. 'You're trespassing.'

'You must have known Dagbjört,' said Erlendur.

'That's none of your business,' said Rasmus. 'Get out of my garden. Get out before I call the police!'

'I *am* the police,' said Erlendur.

'What?'

'I'm a detective. All I want is a few words with you about Dagbjört, though I have to say your attitude is very peculiar.'

'How do you mean peculiar?'

'Or perhaps I should return with backup, as well as a court order and an arrest warrant.'

'Arrest warrant? What do you mean? For me? Backup?'

Erlendur nodded, feeling ashamed of himself. It was so easy to work on the recluse's fears. To take advantage of the vulnerability that he detected in the man's bulging eyes and flat, lifeless face; the solitude, which he couldn't bear to have violated.

'You were Dagbjört's next-door neighbour,' said Erlendur. 'Her bedroom window faces your house. You could have watched all her comings and goings.'

Rasmus retreated into the house again.

'Did you know her well?' asked Erlendur.

Without another word, Rasmus Kruse closed the back door and pulled the curtain over it. Erlendur stayed where he was, showing no sign of leaving. Minutes passed until he saw the curtains stirring again, then the door opened and Rasmus's head popped out.

'I told you to get out of my garden,' Rasmus called, sounding distressed. 'Get out. Get out of here!'

Erlendur stood firm.

'You're not coming inside,' cried Rasmus.

'We can just as easily talk out here in the garden,' said Erlendur, trying to sound amiable. 'I don't mind. I only want to ask you a few questions, that's all. I don't know why you're reacting like this.'

'I'm not used to visits,' said Rasmus, a little less agitated now.

'That's obvious. And I do understand.'

'Then won't you please go away? I really don't think I can help you.'

'Do you remember Dagbjört well?'

'Yes, I remember her.'

'Couldn't I talk to you about her for a moment?' asked Erlendur. 'It won't take long.'

Rasmus stood in the doorway, paler than ever, considering this. Erlendur had no idea what he lived on but judging by his appearance and the state of the house he couldn't be particularly well off.

'What do you want to know?'

'Anything you can tell me.'

Rasmus thought again. 'I noticed her as soon as Mother and I moved here,' he said. 'That was about two years before . . .'

'Before she vanished,' finished Erlendur.

Rasmus nodded. 'She was always surrounded by life. She had lots of friends and they used to play music and go out, to parties and things. They had so much fun but Mama . . . my mother said they were –' He broke off, apparently feeling he had said too much.

'What did your mother say?'

'It doesn't matter.'

'Didn't she approve of Dagbjört?'

'She didn't like all the fun and games they had,' said Rasmus. 'That's just the way it was. She had no time for that sort of thing, Mrs Kruse – my mother. Didn't think it was appropriate for young girls to go out on the town so much. She wasn't like that herself, you see. She saw things rather differently.'

'But Dagbjört and her friends weren't that young, were they?' asked Erlendur.

'Mother thought they were. She said they were tarts and sluts and forbade me to have anything to do with them.'

'Did you have anything to do with them?'

'No, never,' said Rasmus emphatically. 'I never did.'

'Didn't you and your mother have any contact at all with your neighbours?'

'Yes . . . that is, we used to say hello, but my mother didn't want too much contact. Mrs Kruse preferred to be left alone.'

'So you never talked to Dagbjört?'

'No. Not often.'

'Were you and your mother the only ones living in this house at the time?'

'Yes.'

'Just you and your mother?'

'Yes. No, that is, my mother died about six months before that business with the girl.'

'And you've lived alone here ever since?'

'Yes.'

'What about your father?'

'They split up when I was a child. I can hardly remember him except as a guest in my mother's house. Then we didn't hear from him any more. My mother told me he'd moved abroad.'

'Is he alive?'

'Quite possibly. I don't know.'

'Don't you have any interest in finding out?'

'No. None at all. Are you done?'

'Yes, almost,' said Erlendur. 'Were you at home the morning Dagbjört vanished?'

'Ye-es,' said Rasmus slowly.

'Did you see her leave for school?'

'No.'

'Positive?'

'Yes.'

'But you sometimes saw her, didn't you? Leaving for school?'

'Sometimes.'

'But not that morning?'

'No.'

'Is your memory that good? After all, it was a long time ago and –'

'Yes. It's not easy to forget. When people vanish like that.'

'Did you know if she had a boyfriend?'

'A boyfriend? No.'

'Did you ever see anyone hanging around outside, watching her house in the evenings?'

'No. I never saw anyone. Why, do you think . . .? Was someone watching the house? I never noticed.'

'Did you ever see any of the youths from Camp Knox loitering in the street?'

'No, I didn't see . . . not that I noticed, but it's such a long time ago and everything's . . . you forget . . . and . . . and I didn't know any youths from Camp Knox. Mrs Kruse wouldn't allow it. She said they were no better than scum, the lot of them.'

'What about you?'

'Me?'

'Were you interested in Dagbjört?'

'Me? Oh, no. No, not at all.'

'Did you see what she did in the evenings?'

'In the evenings?'

'Did you sometimes see her in the evenings?'

'No, it . . . I . . . I wasn't interested in her.'

'Did you sometimes see her in the evenings when she was alone in her room?'

Rasmus seemed disconcerted by the question.

'Do you think she spotted you?' asked Erlendur. 'Do you think she saw what you were up to?'

Rasmus had difficulty disguising his dismay when it suddenly dawned on him where all these questions had been leading. His prominent eyes bulged even wider and his face was aghast with surprise and fear. He retreated inside the house.

'I haven't got time for this,' Erlendur heard him mutter, then add, on a low, pleading note, as the door closed: 'Please, just go away and don't ever come back.'

Some time later Erlendur stood on the pavement by a high wooden fence, looking into a playground and watching people coming to collect their children. Grandmothers in overcoats and headscarves, with handbags on their arms. Mothers in anoraks and peasant blouses. They lingered, maybe smoked a cigarette. There was the odd father too. Some of the children were playing with teenage helpers who joined them in the sandpit, on the swings or see-saw, aware that soon it would be closing time and they would be free to go home. He heard the sound of the mothers' voices, the shrieking of the children, and watched the woman in charge comforting a little girl who had hurt herself falling off the see-saw. The woman dusted the dirt from her red waterproof trousers and told her she was all right, then took her to the sandpit and encouraged her to play with the children who were building a sandcastle there. The little girl, who was five years old, instantly forgot her woes and started patting sand into a green plastic bucket. He saw that the woman in charge was keeping an eye on her as if she didn't want the girl to be left out. Erlendur had noticed that she had a tendency to wander about on her own.

He watched her pottering about in the sandpit for a while, then turned away and walked off with a heavy heart. He knew the little girl well but thought she was probably starting to forget him. He had only himself to blame. One day he hoped they could be friends, so he wouldn't have to watch her from afar, like some kind of outcast. Every so often he stopped by, like now, but didn't talk to anyone, especially not to the little girl, because he didn't want to cause any trouble. Nor did he hang around long, for fear people would mistake him for some kind of pervert.

Erlendur hunched his shoulders against the cold and headed back to his car, thinking about the little girl and himself and what a mess he had made of things. One day he hoped he would have a chance to explain to his daughter who he was and why he'd had to leave.

29

When Erlendur returned to the office in Kópavogur, he was informed that Marion wanted to see him. Marion was still ill in bed, and Erlendur had to get directions to the house since he hadn't been there before. It was unusual for people to be invited round. At least, this was the first time Erlendur had heard of it and he didn't know what to expect. He had always had the sense that, like him, Marion preferred to keep private life and work separate.

It was nearing supper time and Erlendur was starving since he hadn't eaten lunch, so before heading over to Marion's he swung by Skúlakaffi and bought a takeaway of salted lamb with potatoes and swedes. He was back in his car before it occurred to him that Marion might like something to eat too, so he returned and ordered a sandwich in a box. This offering seemed to meet with approval.

'Thank you, you shouldn't have,' said Marion, accepting the box.

'I thought you might like something to eat,' said Erlendur. 'The only sandwiches they had were prawn.' He glanced around the flat and noticed an open bottle of port on the table. 'Feeling any better?'

'Getting there.'

As was evident from the bookshelves, Marion was an insatiable reader. Every wall was lined with books, from large foreign reference works in many volumes to slender collections of Icelandic verse that marked themselves out here and there by their tatty paper spines. Icelandic sagas rubbed shoulders with love stories; Icelandic folklore mingled with foreign biographies and translated detective stories, works on natural history and every kind of art form, from ballet to baroque music. Everything was neatly ordered on the shelves, the perfectly even rows a pleasure to the eye, testimony to the fact that Marion had once worked at the City Library. The overall effect was only enhanced by the myriad small figurines arranged in front of the books, some made of delicate painted porcelain, others of cruder pottery or carved wood, resulting in the most varied collection. Marion noticed Erlendur's gaze pause on these knick-knacks.

'An old friend of mine, a woman who used to travel at lot, sent me those ornaments over many years,' said Marion. 'No two are alike or come from the same place.'

'Used to? Has she given up now?'

'I got a letter the day before yesterday informing me that she was dead,' said Marion. 'It came as quite a shock. I . . . I wasn't expecting it.'

'I see,' said Erlendur. 'You can't have felt like coming into work.'

His eyes fell on the photograph of an older man in a black

suit, which stood on a table. Beside it burned a candle in a small holder made of lava.

'A friend of mine,' said Marion. 'He rejoiced in the unusual name of Athanasius. Died years ago. Did you see Caroline? I hear you've been out to the base.'

Erlendur nodded and put Marion in the picture about his meeting with Caroline, the cocktail waitress Joan and her relationship with Kristvin, and the fact that Kristvin had in all likelihood been with her the evening he fell to his death. He wouldn't have been able to use the Corolla, so would have had to walk and might conceivably have been attacked by the same individuals who had sabotaged his car. Erlendur admitted that he and Caroline had had a difference of opinion about the presence of the army and that he wasn't sure she would offer them any further help.

'It was clever of her to find that woman, that Joan, so quickly,' said Marion. 'She's done us a good turn. We should try and keep her happy. Try not to quarrel with her unnecessarily.'

'Of course. I did try not to, but she's got quite a temper on her and knows her own mind. I'm hoping she's going to check a name for us — the man Joan mentioned, who was at the Animal Locker with Kristvin. Well, I say "name" — Kristvin referred to him as "W".'

'Dubya?'

'That's all we've got,' said Erlendur. 'Caroline said it wasn't much to go on, but the odds are that he's a member of the Defense Force, or at least associated with it.'

'And Joan's husband wasn't in the country?'

'So she claims. Caroline was going to check up on that too. His name's Earl Jones, and if Joan's to be believed, he doesn't pay her much attention. She's pretty outspoken.'

'Like a lot of Americans,' said Marion.

'Probably a racist too, judging by the way she went for Caroline,' said Erlendur.

'Oh?'

'They almost came to blows. Joan thought she was talking down to her.'

'Caroline must have had her hands full with you two,' said Marion. 'I feel quite sorry for her.'

'Hmm. So, do you reckon Kristvin was already being watched on the base? That people were aware of his movements? Knew about Joan?'

'I've been thinking about what that freak Rúdólf told us. What if Kristvin had uncovered evidence relating to arms shipments in that hangar? Something earth-shattering that would really cause a stir if it leaked out. What if he drew attention to himself by asking questions? Could information about the shipments be so sensitive that they'd actually be prepared to kill Kristvin to shut him up?'

'It's like a whole different country out there on Midnesheidi,' said Erlendur. 'What do we know about how they do things? Look at Vietnam. Or Watergate. What are we supposed to think?'

'Do you drink port, by the way? It's all I have,' said Marion, pouring another glass.

'No, thanks.'

'They put a man on the moon,' Marion pointed out.

'Sure, I'm not knocking their achievements.'

Erlendur had a lot of time for Marion, though he never admitted as much. Since joining CID he had been given a completely free hand, though Marion kept an eye on what he was doing and at times criticised his work in a manner that Erlendur found pedantic, even downright harsh. So it was a surprise to find himself sitting in Marion's living room all of a sudden. He didn't know what he'd done to earn this honour and didn't enquire.

'How's your other case progressing?' asked Marion.

'Dagbjört, you mean?'

'Yes.'

Erlendur delved in his pocket for the pages he had found in the girl's bedroom and handed them over.

'I found these hidden in her room. The house is for sale and they let me look round. The neighbour she appears to be referring to still lives next door. Bit of an oddball. Grew up alone with his mother – Mrs Kruse, as he calls her.'

Marion read the pages twice.

'Was he the peeping Tom?'

'I asked him straight out,' said Erlendur, 'and he shut the door in my face. Name's Rasmus. Rasmus Kruse. Mother was Danish. He doesn't have a police record, not that that tells us much. I want to give him time to think it over before I pay him another visit.'

'She was scared of him,' said Marion, looking at the pages, 'but didn't want to tell anyone.'

'She must have been embarrassed.'

'She was obviously pretty innocent. She sounds so bewildered.'

'Yes. She doesn't understand what he's up to. Mind you, a brief comment like that's not much to go on.'

'So no one knew? That this man was spying on her?'

'No, I doubt it,' said Erlendur. 'I'm guessing Dagbjört never let on to her parents or friends. And the man's name doesn't crop up anywhere in the case files. No one seems to have interviewed him or, if they did, there's no note of it.'

'Of course you can never interview everyone.'

'No, true.'

'This is quite a significant discovery,' said Marion, handing back the pages. 'Have you told her aunt?'

'No, not yet. I want to look into it a bit more before I start raising any false hopes.'

'You're right,' said Marion, eyes resting meditatively on the little figurines on the bookshelves. 'It's not fair to go around raising false hopes.'

30

There seemed no point in detaining Ellert and Vignir any longer. Despite their continued denials of any wrongdoing, they were going to be charged, so there were no further grounds for keeping them locked up. They would be placed under a travel ban until their case came to court. They smirked at Erlendur as they walked out of Sídumúli Prison, as if they had won a major victory against the police. Erlendur was only too glad to see the back of them.

When he returned to Kópavogur, there was a message for him to call Caroline. He knew the number of her workplace but didn't recognise the one she had given this time. It turned out to be her home phone. She answered after one ring.

'What the hell have you gotten me into?' she said the moment she heard Erlendur's voice.

'Why, what's the matter?'

'I need to see you. Not here on the base. Down in the village.'

'The village? You mean Keflavík?'

'Yeah, Keflavík. Know the place?'

'Not very well,' Erlendur admitted.

'Meet me by the soccer field,' said Caroline. 'In the parking lot. You ought to be able to find that. Get going. Now!'

She hung up and Erlendur was left staring at the receiver, not knowing what had hit him. Caroline had sounded in a real state, spitting out the words in a frantic whisper. He thought he had detected genuine fear in her voice.

This was the day after his visit to Marion, who still didn't feel up to coming into the office, so Erlendur drove out to Keflavík alone, ignoring the speed limit. He hadn't been lying when he said he didn't know the town, so after driving aimlessly up and down the main street, he stopped a pedestrian who directed him to the football ground. When he arrived, there were only a handful of vehicles in the car park and he saw Caroline step out of one and walk towards him. She jerked open the passenger door and got in.

'Drive somewhere out of town,' she said.

'What's wrong? What are you afraid of?'

'Just drive!'

Caroline was wearing an army jacket with the hood up. It had a fur ruff that almost completely hid her face. Neither said a word while Erlendur found his way to a road leading west out of town and eventually came to a sign pointing to Sandgerdi and Gardur. He opted for Gardur and they drove in tense silence until finally he pulled up beside the Gardskagi lighthouse. Beyond it, foaming white breakers were crashing onto the rocks and they could hear the booming as the waves rolled up the shore.

'Is everything all right?' asked Erlendur warily, once he had switched off the engine.

'I should never have gotten involved,' said Caroline.

'With what?'

'Your case – what do you think? I should have left well alone.'

'What's going on?'

'The shit's hit the fan, that's what,' said Caroline, twisting in her seat to look through the back windscreen in case they'd been followed. She'd done this several times on the way. 'I have a friend in Military Intelligence in Washington,' she explained. 'I called him up because he's an old boyfriend of mine and I trust him, and anyhow I didn't think the information I was requesting was anything special. But he got real jumpy and started demanding to know why I was calling him from Iceland to ask about an airline called Northern Cargo Transport. He wanted to know where I'd come across the name, why I was asking about it, what I intended to do with the information and whether my superior officers knew about my enquiries. My superior officers! And he's my friend! I asked if he was going to report me. That stopped him in his tracks.'

'Did he know right away what you were talking about?' asked Erlendur.

'Right away. He's quite high up and he's told me before that he has access to all kinds of information. He wanted to know if I was in the office and when I said I was, he told me to go home. Took my number and said he'd call me there. See what I mean? It's that kind of situation. We had to change phones. He's worried about wiretapping and all I did was mention the name of that airline.'

'Did you call him at work?'

'No, at home. He was about to go to the office.'

'Did he call back?'

Caroline nodded and adjusted the rear-view mirror so she could see out of the back.

'When he arrived at the office. I told him that –'

'Hang on a minute, do you think you might actually be in some kind of danger?' asked Erlendur.

'I don't know. He told me to watch my back and steer clear of you guys. To forget about Northern Cargo Transport and all that crap.'

'Your boyfriend?'

'He's not my boyfriend,' said Caroline. 'He's my ex. Try to keep up.'

'Who's supposed to be following you?'

'I've been real careful. I didn't tell anyone I'm helping you except my friend in Washington this morning. Not even my superior officer. My friend told me to keep it that way and to stop helping you right now. And that all phones are risky. I didn't know that. I took mine apart – couldn't find anything but that's not saying much because I don't even know what I'm looking for. I'm not sure about my work phone. Haven't checked that yet. But you have to stop calling me. We can't talk on the phone any more.'

'What did you tell your man in Washington?'

'I told him an Icelandic civilian had been killed, most likely murdered, and that you believe it happened in one of our hangars. I told him the man was a flight mechanic with temporary access to Hangar 885 where the Icelandic airline's permitted to use the facilities from time to time. That he'd serviced a C-130 Hercules for a company called Northern Cargo Transport and discovered that it was carrying artillery. And that he found it kind of strange that a civilian operator should be involved in arms shipments so he started asking around about the company, and that you guys believe this might have cost him his life. That he'd been pushed off a platform in the hangar and afterward his body had been taken off base and dumped in a lava field.'

'And what did he say?'

'He asked me how the hell I'd gotten dragged into this,' said Caroline. 'I told him I was ordered to assist you and that you'd asked me to run a few checks to save you the time and paperwork and avoid unnecessary political hassle or however it was you sold it to me. He said you were just using me and that I shouldn't be doing this and must stop at once.'

'Did he imply you'd lose your job?'

'I guess so. Or worse. Actually I think he was talking more like treason and court martial and all that shit.'

'But you managed to persuade him to help you in spite of that?'

'Yes, in the end. We . . . let's just say he decided to do me a favour.'

'What about Northern Cargo Transport? What did he say about that?'

'He said it was run by the CIA.'

'Did you say CIA?'

'You heard me.'

'Of course, that explains it,' said Erlendur.

'What? What does it explain?'

'The company uses the same call sign as the American air force when they land at Keflavík,' said Erlendur, remembering the conversation with Kristvin's boss, Engilbert. 'Their planes land here under cover of the army. When they enter Icelandic airspace they're not distinguished in any way from the military jets. That's how they slip in and out of the country unseen.'

'That's exactly what my friend said. How did you know?'

'I gather that Icelandic air traffic control has noticed. But I don't think they realise the CIA are using the company as a front to fly in here under military call signs. They'd be bound to comment on that. Especially if a civilian airline's being sheltered by the military.'

'Yeah, they would, right?'

'Though I can't be certain,' said Erlendur, a little shamefaced. 'Our relationship with the army is a bit unusual, as we've been trying to explain. It's all tied up with money and Cold War politics and the fight for independence, and everyone's at each other's throats.'

Caroline gazed at the surf by the lighthouse, listening to the boom and hiss as the waves rolled ashore, then were sucked back out again. She wound down the window to hear better as they rose and fell as rhythmically as if the sea were breathing. She seemed much calmer now and had stopped checking the rear-view mirror.

'But that's the least of it,' she said at last.

'What?'

'I heard some news about the Hercules that landed here in transit two weeks ago,' said Caroline. 'I found out that three men boarded the plane and travelled on to Greenland. After we . . . parted yesterday, I tried to find out what was going on, the little information that exists. Called up a couple people I know. Tried not to seem too interested. Said I'd received a request about a package for the States that was supposed to go by military transport.'

'I'm sorry I upset you,' said Erlendur. 'I have a habit of saying the wrong thing, but I didn't mean to make you storm off like that.'

'Forget it,' said Caroline briskly. 'The plane was operated by NCT and was given special express treatment, according to a colleague of mine. The hold was never opened. It refuelled in a hurry and was back in the air in no time, headed for Greenland, possibly en route to the States. I don't know what its final destination was. Could have been Greenland, for that matter.'

'And you find that suspicious? Isn't it standard?'

'I've no real experience in this area but you were asking about the airline and its planes, so I got curious. Especially after I found out who hitched a ride on the Hercules.'

'You mean one of the three passengers?'

'Yes.'

'Who was it?'

'On the passenger list I was shown, which is a restricted document, it said "W. Cain". And it occurred to me it could be the "W" Joan said was Kristvin's sponsor at the Animal Locker. In this case the "W" stands for Wilbur.'

'The man Joan . . .? Was it this guy Wilbur?'

'I looked him up. Wilbur's not a common name. It turns out there's only one man with that name at NAS Kef at the present time.'

'Wilbur Cain?'

'Yeah. I ran it by my friend in Washington but he didn't recognise it and said he'd check it out when he got to the office. He called me back earlier. Turns out Wilbur Cain's employed by Military Intelligence. He was sent to Iceland about four months ago on assignment but my friend doesn't know what it entails. He told me to watch my back with him – Cain's the reason my friend's now trying to find out just what in hell is going on here. He told me to quit making all these enquiries and sit tight till I heard from him.'

Caroline was growing jittery again. She fiddled with the mirror and stared frowning out of the rear windscreen.

'Wilbur Cain's most likely an alias. Cain's an experienced agent, he's worked on all kinds of covert missions for the military, and he's an expert in making assassinations look like accidents.'

Caroline looked at Erlendur.

'It's him I'm afraid of.'

31

They sat perplexed, listening to the pounding of the waves below the lighthouse as the early darkness of winter closed in. Erlendur glanced up at the lamp that came to life and died at regular intervals as a warning to seafarers. He felt completely out of his depth.

'What's a man like that doing here of all places?' he asked after a long pause.

'I have no idea.'

'And what on earth was he doing with Kristvin at the Animal Locker? How could they have met?'

'Who knows?' said Caroline. 'Maybe Kristvin drew attention to himself by asking questions about the Hercules and NCT. Somebody was alerted, who alerted somebody else and Wilbur Cain was tasked with making enquiries about the man.'

'But he went to the club with him,' said Erlendur. 'That's hardly discreet. And Joan knows he's called "W". Would Kristvin have known his name? If this man's a Military Intelligence agent as you say?'

'I think –'

'Not that I have a clue how these people work.'

'Apparently it's just one of the aliases he uses,' said Caroline. 'Wilbur Cain's on home turf. He has no reason to go to ground when he's on the base. He can leave the country at an hour's notice and the authorities can deny that anyone of that name ever set foot in Iceland.'

'So it's possible that Kristvin wasn't careful enough – he mouths off about arms shipments and private airlines and this Wilbur Cain is sent to find out what he's up to?'

'Maybe.'

'He seems to have been quick to befriend him.'

'Wasn't Kristvin after something? Vodka? Cigarettes?'

'Marijuana.'

'Then it wouldn't have been hard for Cain to strike up an acquaintance with him.'

'Are you sure this Wilbur Cain is the same man as Kristvin's "W"?'

'Of course I can't be sure, but it seems likely,' said Caroline. 'The airline's a link – Kristvin's enquiries about the NCT planes. And we know that someone called "W" was in Kristvin's company on at least one occasion. Cain's a member of special forces, so he must have been sent here on a specific assignment. I don't think we should dismiss the possibility.'

Erlendur sat silently for a long time and found himself inadvertently comparing the two cases that were occupying all his thoughts at the moment. On the one hand Kristvin's death, in which a superpower might have played a part, with its military installations and special-forces agents, and on the other the

Dagbjört affair, the tale of a lone individual going missing on a remote little island in the North Atlantic. Caroline asked what he was thinking and Erlendur started to tell her about the girl who had vanished so inexplicably on her way to school in 1953, about the unsuccessful search for her, and all the years that had passed since then with no news of her fate. There was no way of telling – probably never would be – if a crime had been committed. He said Kristvin's case presented such a stark contrast.

'The odd thing is,' Erlendur added, 'that both cases have a connection to the American occupation. The girl's route passed by Camp Knox, an area of old barracks built by the US garrison in Reykjavík. It's rumoured she knew a boy there.'

'An American?'

'No, the soldiers were long gone by then, moved out here to Midnesheidi. No, a local boy. What I'm trying to get across is that we Icelanders just don't know how to deal with what's happening on the base.'

'Nor me,' she said. 'You can take that as read.'

'I mean, this is your world but it's a world we simply don't understand. As a nation we emulate everything you do without really knowing why and forget that we're just a bunch of poor farmers, forced by modern life to live in blocks of flats. You're the richest nation on the planet. The biggest military power in history. For most of our existence we've been fighting a losing battle against starvation.'

'That sucks,' said Caroline, momentarily forgetting her anxiety. 'What . . . why . . .?'

'Oh, a combination of factors. Volcanic eruptions. Earthquakes. Sometimes epidemics. But mostly bad seasons with prolonged periods of arctic conditions. Sometimes all of them rolled into one. But in spite of that we've managed to scrape some sort of living up here, and our generation and the generations to come will reap the benefits and be better off than they'll ever realise.'

Erlendur pulled out a packet of cigarettes, lit one and inhaled. He wound down the window on his side to let out the smoke.

'As a result our crimes tend to be rather old-fashioned and provincial,' he continued. 'Murders are rarely premeditated, though of course we have our share of notorious cases and mysterious disappearances, like any other country. But what I wanted to say is that they seldom have any international context. Perhaps that's changing now. Of course there's a Cold War going on in the outside world and it affects us here with its spies and undercover shenanigans. We know the Soviets have tried to recruit Icelanders and there have been incidents related to international politics, but, I don't know . . .'

Caroline allowed herself a faint smile.

'Times change,' she said.

'Yes, times change.'

'Someone told me you can drive round the whole island in twenty-four hours. Is that true?'

'Yes, it's true. There are only 230,000 of us living here, speaking our funny language. Descendants of the Vikings. Once, the worst humiliation anyone could conceive of in this country was if a woman slapped a man across the face.'

'And now?'

'Now, like other dwarf nations we're desperate for recognition that we have something to offer, trying to prove that we can play with the big boys on the world stage. That's why we've got this socking great naval base here. We long to be important in some way. But of course we're not. We're of no importance to anyone.'

'Sounds like me in high school,' said Caroline, smiling. 'I was always a bit of an outsider. Never managed to fit in. And now here I am, stuck in the middle of nowhere.'

'Are you from Washington like your boyfriend?'

Caroline gazed out over the dark sea.

'We met in the marines. I didn't know what to do after high school and my dad suggested I try the army. He'd fought in the war and stayed in the army afterward and loved it. That's where I met Brad. We were together for several years until it just wasn't working any more. He was . . . I don't know. I applied to be transferred somewhere far away. Wanted to high-tail it out of Washington as soon as possible. See the world. I thought Iceland would be a choice assignment. I didn't know it was a windswept rock in the middle of the North Atlantic and that I'd end up helping out the Icelandic police. Don't misunderstand me, I'm not unhappy here. I travelled round the country a bit last summer. The scenery's incredible. And I like the midnight sun. When the sun doesn't go down in the summer and the nights are as light as day.'

'Not everybody's keen on that,' said Erlendur. 'So you don't regard Iceland as a hardship post?'

'Hardship post? No, I don't think of it like that.'

'Anyway what do you want to do now?'

'Brad told me to lie low till he'd had a chance to look into the matter at his end,' said Caroline. 'So perhaps I'd better take it easy till I hear from him again. All that stuff about farmers and famine has soothed my nerves a little.'

Erlendur smiled. 'Do you trust him, this Brad?'

'Yeah. Brad's OK – he'd never get me into trouble.'

'Did you tell him about me and Marion?'

'Sure. Wasn't I supposed to?'

'Yes, of course. Look, wouldn't it be best if you went straight to Fleet Air Command? Is there any reason to wait? Marion and I could go with you, if you like.'

'Brad told me not to trust anyone or talk to anyone till I'd heard back from him,' said Caroline. 'He's going to try and find out what Wilbur Cain's up to in Iceland. Chances are he's here with the knowledge and at the request of the military authorities. Brad told me that when the time came, I should go directly to the Rear Admiral and take you both with me.'

'Good,' said Erlendur. 'In the meantime, you can come with me if you want. We could put you up in a hotel in Reykjavík or –'

'No, thanks all the same. But it was good talking to you. I feel a bit less stressed. I'll be fine. I have friends here I can turn to.'

'Sure?'

'Yeah.'

'You won't go back to your apartment, will you?'

'No, not till I hear from Brad. Maybe the whole thing's a big mistake and Wilbur Cain has nothing to do with Kristvin's death. That's what Brad said. But I think he was just trying to reassure me.'

'And you definitely trust him?'

'Yes, I trust him,' said Caroline firmly. 'You'd better not talk to anyone about this either until you hear from me. You never know by what route information reaches the base. If something's happening here that's costing the lives of innocent civilians, the Icelandic government might well be in on it. Brad told me to trust nobody. Nobody at all.'

'I don't believe the Icelandic government could be –'

'Everyone has their price and it was you who told me that the defence question here revolved mainly around money.'

'All right,' said Erlendur, 'though I hope you trust me and Marion, if no one else.'

'Yes, maybe you two. But not many others.'

Caroline looked despondently out into the gloom. Erlendur sensed that she had not quite finished. Something remained to be said. Not wanting to put pressure on her, he let time pass without breaking the silence.

'Marion asked me to check who could have been in the hangar the night Kristvin was killed,' said Caroline at last.

'Oh?'

'Work's been suspended for the most part because of the construction, but the hangar's guarded twenty-four/seven. I discovered that one of the security guards is called Matthew Pratt. A private. Young. Only twenty-two. A friend of mine who works on the airport gate knows him but he didn't recognise the names of the other guards. There are several, apparently, and they patrol it in shifts.'

'Have you spoken to him? This Pratt?'

'That's the strange part.'

'What do you mean?'

'I can't trace him,' said Caroline. 'He's not at home. His neighbours haven't seen him for forty-eight hours. He hasn't been on duty and I'm told he reported in sick several days ago. He hasn't left the base, to the best of my knowledge, but he seems to have vanished off the face of the earth.'

32

Erlendur couldn't persuade Caroline to change her mind about returning to the base, so he left her in the car park by the Keflavík football ground. She gave him the phone number of some people she was going to take refuge with and said she would be in touch soon.

'Be careful,' Erlendur said in parting. 'The fewer people you tell, the better. Are you sure you can trust them?'

'Don't worry,' said Caroline. 'They're the kind of friends who'll help without asking any questions.' She pulled up the hood of her jacket and got out of the car.

As Erlendur drove back along the Keflavík road he looked over at the billows of steam rising from Svartsengi and felt as if many weeks had passed since he saw Kristvin's body floating in the lagoon. Since then the inquiry into his death had almost entirely focused on the naval air station on Midnesheidi, and now both the CIA and Military Intelligence had become tangled up in it.

Erlendur found it highly unlikely that a nobody like Kristvin could have constituted a serious thorn in the side for a powerful nation like the US, but then again Caroline was clearly rattled, and maybe Kristvin had as much chance as anyone else on the base of stumbling on classified information. He had access to the largest hangar on the site, after all, so he could have witnessed something he wasn't supposed to.

As Erlendur wrestled with this question on the drive back to Reykjavík, he reflected on what he had told Caroline about the difference in scale between their two nations. From there, his thoughts wandered back to Dagbjört and what the old woman, Baldvina, had told him about Camp Knox. Erlendur had made casual enquiries about where he might find her son Vilhelm these days. All he had learned was that the tramp was still alive and occasionally showed his face at the shelter for alcoholics and home-less men on Thingholt.

When Erlendur got back to the office he found Marion sitting at the desk, apparently sufficiently recovered to return to work. Erlendur gave a detailed account of his meeting with Caroline out at Gardskagi and how her investigations had put her on the trail of Wilbur Cain, who scared her.

'But she insisted on going back to the base in spite of that?' said Marion, once Erlendur had finished.

'She said she was going to stay with friends and would be in touch when she had more information. Let's just hope she knows what she's doing. I told her we're a bunch of clueless bloody amateurs when it comes to the world she moves in.'

'Maybe not such a bad thing to be, in the circumstances,' said Marion.

'No, true.'

'What can we do at this end to help her?' asked Marion. 'Anything practical?'

'She said she didn't trust the Icelandic government any more than the military authorities. One option would be for us to issue a warrant for Wilbur Cain's arrest, but we can't produce any evidence to back it up. Caroline said they could whisk him away at a moment's notice and claim ignorance of his existence.'

'What are the chances he killed Kristvin – realistically?'

'I don't know,' said Erlendur. 'Caroline thinks it's possible Wilbur knew him and was with him at that club or bar or whatever it is, the Animal Locker. We have Joan's word for that. She referred to Kristvin's companion as "W". Admittedly it's not definitely "Wilbur", but it was enough to spur Caroline to talk to her contact in Washington, who told her to watch out for this Cain character.'

'I hope we're not going to live to regret the fact we persuaded her to help us,' said Marion.

'She can look after herself.'

Erlendur announced that he had a brief errand to run. Marion promised to stay by the phone in the meantime in case Caroline rang. Saying he would call in regularly to check if there were any developments, Erlendur left and drove down to the homeless shelter on Thingholt. He spoke to the warden who knew Vilhelm well and said he had spent the previous night there, but he didn't know whether to expect him back that evening.

'The poor bloke's in pretty bad shape,' said the warden.

'Well, it's a dog's life.'

'You could try the centre of town – they sometimes gather in Austurvöllur Square in spite of the cold. Or up on Arnarhóll. Or by the bus station at Hlemmur.'

Erlendur drove through the centre of town without seeing Vilhelm. During his years on the beat he had become acquainted with the desperate lives led by the city's homeless and knew the names of many of the men and women who roamed the streets, in varying states of intoxication. Among their number was a woman called Thurí and he spotted her now, standing on the corner by the post office, wearing a thick anorak, two scarves tightly knotted round her neck and a torn hat on her head, the ear flaps fluttering in the wind. She recognised him immediately when he drew up beside her. They were old friends.

'Fancy seeing you, mate,' she said.

'I'm looking for Vilhelm. Seen him around?'

'No,' said Thurí. 'Why are you looking for him?'

'Any idea where he might be?'

'Has he been a bad boy?'

'No, I just need a word with him.'

'Are you sure?'

'Yes, I'm sure.'

'He hangs out in the Central Bus Station sometimes, but I don't know if he's there now.'

'I'll check. How are you, by the way?'

'Ah, you know,' said Thurí, 'same old shit.'

He didn't see Vilhelm at the bus station. Two coaches were waiting out on the tarmac behind the building, one marked 'Akureyri', the other 'Höfn in Hornafjördur'. Passengers were handing their bags to the driver to stow in the baggage compartment. A third coach drew up and the passengers climbed out, stretched their limbs, then went to retrieve their luggage. Erlendur hung around, watching people going in and out of the station building. He had searched the gents, the cafe and the waiting area, and done a circuit of the building, but Vilhelm was nowhere to be seen.

Finding a payphone, he rang Marion, who hadn't heard from Caroline and was growing increasingly anxious.

33

Erlendur was back in his car, pulling away from the bus station, when he caught sight of a figure loitering by the dustbins at the eastern end of the building. The man lifted the lid of a bin, examined its contents and rooted around inside, then replaced the lid and moved on to the next. Having drawn a blank, he was turning to leave when Erlendur walked up to him.

'Hello, Vilhelm,' he said, recognising the tramp at once by the glasses perched on his nose, the thick, domed lenses making his eyes look huge. The frames were broken, stuck together in two places with Sellotape.

'Who are you?' asked Vilhelm, instantly wary.

'I'm Erlendur.'

'I lost my gloves,' said Vilhelm, as if compelled to explain why he had been rummaging in the dustbins. 'Thought maybe they'd fallen in the rubbish.'

'I don't suppose you remember me but we spoke several years

ago about a homeless man who was found in the old peat diggings in Kringlumýri.'

'Oh?'

'Yes, does that ring any bells?'

'You mean . . . do you mean Hannibal?'

'Yes, Hannibal.'

'Didn't someone drown him?'

'Yes, that's right. A nasty business. Feel like a coffee or a bite to eat inside? Warm up a bit?'

Vilhelm subjected Erlendur to a suspicious, magnified gaze.

'What . . . what do you want from me?'

'I want a chat about the old days,' said Erlendur.

'The old days? What do you mean?'

'I want to talk to you about Camp Knox,' said Erlendur. 'I know you grew up there and I wanted to ask a few questions about the old barracks neighbourhood.'

'Bollocks,' said Vilhelm. 'Like anyone's interested in Camp Knox. Who cares about Camp Knox nowadays?'

'I had a chat with your mother – with Baldvina – the other day. She told me about life in the camp. Said you might be able to help me.'

'You spoke to my mother? Why the hell would you do that? What did you want? What did you have to go and do that for?'

'I'm gathering information. I've spoken to her and various other people and now I'd like to sit down for a chat with you. It won't take long.'

'I don't know . . . I wouldn't mind a coffee but I doubt I can help you with anything to do with the camp. I've forgotten all that, not that there was anything to remember. Nothing you'd want to remember.'

Erlendur escorted him into the bus station cafe and chose a table as far from the other customers as possible since Vilhelm gave off a foul odour that came into its own indoors. He was wearing rubber waders laced up his calves, a coat tied around him with a belt, and several layers of jumpers. Erlendur had read descriptions of the old vagrants who used to tramp the Icelandic countryside, travelling from farm to farm, often welcome visitors for the news they carried which livened up the monotony of life. Vilhelm reminded him of these old gentlemen of the road.

'How is she then?' Vilhelm asked when Erlendur returned with a large mug of coffee and a tasty-looking Danish pastry which he placed before him. There was a chaser of *brennivín* that Vilhelm had asked him to buy. Vilhelm downed it in one and wiped his mouth.

'Who?'

'Thought you said you'd talked to my old mum.'

'Oh, yes. I had a good chat with her. She's a tough old bird,' said Erlendur.

'Yes, she always knew how to fend for herself,' said Vilhelm. 'I haven't . . . haven't been to see her in ages.'

'You should go round,' said Erlendur.

'It's coming back to me now,' said Vilhelm. 'You're a cop, aren't you?'

'Yes,' said Erlendur. 'That's right.'

'What does a cop want with Camp Knox? I thought everyone'd forgotten about that shithole.'

'I don't know if you recall but back when you were living there with your mother, a young girl, a pupil at the Women's College, went missing on her way to school and was never found. Her name was Dagbjört and her route to school in the mornings passed by the camp. There was a rumour she knew a boy who lived in the huts but he never came forward and in spite of inquiries he was never found. Baldvina told me you might know about a boy who moved out of the camp at around the same time. His mother was called Stella.'

While Erlendur was speaking, Vilhelm sipped his hot coffee impassively. Then he extracted a dirty rag from his coat, wrapped the Danish pastry in it and returned it to his pocket. Saving it for later, no doubt.

'So what if he moved out?' said Vilhelm. 'Nothing odd about that, is there?'

'Do you know why he left?'

'People moved out of Camp Knox because they'd found something better, I can tell you that for nothing. From there you could only move up in the world.'

'Do you remember Dagbjört's disappearance?'

'Yes, I do, as it happens,' said Vilhelm.

'And Stella's son?'

'Stella had three sons,' said Vilhelm, brushing his hand over the shot glass. 'One drowned in Skerjafjördur. He was only thirteen. Fell in the sea. His name was Tobbi. Bloody good lad. Used to play together all the time. Same age as me. He was an ace footballer. That was before the thing you're talking about. Then there was Haraldur, known as Halli. Couldn't swear to it, but I think he became a baker. At least he used to talk about it enough and he was a fat bastard, always stuffing his face – I've never known anyone as cunning at shoplifting from bakeries. Haven't seen him for donkey's years. Then there was the eldest. I didn't know him as well. They used to call him Silli, and you're quite right, he moved away. I think it was to somewhere out of town.'

'Any idea what his full name was?'

'Sigurlás.'

'Were they full brothers? Do you know who their father was?'

'Stella was a single mother. Tobbi and Halli shared the same dad, far as I can remember. Silli was their half-brother. Had a different dad. Don't know who he was, though.'

'You don't know what became of Silli? Or why he left Camp Knox right around then?'

'No. Never heard any particular reason. People were generally keen to clear out of there as soon as they could.'

The heavy glasses had slipped down Vilhelm's nose. He pushed them up again and fixed the domed lenses on Erlendur.

'Why are you asking about that girl now?' he asked.

'Her aunt's still looking for her.'

'Isn't that a lost cause?'

'They know she can't still be alive, if that's what you mean. They just want to try and solve the mystery of why she vanished.'

'But why now? Is there some new evidence?'

'No, it's just that time's passing and soon it'll be too late. What did the residents of the camp think of the search? Did they know Dagbjört? Did they know about the lad she was supposedly seeing?'

'I remember that lots of them took part in the search and it was talked about at the time, but I don't think the camp people felt it had anything to do with them. Or that any of them were likely to have harmed her. At least I don't recall any mention of it. I'm not sure anybody knew her.'

'Was it unusual for a lad from the camp to get involved with a girl from outside?'

'How should I know?' said Vilhelm. 'We were no worse than

anyone else. Don't think that. Prejudice is prejudice, whichever way you look at it. OK, there were a few ugly customers around like anywhere else, I'm not trying to make excuses for that, but on the whole we were no worse than other people. I never knew a harder-working woman than my mother.'

Vilhelm nudged the shot glass meaningfully towards Erlendur. 'How's she doing, by the way?'

'She said a lot of people went off the rails. But that it was the children who always came off worst.'

'Did she talk about me at all?' asked Vilhelm. 'Did she mention my name? I haven't seen her in ever such a long time.'

'I got the impression it was you she was talking about,' said Erlendur carefully, taking hold of the shot glass.

Vilhelm gave Erlendur a long look, then rose to his feet, saying he couldn't hang about any longer, he had to be off. He was sorry he couldn't help, he added, then knotted his coat more tightly around himself and said goodbye. Erlendur pursued him to the door of the cafe.

'Thanks for agreeing to talk to me,' he said.

'No problem.'

'I didn't mean to offend you.'

'Offend me? I'm not offended. Don't know what you're on about. So long.'

'Just a minute, Vilhelm, one last thing. Did you know where Dagbjört lived?'

'Where she lived? Yes, the news soon got around because everyone was talking about it. I knew exactly where she lived.'

'Were you familiar with her street at all? With her neighbours?'

Vilhelm thought about this. 'No, can't say I was.'

'You don't happen to remember a half-Danish man called

Rasmus Kruse who lived next door to Dagbjört? Used to live with his mother, though she'd died by that time. Bit of an oddball. At least, not the outgoing type.'

'I remember Rasmus all right,' said Vilhelm. 'Remember him well. Didn't know him to talk to but I remember seeing him around. His mother too. The old bitch. Hated us kids from the camp. We were filth in her eyes. She used to drive a big flashy car, a green Chevrolet, I think. Put on airs like she was a real lady. They beat the shit out of him . . . that Rasmus. Used to call him Arse-mus.'

'What do you mean? Who beat him?'

'Don't know – some lads.'

'When?'

'Suppose it would have been a few years after that girl of yours went missing.'

'Why . . . did it have something to do with her?'

'No, I don't think so. They kicked the shit out of Arse-mus because they thought he was a poof.'

With that Vilhelm darted out of the door and Erlendur watched him stride off towards the town centre, aware he would get nothing more out of him for now.

34

Erlendur went back to the payphone and rang Marion who still hadn't heard from Caroline. Erlendur advised patience, but Marion was all for going out to Keflavík to see if she was all right. After a brief argument, they agreed to give her a little more time before taking action.

'We've got her friends' phone number,' pointed out Erlendur. 'If we don't hear from her soon we can ring and –'

'Already tried it,' broke in Marion.

'You what?'

'I rang the number. It was answered by a member of staff at the Andrews cinema. He'd never heard of any Caroline.'

Hearing the pips, Erlendur hurriedly put more coins in the slot.

'Did she give us a false number?'

'Looks like it.'

'Why? Is she trying to pull the wool over our eyes?'

'Perhaps she just gave you a number to reassure you. I don't know. Perhaps she doesn't trust us any more. Probably doesn't trust anyone.'

'That's what she said. That she didn't trust anyone, but I thought she was making an exception for us. What the hell's she playing at?'

'Maybe she doesn't have any friends there,' suggested Marion. 'Or her contact, that bloke in Washington, put the wind up her and told her not to work with us any more.'

'In that case why would she have met up with you afterwards?'

'Search me,' said Erlendur. 'To bring us up to speed? After all, she could be compelled to leave the country at a moment's notice. Look, I've run out of coins. I'll catch you later. I've just got to drop by somewhere first.'

He hung up and made way for a fat man with two large suit-cases, newly arrived from the countryside, who had been waiting impatiently to use the phone. Erlendur went back to his car, keeping an eye out for Vilhelm as he drove away from the bus station, heading west in the direction of Rasmus Kruse's house. In no time he was entering the street where Dagbjört had once lived and caught her neighbour spying on her in the evenings. He parked in front of Rasmus's house, walked up to the front door and knocked.

He thought he saw the curtains moving upstairs but it could have been a trick of the light. He rapped again, louder this time. He didn't want to alarm the man, mindful of how peculiar and fearful his behaviour had been at their previous meeting. There was no telling if he would open the door to Erlendur now that he knew who he was and why he had come. Erlendur knocked yet again, called the man's name twice, then put his ear to the door. There was no movement. It was as if the house were sealed in silence. No outside sounds reached it. None could be heard from within.

He was turning away when the door opened behind him and a white face peered out.

'I asked you not to come back,' said Rasmus in a high, thin voice, regarding him with his bulging eyes. They reminded Erlendur of Vilhelm's domed glasses.

'Yes, I'm sorry,' said Erlendur, 'but I'm afraid I'll have to disturb you again. I'd be grateful if we could talk, even if only for a few minutes.'

Rasmus Kruse stared at Erlendur for a while, clearly still trying to work out how to keep him at arm's length.

'I've nothing to say to you.'

'I'll be the judge of that,' said Erlendur. 'It might . . . it might actually do you good to talk to someone,' he added.

'Talking to you won't do me any good,' said Rasmus. 'Please go away and never come back.'

'Why are you so unwilling to talk to me? What are you scared of? I know you were acquainted with Dagbjört. It's obvious. You lived next door to her. That's no secret. I know you watched what was happening in the street and saw a good deal. I believe you used to stand in the window facing her house, peering in at her. She as good as said so in a letter I came across recently.'

'What letter?'

'It's actually a page from her diary.'

'Her diary?'

'Please let me –'

'No, I'm sorry, I can't talk to you,' muttered Rasmus, so quietly that Erlendur could barely hear him. 'There's nothing to say.'

He made to shut the door but Erlendur stepped forward and prevented him.

'Get out of the doorway,' cried Rasmus. 'Go away.'

The words burst from between his thin, barely moving lips, and his pale face swelled with the strain of withstanding Erlendur's weight. But Erlendur had no intention of letting him out of his sight this time. Rasmus proved incapable of putting up much resistance and a moment later Erlendur was standing in the entrance hall, the door swinging shut behind him.

'Get out!' shrieked Rasmus. 'You have no right to force your way in here.'

'I'll go in a minute,' said Erlendur. 'I need to know what you saw. I need to ask you a few questions, then I'll be out of here. I promise. A few questions, that's all.'

'No, I want you to leave!'

'It's up to you. The sooner we can have a civilised chat, the sooner I'll be gone. Understand? I'm not going anywhere till you've answered my questions.'

Erlendur couldn't see much of the house from the hall, though he noticed a staircase. A faint light came from the upper floor but otherwise the house was shrouded in darkness. There was a strong odour of mildew. Maybe the roof or a water pipe had leaked at some point in the past. He could see the shapes of paintings on the walls and part of the way into what looked like a study by the stairs. Once his eyes had adjusted to the dark he realised there was a large chandelier hanging over the staircase. If the house had looked gloomy from the street, it was positively creepy inside.

Rasmus was watching him and the stand-off continued until eventually Rasmus dropped his eyes. The tension in his body eased, his shoulders sagged, his face grew blank again and he sighed heavily, as if resigned to this ill-mannered invasion.

'You're not coming any further inside,' he said.

'All right,' said Erlendur. 'I didn't mean to barge in like this, but –'

'I have nothing to offer you,' said Rasmus. 'I don't have any coffee or cakes. I haven't been out recently.'

'Don't worry about that,' said Erlendur.

'I wasn't expecting any visitors.'

'No, I'm aware of that.'

'Or I'd have made arrangements,' persisted Rasmus.

Again Erlendur told him not to worry, puzzled by Rasmus's sudden metamorphosis into an embarrassed host. One would have thought his greatest source of concern was not being able to entertain his guest properly. Perhaps this was a Danish habit instilled by his mother.

'I should have let you know I was coming,' Erlendur said, entering into the social pretence, though he knew it would have made no difference if he had given advance warning. 'Could you tell me when you last saw Dagbjört?'

'I don't know . . . it's been a long time,' said Rasmus, his mouth scarcely moving, his lips pursed together as if he were reluctant to let the words escape. 'I thought it had all been forgotten about years ago but then you turn up and start acting with a disgraceful rudeness I've never encountered before, and start interrogating me about her. It's . . . I've . . . to tell the truth it's come as quite a shock.'

'You'd been living here for two years when Dagbjört went missing,' said Erlendur. 'Did you watch her from your window all that time?'

'No, it wasn't like that. Don't try and make it sound dirty. It wasn't like that.'

'It sounds to me as if she was afraid of you,' said Erlendur. 'She must have found it excruciatingly embarrassing or she'd have told her parents straight away. Or her friends. She hardly dared confide it to her diary. She tore out the pages and hid them.'

Rasmus regarded him expressionlessly.

'No doubt she'd have complained about you if she'd discovered your spying earlier, but this was only two weeks before she disappeared. I want to know if anything happened during that time?'

Rasmus didn't answer.

'Did she speak to you?'

Rasmus shook his head.

'Did you notice when Dagbjört caught you spying on her? Did she spot you lurking here in the dark? Do you remember?'

'She saw me, yes,' said Rasmus after a lengthy pause. 'One evening she saw me and . . . then it was over. I never watched her again. I was so ashamed. She was never supposed to find out. After that she used to draw her curtains. And that was it.'

'How come she noticed you?'

'Clumsiness,' said Rasmus. 'I moved too close to the window and was suddenly visible to her and I realised at once that she suspected this wasn't the first time I'd . . . I'd watched her. I'd been found out and I assumed her parents would be straight round and she'd come with them and point the finger at me, and they'd be outraged because what I'd done was ugly. So ugly I should have gone to prison for it. But then . . . nothing happened. No one came round until you turned up at my door all these years later. She never told anyone.' His words faded to a whisper.

'What made you behave like that?' asked Erlendur.

'I don't know,' said Rasmus. 'I didn't have many friends and . . .'

'Surely you didn't think she'd become your friend?'

'Oh, no, no, I never even dreamt of that. I'd have really liked to get to know her, really, really I would, but it was impossible. Impossible.'

'You said you'd never spoken to Dagbjört. Was that true?'

'Yes,' said Rasmus after a moment's hesitation.

'I find it hard to believe you lived next door to her for two years without ever exchanging a word.'

'No, it . . . perhaps what I said to you last time wasn't strictly accurate but I didn't think it mattered. I did speak to her a handful of times but not about anything important. I feel you're trying to twist everything I say to make it sound suspicious, so I'm sorry if I was cagey. I ran into her once in a shop that used to be near here but closed down ages ago. We were standing in the queue and she was kind enough to spare a few words for me.'

'So she showed you some minor attention? Was that why you used to stand in your window, spying on her and dreaming that you were lovers?'

Rasmus shook his head. 'You're deliberately misunderstanding me,' he said. 'You're trying to get me into trouble. Mrs Kruse said girls were nothing but trouble and that I should watch myself with them, but I knew she was lying. She was a selfish woman. A spiteful woman. Dagbjört wasn't like she said.'

'Did she know what you were up to? Mrs Kruse? Did she know what you got up to in the evenings?'

Rasmus's eyes widened. 'I can't tell you anything else,' he said. 'You mustn't ask me questions like that. Don't ask me any more questions.'

'Did Mrs Kruse catch you acting the peeping Tom?'

'No, don't ask me that,' said Rasmus, shaking his head, visibly agitated. 'You've got no right. You've got no right to judge me. I'm not a monster! I just want to be left alone. I can't help you any more. I don't know what happened to Dagbjört. I'd never have hurt her. Never. And now I want you to leave. You can't stay here any longer.'

'But you were afraid of being found out, weren't you?'

'It was –'

'You were scared out of your wits that Dagbjört would report you,' said Erlendur, moving closer to Rasmus. 'You were terrified she'd tell her parents. Isn't that how it went? You couldn't bear to think of them finding out what you did alone in the evenings while you watched their daughter undress. While you watched her take off –'

'Stop it! Don't say that! Don't say it. You don't know what you're talking about. How could you say something like that?'

'But it's the truth, isn't it?'

'No! No! It's not.'

'Are you sure?'

'I could never have hurt her,' shouted Rasmus, his voice cracking, and retreating from Erlendur further inside the house. 'Never. I used to watch over her so no harm would come to her. I was like her guardian angel, watching over her as she fell asleep. I could never have hurt her. I worshipped her. You've got to believe me,' he whimpered. 'You've got to believe me. I took part in the search too and prayed to God every evening that she'd be found. You've got to believe me. I could never have hurt her. I could never have hurt a hair on her head.'

35

Rasmus retreated down the hall, backing towards the staircase until he stumbled over the bottom step. Recovering his balance, he climbed onto it and paused there. Erlendur could now see better in the gloom and was able to make out the study, a dining room and a kitchen to one side of him. Along the walls stood bundles of newspapers, tied together with string. The floor was strewn with plastic bags of rubbish. He could see the dim shapes of shelves, old furniture and paintings on the walls. There were cardboard boxes and packages on the floor and surfaces. On every side Erlendur was confronted with the clutter and chaos of a man who was trying to keep the world at a safe distance by turning this dark house into a refuge.

'I'm sorry if I went too far,' said Erlendur, feeling pity for the recluse. 'I didn't mean to upset you. Didn't mean to scare you.'

Rasmus was looking at him sceptically.

'I just have a few more questions, then I'll go,' said Erlendur.

'You can't force your way in here and speak to me like that,' said Rasmus, still hurt and angry.

'No, I know. I overstepped the mark. It won't happen again. Just a few more questions, then I'll be gone. When did you last speak to her?'

'What do you mean?'

'You said you'd spoken to Dagbjört several times. Once when you met her in the shop. When was the last time you spoke to her?'

'Shortly before she went missing. It was out here in the street, a bit further down. We got talking. She was having a party that evening and wanted to apologise in advance in case her friends were too noisy. I told her not to worry. I could tell by looking at her how much she was looking forward to it.'

'Do you remember what else you talked about?'

'Yes, I remember it well. Every detail. Every word she said. She told me they had a good gramophone but almost no decent records. And she asked if I could lend her any. I said I was afraid I didn't own any records. The only music I listened to was on the radio. She said they never played anything for young people and I agreed. The State Broadcasting Service put on nothing but symphonies. Still does.'

Rasmus attempted to smile but it resulted in no more than slight tremors of his lips that revealed a hint of teeth. He was recovering his composure after this rude invasion of his property. Erlendur had succeeded in calming him.

'Was that all?' said Erlendur. 'You only talked about music?'

'Yes, that was all.'

'Is it right, what I've heard, that you were the victim of an attack several years after Dagbjört vanished?'

'Where did you hear that?' asked Rasmus, surprised.

'From a man I know who used to live in Camp Knox.'

'I'm not sure I want to talk about it,' said Rasmus hesitantly.

'No, all right,' said Erlendur, keen not to put too much pressure on the man.

'It was an unpleasant experience.'

'I can believe it.'

'A couple of hooligans. They stank of the camp. I was walking home from town and they followed me as if I was some kind of freak. Started insulting me. I'd never seen them before but they seemed to know all about me. That I used to live with my mother and so on. That she was dead. I begged them to leave me alone but they wouldn't listen. They pushed me into an alleyway and hit me. Stole my bag. Then ran away. I was left lying there, covered in blood, but managed to struggle home somehow.'

'Did the police catch them?'

'Police? I didn't bother the police. My mother would have said there was no point making a fuss about a little thing like that. People are just envious of our sort, you see.'

'Tell me more about your conversation with Dagbjört. You discussed the party she was having that evening, and music. That's all?'

'I remember it so well; she wanted to get hold of some new records,' said Rasmus. 'There weren't as many foreign records around then. Not like now, all that terrible racket.'

'And how was she planning to "get hold of" them?'

'She was hoping a friend of hers would bring along some brand-new records from America. The girl had got them through her cousin who worked on the base. Dagbjört wanted him to buy some for her too.'

'So, he worked on the base, did he? This cousin?'

'Yes, that's what she said.'

'Did he live there too?'

'She didn't say.'

'Do you know what he was called?'

'No, all I knew was that he was the cousin of one of her friends.'

'You didn't mention this to the police after Dagbjört went missing?'

'The police?'

'Didn't you think you were in possession of an important piece of information?'

'What information?' asked Rasmus, looking confused.

'I don't think this has come out before. That she might have been intending to meet this man.'

'I wouldn't know.'

'Didn't it occur to you after she vanished?'

'No, I can't say it did. She must have mentioned it to other people too. If she was intending to buy records from this man. What's so remarkable about that? It can hardly have been much of a secret.'

'You're right,' said Erlendur. 'Not everything's reported in the files. Perhaps it wasn't significant.'

'I wouldn't have thought so,' said Rasmus.

'Did you watch Dagbjört and her friends having their party? From your house?'

Rasmus nodded.

'And when the party was over and her friends had left, Dagbjört went up to her room to get ready for bed and saw you peeping through the curtains, watching her undress?'

'Yes,' Rasmus admitted reluctantly.

'You don't like visitors much,' said Erlendur, trying to meet Rasmus's shifty eyes and read the truth from them. 'Especially not from the police. You don't report it when you're beaten up. You talk to Dagbjört shortly before she vanishes but don't tell anyone. Maybe you were afraid your secret would be exposed?'

'My secret?'

'After all, if it had emerged that you used to spy on her in the evenings you might have been suspected of far worse after she went missing. You couldn't take the risk. Unless you were afraid of something quite different. Have you got other secrets, Rasmus? Something you're hiding here in your house?'

'I didn't touch her,' protested Rasmus. 'I could never have hurt her. You've got to understand that. Never. Never. Never.'

36

Caroline still hadn't made contact by the time Erlendur returned to CID headquarters. Marion was sitting by the phone but said it was unlikely they would hear from her any time soon, given that she had fobbed them off with a false number. There was no telling what she was thinking or what her next move would be. It seemed obvious to Marion that she didn't want any further dealings with the Icelandic police for now and that she would get in touch when she felt the need. Erlendur countered that she could be in real danger if Kristvin's death was linked to Wilbur Cain, CIA transport aircraft and arms dealing.

'Hadn't we better go back out there?' said Erlendur. 'Do something?'

'You're right. There's no way I can sit here and wait for her to make contact if there's the slightest chance she's in danger,' said Marion. 'The question is, should I go alone this time?'

'Hmm, second thoughts, I'm not sure she'd want that. I'm sure she'd let us know if she uncovered something major.'

'Still, it couldn't hurt to take a trip out there,' said Marion, standing up. 'I'll try to be discreet. You wait by the phone and talk to her if she calls. What have you been up to, by the way? Ringing from payphones, charging around town.'

'Dagbjört,' said Erlendur.

'Making any headway?'

'Not sure. Could be.'

Erlendur outlined what he had found out since he discovered the diary pages in Dagbjört's room. He described his visit to Rasmus Kruse who had admitted spying on Dagbjört across the garden in the evenings. And his encounter with Vilhelm at the bus station. And the news about the friend's cousin who worked on the base and supplied the latest records from America and possibly a variety of other sought-after items that teenage girls would have coveted in the post-war years.

'You mean the cousin may have been using that as bait?' said Marion.

'It crossed my mind.'

'Of course there was nothing in the shops after the war,' said Marion. 'We had import restrictions and acute shortages for years, right around the time your girl went missing.'

Erlendur was aware of the import restrictions in those days. Special licences were required to ship any kind of goods into the country. Not even a holey sock could be brought in unless a rationing clerk had approved the request. Long queues would form if people got wind of some new product arriving in the shops; they were prepared to camp outside all night if necessary, waiting for the doors to open. There was a flourishing black market too and corruption was rife. The restrictions spawned all sorts of smuggling rackets and under-the-counter trade.

'And profiteering from the army was at its height,' said Erlendur.

'You can say that again.'

'There's a passing reference to the gramophone records in the files containing interviews with the girls who were at Dagbjört's party, but the police saw no point in following it up. They never made any connection between this man and Dagbjört – perhaps for a good reason. Perhaps they didn't know each other and never met. But it would be interesting to talk to him. If he's still alive.'

'You should try and trace him,' said Marion. 'Meanwhile, I'm going to pay a visit to the base and see if I can make contact with Caroline.'

Marion left and Erlendur sat down by the phone and dialled the number of Dagbjört's friend Silja. When she eventually picked up, Erlendur launched straight in, asking if she knew which of Dagbjört's friends used to have a cousin who supplied the latest American records from the base.

'I'm sorry?' said Silja, unprepared for the question. It occurred to Erlendur belatedly that he might have interrupted her supper.

'You and your friends went to a party at Dagbjört's house shortly before her disappearance. One of the girls had got hold of some new records. She'd obtained them from her cousin who worked at the air-force base in Keflavík. I need to know which friend that was.'

'I've completely forgotten.'

'Would you be able to find out for me?'

'I could try,' said Silja. 'Why's it important?'

'I can't tell yet but I'd like to know who the man was.'

'What's so interesting about this man? Have you discovered something?'

'No,' said Erlendur, to discourage her from getting ideas, 'I'm no closer. I just want to know who he was.'

'My mind's a blank,' said Silja, the surprise still lingering in her voice. 'Records from the base?'

'He may have been living there at the time,' said Erlendur. 'Could you track down the friend for me?'

'I'll try.'

'Good,' said Erlendur. 'Thanks. I'll be in touch.'

There was little traffic on the road to Keflavík. The weather was still and the rising moon shed a cold light over the surrounding lava field and the pyramid form of Mount Keilir. At the gate Marion was given directions to military police headquarters and a few minutes later drew up in front of the building. There were grey jeeps parked outside. In addition to maintaining law and order among the Defense Force personnel, the police were responsible for patrolling the perimeter fence and deterring intruders.

Marion went inside and approached the reception desk. The young man standing behind it asked if he could help. Marion explained that the Icelandic police had recently received assistance from a liaison officer, Sergeant Caroline Murphy, and –

'Are you from the Icelandic police?' interrupted the young man.

'Yes,' said Marion, smiling. 'Didn't I mention that? I just wanted to thank her for her help.'

'I'm afraid Caroline's taking a few days' leave,' said the young man, turning over the pages in front of him. 'But I'll tell her you dropped by.'

'Thank you,' said Marion. 'But I won't be back this way any time soon. You couldn't tell me where she lives? I only want to say a quick hello. It won't take long. She really was extremely helpful.'

The man was not yet twenty, with red hair and skin, freckles, and a fine down on his cheeks. Marion noticed that his uniform was crumpled, which seemed consistent with his general air of apathy with regard to his job and assisting those who came into the station.

'May I see some ID?' he asked as he unhurriedly looked up the address.

'Of course,' said Marion and handed him a warrant card.

After giving it a sidelong glance, the young man read out Caroline's address. Marion thanked him effusively for his helpfulness, then got behind the wheel again and a few minutes later stopped in front of a two-storey barracks. The car park was chock-full of cars and trucks which spilled out into the street as well. Finding Caroline's name on a bell in the lobby, Marion rang it several times without getting any response. The door to the stairwell was open. There was a cigarette vending machine by the wall and another selling soft drinks and beer. Marion entered and climbed the stairs to the first floor.

This must be it, thought Marion, walking up to an unmarked door on the right-hand side and knocking. Marion waited, and knocked again, with no more success than before, then started hammering on it, calling Caroline's name. The only result was that the door of the flat opposite opened and a man emerged onto the landing.

'Do you have to make such a goddamn racket?' he asked.

Marion swung round. 'Sorry, I'm looking for Caroline. Do you have any idea where she might be?'

230

'Who are you?' asked the man, who was clad in jeans and a college sweatshirt and had a beer can in his hand. A woman peered out inquisitively from behind him.

'I just wanted to say hello,' said Marion. 'We worked together recently and she was going to . . . er . . . take me to the officers' club.'

'You Icelandic?'

'Yes.'

'You here to buy something?'

'Buy? No.'

'So you weren't helping yourself to cigarettes downstairs?'

'No,' said Marion. 'No cigarettes.'

'Like a beer?' asked the man, waving the can.

'No, thank you,' said Marion, unsure if the man was joking.

'Is it you who's always cleaning out the machines downstairs?'

'I've never touched them,' said Marion. 'I've never been here before.'

'You're all the same, you Icelandics. Goddamn parasites.'

'Well, it –'

'We haven't seen Caroline today. I reckon she'd have answered by now if she was home, so you can stop banging on her door.'

The woman retreated further into the flat behind him. Marion heard the phone ringing inside.

'Do you know where she might be?'

'She sometimes goes to the Animal Locker in the evenings,' said the man. 'But never to the officers' club. Though maybe with you. She your sponsor?'

'The Animal Locker?' said Marion, remembering that this was the place Erlendur had mentioned in connection with Joan; it was where she worked. Kristvin had gone there with a sponsor who may or may not have been called Wilbur Cain, and it was a place Caroline sometimes patronised herself. 'Isn't that . . . is it a . . .?'

'It's a bar,' said the man.

'Known as the Zoo?'

'That's the one.'

'Oh, right, that's where we were supposed to be going,' said Marion. 'She's probably there already. I'm sorry about all the noise; I didn't mean to disturb you.'

'Just remember that other people live here too,' said the man and took a swig from his can.

Marion smiled apologetically, said goodbye and headed downstairs, out to the car and drove away. It was like being a foreigner in one's own country. After a few minutes Marion stopped a soldier who was passing and asked if he could point the way to the Animal Locker.

37

Erlendur heard the phone ringing in the office. He had stepped out
to fetch a coffee and, hurrying back inside, snatched up the receiver.

'Caroline?'

'Er, no . . .? Who's this, please? Is Erlendur there?'

He recognised Silja's voice.

'Yes, sorry, hello again, this is Erlendur speaking. I was
expecting another call.'

'I found out who had the cousin with the records. Would you
like her number?'

'Yes, please,' said Erlendur, grabbing a pen and paper. 'That'd
be great.'

'It's Rósanna,' said Silja and reeled off her number. 'Just give
her a call, she's expecting to hear from you. She was astonished
to be asked about the records, as you can imagine. Of course all
I could tell her was that you were trying to get to the bottom of
the case. Are you making any progress?'

'Not really,' said Erlendur, sipping his coffee. He didn't think Rasmus's peeping Tom activities were worth reporting at this point.

'Well, let me know if I can be of any more help.'

'Thank you.'

Silja hung up and Erlendur phoned Svava, Dagbjört's aunt, and asked if she remembered her brother's next-door neighbours: a Danish woman and her son — name of Rasmus. Half Danish. His father was Icelandic but didn't live with them.

'Do you remember them at all?' asked Erlendur. 'The mother died years ago but the son still lives there.'

'Not really,' said Svava. 'As far as I know, they kept themselves to themselves, the mother and son, and my brother didn't have much to do with them.'

'You never heard him complain about them?'

'Not that I can remember off the top of my head.'

'Not about the man, Rasmus?'

'No – or only that my brother thought they didn't look after the garden properly,' said Svava, 'didn't take care of it at all, just let it go to seed. The mother may've been a bit odd. Not that I want to judge anyone. But now you come to mention it . . .'

'Yes?'

'My brother once fell out with her because she claimed he'd killed her cat. Which was absolute rubbish, of course. My brother would never have hurt a fly. He couldn't bear to see anything suffer. The woman obviously doted on the animal because she actually rang the police and sent them round to my brother's. He had a terrible time with the old bat.'

'What happened to the cat? Did it ever turn up?'

'Yes, it did. My brother said it probably just needed a break from her. Why are you asking about them?'

'No real reason,' said Erlendur, to deflect suspicion from Rasmus. 'I was checking who lived next door at the time and wondered about those two, that's all. Do you recall the other neighbours at all?'

'No, no one in particular. It was a good area. There was nothing wrong with it. As far as I know they were decent types, the people who lived there.'

They quickly wrapped up their conversation after that, then Erlendur dialled the number Silja had given him. After several rings the phone was answered, by a teenage boy, Erlendur thought. He introduced himself and asked to speak to the boy's mother, Rósanna. Erlendur heard him call her and she picked up the phone almost immediately. He introduced himself again and Silja was right, she had been expecting to hear from him.

'This is about Dagbjört, isn't it?' she said, the wonder apparent in her voice.

'Yes, that's correct.'

'Are they still investigating her case?'

'No, there's no real investigation, I'm just taking a look at it for Dagbjört's aunt.'

'It must be twenty-five, twenty-six years ago?'

'Yes. I hear you have – or had – a cousin who used to work on the base in those days and could supply this and that – records, for example.'

'What about him?'

'Is it right that he used to help out with that sort of thing?'

'Well . . . I . . . I'm a bit uncomfortable discussing this over the phone,' said Rósanna. 'You couldn't pop round, could you? It's not that late.'

'I'm afraid I'm rather tied up,' said Erlendur, thinking of

Caroline. He needed to stay by the phone in case she or Marion called.

'Well, what about tomorrow, then?' said Rósanna. 'No, come to think of it, I'm quite busy tomorrow, and after that it's my son's birthday . . .'

'Maybe I will come over, if that's all right,' said Erlendur, unwilling to lose this chance. 'It won't take long.'

'Right, good,' said Rósanna, and gave him the address. 'See you soon, then.'

Acting quickly, Erlendur told reception that he was expecting a phone call and wanted it forwarded to the place where he was going. It was absolutely vital. Then he ran down the stairs, drawn to this encounter with the past, a past that had got its hooks into him so tightly that everything else had to take second place.

38

Marion surveyed the bar known as the Zoo. Things were unusually slow, if the nickname was anything to go by. A few tables and bar stools were occupied by enlisted men in uniform or men in civilian dress, some with a beer glass in front of them, others with something stronger. Country music was playing quietly from invisible speakers. Cigarette smoke curled up from the tables. All the customers looked American to Marion; one was actually wearing a cowboy hat. The only women were the two waitresses, one blonde and one brunette, who were chatting to the older guy behind the bar. He cracked a joke and they shrieked with laughter, then quickly scanned the room in case anyone needed a drink.

Marion sipped at a beer: it tasted like watered-down Pilsner. Either the entrance policy was unusually lax or they didn't take the need for an American escort seriously here. At least there was no doorman and no one had asked for a sponsor. The bartender probably assumed Marion belonged to the horde of civilian contractors, inspectors, engineers and technicians who worked for the army and lived on the base for a while. More likely he simply couldn't be bothered with an interrogation, though no one could have failed to notice that Marion stuck out like a sore thumb from the regulars.

Marion had asked the blonde waitress about Joan and learned that it was her evening off. The woman turned out to be acquainted with Caroline too and said she dropped in from time to time. Apparently she was a red-hot bowler and belonged to the number-one team on the base. That explained her choice of venue for her meeting with Marion the other day. The waitress was also able to supply the information that Caroline was single, not very open or chatty, and a bit of a loner.

A man rose from one of the tables and walked over to the bar, casting a glance at Marion as he did so. He was fleshy, wore a workman's checked shirt, jeans and sneakers, and his dark hair and skin gave him a Latino appearance. He grinned at some comment of the blonde's, then approached the table where Marion was sitting.

'You Icelandic?'

Marion admitted as much.

'Mind if I take a seat?' he asked, and without waiting for an invitation pulled up a chair. 'Haven't seen you around here before. Do you work on the base?'

'I'm waiting for a friend,' said Marion.

'You mean Caroline?'

'Yes.'

'I know Caroline,' said the man with a grin. 'The name's Martinez. Carlos Martinez, from New Mexico. Me and Caroline go bowling together. They told me at the bar you were asking questions about her. How do you know Caroline, if you don't mind my asking?'

'She's been helping us with our inquiries in connection with a man who used to work here,' said Marion. 'I'm with the Icelandic police.'

'She doesn't talk about work much. We heard about the death . . . that you think the Icelandic man whose body was found in the lava field was killed here on the base. Is that true?'

'The matter's under investigation and we can't –'

'No, sure. I understand. Been here before?'

'No.'

'How do you like it?'

'I feel as if I'm in Texas,' said Marion. 'Though I'm only fifty kilometres from home.'

Martinez laughed. 'This is the liveliest bar,' he said, grinning. He seemed a very good-natured, talkative man. 'I don't go anywhere else if I can help it.'

'Do you get many Icelanders in here?' asked Marion.

'Yeah, sometimes. I know a few. They're usually pretty fun, lively guys and I have to say you have some real good bands who come and play in the clubs. Real good musicians.'

It soon emerged that Martinez had been on a duty tour in the Philippines before coming to Keflavík; he'd been in the marines for three years, eight months of which had been spent in Iceland. He knew nothing about the country other than it was cold, bleak and remote; still hadn't ventured outside the military zone and wasn't sure he wanted to. He'd been very happy in the Philippines and couldn't imagine two more different countries. It had been warm and sunny there; good weather every day, beautiful girls, friendly locals. Here it was freezing and dark and the wind never stopped howling. Coming from a hot climate himself, Martinez couldn't take the arctic temperatures. It hadn't been his decision to come to Iceland: he'd been posted here.

'You people don't much care for us being here, do you?' he said.

'I wouldn't say that,' said Marion. 'Depends who you ask.'

Martinez nodded and said that when he first arrived here, he had soon learned that many Icelanders were opposed to the American presence in Iceland and that the issue split the nation down the middle. The military zone was securely fenced off and communications with the locals were kept to a minimum. But a large number of Icelandic civilians worked inside the area during the day, since all construction and maintenance projects on the site, from the building of accommodation or hangars to the upkeep of roads, were in the hands of Icelandic entrepreneurs who had no scruples about lining their pockets at the military's expense. Martinez said he couldn't get his head round the double standards.

'People here disapprove of the military and find fault with everything it does but somehow it's OK to make money out of it,' he said, lighting a cigarette.

Marion had no answer to this.

'Hey, I didn't mean to sound like an asshole,' Martinez added. 'Sorry. I'm quitting the marines when I finish my tour over here. Going home to New Mexico. It's about time. Want another beer? I'll get this one.'

He was back at the bar before Marion could respond and returned with two beers.

'You don't happen to know a man who used to drink here, an Icelander called Kristvin?' asked Marion. 'He worked on the base. Flight mechanic.'

'Who's he? Is he the man who was murdered?'

'We don't know if he was murdered,' said Marion. 'Do you remember him in here? He was known as Kris.'

'Kris? No, I don't recall anyone by that name. How did he die?'

'We don't know the circumstances,' said Marion. 'We're trying to piece them together and find out who he associated with on the base, what he did here and what he was working on before he died. It's just part of our routine investigation. Caroline's working with us because the military police need to be kept in the picture.'

'I see.'

'There's another thing. I don't know how to put this so I'll just ask you straight out. If I wanted to score marijuana here, who would I go to?'

'Marijuana?' repeated Martinez warily.

'I'm not trying to insinuate that you or anyone else in here's involved in dealing.'

'I don't know. Was your man mixed up in that?'

'Possibly. These are the kinds of questions we're grappling with, you see, and we hardly know where to begin. We know so little about the set-up here. If I were an Icelander who purchased drugs regularly from someone on the base, who would I be dealing with? Enlisted men? Officers? Pilots? Where would the deal take place? At their homes? In a public place? Say I owe someone money and I'm in trouble because I can't pay up. Do you have any idea who might be after me in a situation like that?'

Marion ploughed on with the questions, though Martinez was clearly ill at ease.

'I'm not the right man to help you with this,' he said cautiously. 'I'm not into that scene.'

'How about Wilbur Cain?' asked Marion. 'Do you know him?'

'Never heard of him,' said Martinez. 'Wilbur Cain? Who's he?'

Marion could only reply that the investigation was focusing on this bar because the Icelander used to drink here and that the name Wilbur Cain had cropped up in connection with Kristvin, but so far they had failed to track the man down. Martinez listened attentively.

'There's a woman who works here, Joan. Maybe you should ask her about the dope,' he muttered in a low voice.

'Joan? Who works here?'

'I shouldn't . . . Is Caroline in some kind of danger?' asked Martinez.

'Hopefully no more than you'd expect in her line of work,' said Marion, worried now about having gone too far and blurted out too much information in a soldiers' bar.

'The thing is, she didn't turn up to bowling practice this evening,' said Martinez. 'I called her at home but no one answered. Then you show up and say you're waiting for her. I'm getting kind of worried. That's all.'

'What about Joan? Can she supply drugs?'

'I know her husband does. But you didn't hear that from me.'

'Does he sell to Icelanders?'

'That's what I heard. She works here and people gossip, you know how it is. I don't like to spread rumours but if it might help Caroline . . .?'

'Don't worry about Caroline,' said Marion. 'Have you any idea where I might find her?'

'No, she's kind of reticent, doesn't talk about herself much.'

'Is she happy here?'

'Yes, I think so. Plenty of people are. In spite of the weather.'

Martinez grinned. 'Actually, she told me she goes to the movies a lot. I think there's something going on between her and Bill. Or that's what a little bird told me recently.'

'Bill?'

'He runs the movie theatre.'

'The movie theatre? You mean the Andrews cinema?'

'Yes. It's the only one on the base.'

Having thanked Martinez for the beer, Marion left the bar, got back in the car and headed for the cinema. Taking out the scrap of paper with the phone number Caroline had given them that had turned out to be for Andrews, Marion wondered if she had in fact been directing them there all along.

Marion was now assailed by doubts, by the fear of having revealed too much at the bar. Had mentioning Wilbur Cain by name been a mistake? On the other hand, it wouldn't hurt to make their presence felt and shake people up a bit. Perhaps word would get back to Cain that a detective had been asking questions about him. How would he react? Make a run for it? Leave the country? The Icelandic police were powerless to prevent him, Marion thought. The Americans could do what they liked in the military zone.

'They can throw us off the base any time they want,' Marion muttered aloud in the car, then caught sight of the Andrews cinema ahead.

39

Rósanna was a single mother of three, who lived in a basement flat in the Laugarnes area. A flight of stairs led down to the front door, and Erlendur was on the bottom step when the door flew open and the eldest boy, who had answered the phone earlier, appeared, took one look at Erlendur and yelled to his mother as he shot past and up the steps: 'That old bloke's here.'

Erlendur was disconcerted. Never, to his knowledge, had he been described as an old bloke before; he was only thirty-three. He watched the boy's retreating figure, wondering if that was how he looked to him. When he turned back, Rósanna had come to the door. She was quite short, looked careworn, and was regarding Erlendur with an enquiring expression.

'I expected you to be older,' she said.

'Ah, is that . . . was that your son?'

'Is there someone else with you?'

'What? No, I'm alone.'

He saw that she was trying to suppress a smile. She invited him in, apologising for the mess. She'd been working late and had had no time for housework all week. 'The kids don't lift a finger,' she added. Erlendur said he quite understood and they chatted for a while, mostly about her friends at the Women's College and what had become of them. This led her to talk about herself and what she had been up to in the intervening years. She was not in the least shy, took a matter-of-fact view of her circumstances and had not an ounce of self-pity. She ran a small shop near the top of Skólavördustígur which stocked a variety of health foods, though she said that business was slow. The Icelanders were only interested in red meat and stodgy sauces but she had taken a gamble on health food being the future. Erlendur admitted that he ate little but fatty meat in gravy and fermented fish with melted dripping, but pretended to be interested in improving his diet. This provoked another smile.

'People are more interested in their health than they used to be,' Rósanna said optimistically. She hadn't gone on to higher education after leaving school but had met a man and got married instead. Her husband had set up a small company and she'd worked for him until their children were born and she became more involved in running their home. But over time the company had started losing money and they'd ended up badly in debt. Then her husband had fallen ill. It transpired that he had pancreatic cancer and he died within the year. She had sold the company, their house and two cars, which left her largely debt-free, and moved into this basement flat with her children.

'I wasn't the one who knew Dagbjört best,' she said, thinking back, 'but of course I remember what a shock it was for us girls in her class when it happened. We couldn't believe it. We thought she must have gone off somewhere without telling anyone and that she'd turn up at school next day and it would all have been a misunderstanding. Of course that didn't happen. I was a bit taken aback when Silja rang and then you.'

'There are no new developments,' said Erlendur. 'I don't know if Silja explained but Dagbjört's aunt wants to know if it's possible to draw any conclusions, although it was a long time ago, and I agreed to look into it. It's a last-ditch attempt, I suppose.'

'It must have been devastating for the family. We were all given the third degree by the police at the time. But I don't know if I can add anything, and I really don't see what it's got to do with my cousin.'

'It's just one among a number of details that have cropped up,' said Erlendur, trying to reassure the woman. 'At the time it was rumoured that Dagbjört had a boyfriend. Were you aware of that?'

'You mean the boy from Camp Knox? Wasn't that just idle gossip?'

'Maybe.'

'I remember people talking about it but I can't tell you if it was true or not. We weren't that into boys at the time. One or two of the girls may have been in relationships – I really can't remember.'

'What about Camp Knox? Did she ever talk about it?'

'She may have done but if so I've forgotten. I lived on the opposite side of town and didn't know the west end. Though of course I knew about life in the camps. It certainly wasn't easy. One of my mother's sisters lived in Múli Camp.'

'I gather your old class still keeps in touch,' said Erlendur.

'Yes, we do. We have a reunion at least once a year and I know it's probably a bit morbid but we always raise a toast to Dagbjört. She's never far from our thoughts. Then we play popular hits from the time. Dean Martin and so on.'

'Doris Day?'

'Yes, and Doris Day,' said Rósanna, smiling.

'I know it's a long time ago, but did you ever hear Dagbjört mention her next-door neighbours?'

'No, not that I recall.'

'The thing is, I spoke to one of them the other day and he told me he'd bumped into Dagbjört shortly before she went missing and that she'd been talking about wanting some new records from America. She mentioned your cousin. Said he worked out on the air-force base and supplied you with the latest hits, Doris Day and so on. You were going to bring some to her birthday party. Does that jog your memory? Do you know if Dagbjört ever got in touch with your cousin?'

Rósanna listened intently, trying to cast her mind back to what had been said and done in the lead-up to the tragic event.

'Wouldn't she have had to go through you?' asked Erlendur. 'If she wanted to contact your cousin?'

'I only have one cousin who worked on the base,' said Rósanna thoughtfully. 'Our fathers are brothers. He's about ten years older than me. His name's Mensalder. I'm trying to think if Dagbjört ever asked me about him or if I gave her his phone number. My mind's a blank. At least I wasn't aware that they ever met or spoke to each other. Mensalder lived out at Keflavík and worked for the army; he was always bringing home stuff he bought there or picked up for free. Cigarettes, turkey, steak, jeans. They were real luxuries in those days because you couldn't get them for love or money in Reykjavík. It was a way for him to earn a bit on the side. But he mostly gave us things or my dad paid a token amount. Mensalder always had dollars and the latest records and I clearly remember borrowing three or four from him for Dagbjört's party. It's quite possible I gave her his number. Or perhaps she got it from someone else. But I never heard if she rang him.'

'So you didn't act as go-between?'

'No. I didn't order anything for her, if that's what you mean. But . . . it was . . . hang on a minute . . .'

'What?'

'I do believe he took them round himself.'

'The records?'

'No, he picked them up from hers the next day. That was it. I remember now. He lent me the records and wanted them straight back because he'd already sold them to somebody else, but I forgot them at Dagbjört's house and didn't have time to fetch them, so I told him where she lived and he was going to drop round for them. That was it, if I'm not mistaken. He was in a bit of a hurry.'

'So they would have met?'

'Yes, of course.'

'And it's possible she asked him if he could get her some stuff from the base?'

'Yes, but wait a minute, surely there's nothing suspicious about that? It's got nothing to do with . . . with what happened to Dagbjört?'

'What does he do now? This Mensalder?'

'Last I heard he was working at a petrol station,' said Rósanna.

'Here in Reykjavík?'

'Yes.'

'Is he married? Any children?'

'No, no wife, no children,' said Rósanna, and Erlendur saw it gradually dawning on her, the real reason he was here in her flat this evening, a complete stranger, asking questions about Dagbjört. 'Mensalder's always lived alone,' she said hesitantly. 'Why are you dragging him into this? What's he done?'

Erlendur didn't know how to answer.

'I don't believe . . . no, Mensalder's totally harmless. He could never have . . . are you implying he's linked to Dagbjört's disappearance? Is that what you're insinuating?'

'I have absolutely no idea,' said Erlendur, observing Rósanna's dismay. 'Honestly, I don't know.'

40

Marion drew up in front of the Andrews Movie Theater. The car park was quite busy. *Apocalypse Now*, the film currently showing, appeared to be very popular. The area was poorly lit and Marion switched off the ignition on the side furthest from the cinema and was just wondering how best to conduct an unobtrusive search for Caroline inside the building when the rear door of the car was torn open and Caroline herself climbed in. Marion jerked round.

'Why didn't you call to say you were coming?' Caroline asked, nervously scanning their surroundings. 'Are you being followed?'

'Followed . . .?'

'Well?'

'Not that I've noticed,' said Marion, starting the car and preparing to reverse out of the space.

'No, stay here,' said Caroline. 'We're OK here in the parking lot.'

'We rang the number you gave us and thought you were trying to trick us when the cinema answered,' said Marion.

'Trick you? Why did you come here if you thought I was trying to trick you?'

'Because then I heard about Bill,' said Marion, switching off the engine again.

'Who from?'

'I bumped into a friend of yours, Martinez. A very friendly guy, I must say.'

'Carlos Martinez?'

'Yes,' said Marion. 'He was at the Animal Locker. I thought he'd never stop talking about himself.'

'Bill works here at the movie theatre. He's a friend. He let me use the office after he went home. I've been making calls all day.'

'Are you all right?'

'Yes, I'm OK, though all this secrecy's making me jumpy. Did you go round to my apartment? I haven't been back there yet.'

'Yes, I did.'

'Was the dorm being watched? That you noticed?'

'I didn't see anyone,' said Marion. 'But it's possible. This is all rather new to me.'

'Yeah, yeah, Erlendur's already given me the speech about how you guys are clueless when it comes to this place, how it's a whole new world to you and all that bullshit. I wondered what the hell he was talking about.'

'I met your neighbour. He mentioned the Animal Locker, and Erlendur had already told me you sometimes went there. Do you realise you missed a practice?'

Marion caught the flash of Caroline's grin in the mirror.

'Tell me about Martinez.'

'I don't know him that well,' said Caroline. 'He's a sergeant in the marines. We go bowling together. He's OK. Quite a hotshot at bowling too.'

'I asked him about Kristvin and if he was acquainted with a man called Wilbur Cain.'

'What did he say about Cain?'

'He didn't recognise the name.'

'I heard earlier that Cain spent a lot of time in Greenland before he came here,' said Caroline. 'He still goes there on regular assignments. And NCT planes stop there fairly frequently too, en route from Europe to points west. They land here at Keflavík to refuel and sometimes take on cargo, and every now and then Cain joins them to travel to Greenland and back.'

'What's in Greenland?'

'Thule,' said Caroline. 'Our biggest military installation in the northern hemisphere.'

'Where did you learn this?'

'Here and there. My buddy in Washington. Also a woman I know quite well who works for air traffic control here on the base. I helped her out once. Her husband used to knock her around. She left him and they're getting a divorce now but the jackass couldn't leave her alone whenever he had a drink inside him. He wasn't a bad person apart from that. Just a loser, like so many of those guys. Anyhow, I pulled a few strings to get him transferred so she could get rid of him. All without his knowledge. The first he knew about it was when he landed in his new station. And guess where that was?'

'Thule?'

'You got it. She called him for me. He works in air traffic control too and she got the lowdown from him about NCT at that end, who travels with the planes, and so on. He always used to come crawling back to her after he'd hit her, so he'll do anything for her now.'

'What's going on in Greenland? Why should a Military Intelligence agent be travelling back and forth between Keflavík and Thule?'

'I still haven't been able to dig up any information on that.'

'Do you think Kristvin might have known?'

'I don't see how,' said Caroline. 'These are covert flights. Your air traffic control is unaware of them. He'd have had to speak to someone who was well informed about these matters and, what's more, was prepared to talk about them.'

'Like who?'

'I have no idea. The aircraft generally stop very briefly here and don't attract any special attention.'

'But then one develops a fault,' said Marion, 'and they have to call in the mechanics. And one of them sees enough to make him curious and starts asking questions and before you know it he's dead. We've established that he almost certainly died as the result of the impact from a big drop. And we're told there are some very high work platforms in Hangar 885. Kristvin could have climbed up them and fallen off.'

'Been pushed off, you mean?'

'We've been denied access to the hangar, in addition to everything else. Chances are he took refuge in there while trying to escape, fled up the scaffolding and was trapped there. What do you know about the airbase at Thule?'

All was quiet in the car park. The Andrews cinema was a splash of neon in the winter darkness. It was named, Marion knew, after an American general who had died in a plane crash near Keflavík during the war. Posters advertising the latest Hollywood films hung either side of the entrance: *Kramer vs. Kramer*, *Alien*, *The China Syndrome*.

'Not much,' said Caroline. 'It's strategically important as part of the defensive line against the Russians in the northern hemisphere. From there it's possible to enter Soviet airspace via Siberia where there are far fewer defences than if we fly from our bases in Western Europe over the heavily fortified areas of Eastern Europe and Russia. Thule's vital in that context. Even more significant than this little installation here.'

'Talking of hardship posts,' said Marion. 'Iceland must seem like a tropical paradise compared to Thule.'

'You bet.'

'The Danes are about as happy with the base at Thule as we are about our "little installation",' said Marion, and went on to explain that there had been a major debate in Denmark in recent years about the fate of the Inuit in the vicinity of Thule. When the base was built, the Greenlandic hunting settlement was uprooted and moved north to a place called Qaanaaq, without reference to their wishes, with unforeseen consequences.

'You must think we're complete monsters,' said Caroline.

Marion was silent. Taking this as assent, Caroline saw red.

'Jesus, I don't know why the hell I'm doing this. You hate literally everything I stand for. Everything we do looks suspicious to you.'

'That's not true,' protested Marion. 'Your help's been invaluable and we're very grateful, even if we do have our doubts about your country's military activities. You've done more for us than we could have dared ask and I get the impression that's because you yourself want to know what's going on here.'

Caroline didn't answer. The cinema doors opened and people began to pour out. The crowd quickly dispersed homewards, some on foot, others in cars. There was only a short interval before the next screening and a new audience was already gathering. Occasional shouts, the honking of car horns and laughter carried through the darkness.

'Thule's a top-secret installation, of course,' said Caroline. She had slid down in her seat and was peering out of the window at the cinema-goers as if they belonged to a different, more benign world. 'Not many people know this but I'm told that B-52 bombers used to be kept aloft in a holding pattern over the area at all times, one taking over from the other so the chain was never broken. That was to ensure the fastest possible response in the event of a Soviet strike. They assumed it would be one of the first places to be flattened in a nuclear attack. By keeping the B-52s constantly airborne they made sure that at least one would escape being destroyed in the attack and make it over the Soviet frontier with its payload of bombs.'

'What kind of bombs?'

'Hydrogen bombs. Four to a plane. Each one a hundred times more powerful than the atom bomb that destroyed Hiroshima.'

'Are you telling me there are nuclear weapons in Greenland?' said Marion.

'Apparently. About a decade ago a bomber crashed in one of the violent blizzards you get in the region. The wreckage was found about six miles from the base and the bombs were removed. After that they abandoned the policy of keeping B-52s airborne. But the weapons are still stored on the base.'

'The Danish government has always denied the presence of nuclear weapons in Greenland,' said Marion. 'It's a highly controversial issue over there. Was it your friend in Washington who told you this?'

Caroline nodded. 'He feels he owes me,' she said quietly.

'Oh?'

'It was hard for me to turn to him for help but he's behaved honourably. And I didn't know what else to do.'

'What . . . in what way does he owe you?'

'He feels guilty.'

'About what?'

'Another woman.'

'Another woman?'

'Not that it's any of your business.'

'No, fair enough.'

'I thought we had a good relationship until he started cheating on me,' said Caroline. 'I guess he's still trying to make up for it. He's the reason I'm here. I wanted to get as far away from him as I could and now he thinks it's his fault that I'm in deep shit out here at the ends of the earth.'

'What's all this got to do with Hangar 885 and Wilbur Cain?'

'I wasn't supposed to tell you but it's conceivable, just conceivable, that the NCT Hercules transports have been ferrying nuclear weapons from Thule and establishing them here. It's also conceivable that the person responsible for security matters on this operation is none other than our friend Cain.'

'Wilbur Cain?'

'You got it.'

41

There were two men on duty at the filling station, one of whom looked to be in his late fifties. Rósanna's cousin, presumably. The age was right at any rate. Erlendur sat in his car, trying to be inconspicuous, and watched the garage. The occasional vehicle pulled up by the petrol pumps and the men would fill it up and, if required, perform small additional tasks such as topping up the antifreeze or cleaning the windscreen. The older man, the cousin, pumped petrol and exchanged pleasantries with the customers while the younger one mainly took care of the till. The weather was cold, as it had been for several days now, and the pump attendant was wearing a down jacket and a baseball cap, both branded with the petrol station logo. He was round-shouldered and moved with slow deliberation as was common with manual labourers his age. In between customers, he took a seat behind the counter and whiled away the time with some activity that Erlendur couldn't make out.

A car drove into the forecourt and the older man stood up and drew on his gloves. Rósanna had told Erlendur that Mensalder worked at one of the few garages in the capital that stayed open late. She didn't know much about him as they hadn't been in contact for years. Although they were first cousins, their families didn't get along so they weren't close. Erlendur had gone round to his flat first but, finding nobody home, had swung by the garage Rósanna mentioned. She had been keen to come too but Erlendur had dissuaded her, telling her not to worry. All he was doing was gathering information about Dagbjört's case and the fact that her cousin had come into the picture wasn't necessarily significant.

The garage, one of the largest in the city, was located on its eastern outskirts. After watching the place from a discreet distance for a while, Erlendur drove up to one of the pumps. He went into the shop and asked for petrol. The attendant he took to be Mensalder stood up and Erlendur saw that he had been playing patience. Mensalder asked if he should 'fill 'er up'. When Erlendur said yes, the man put his gloves on again and went out to the pump. Erlendur looked around the shop which sold newspapers, magazines and a variety of motoring accessories such as windscreen wipers and ice scrapers, as well as shelves of cigarettes, cigars and sweets. Then he went outside in the wake of the attendant who had started filling his car. There was a rumble of traffic from the road. The man leaned against the car while the pump was working, glancing every now and then at the litre counter and price.

'Quiet this evening,' remarked Erlendur, automatically reaching for his cigarettes, then remembering where he was.

'Yes,' agreed the man. 'It's been pretty quiet. We were busier yesterday. It varies. Every day's different, like anywhere else.'

'I suppose so,' said Erlendur.

The pump churned away and the man checked the litre counter. As he did so, Erlendur caught a glimpse of his face. He had several days' worth of stubble on his lean cheeks, a small nose and bushy eyebrows. His nose was running.

'Was she totally empty?' asked the attendant.

'Yes, almost.'

'Nearly there, though it's surprising what big tanks some of these little cars have.' He wiped his nose with the back of his hand. 'Need any new windscreen wipers or anything like that?'

'No, thanks.'

'We have to ask,' said the man apologetically. 'New rules. We have to ask the customers if they need anything else.'

'I understand.'

'We're always learning something new.'

'By the way, you wouldn't be Mensalder, would you?' asked Erlendur casually.

'Yes, that's me. Or that's my name, anyway. Do we know each other?'

'Rósanna's cousin?'

'I've got a cousin called Rósanna, yes. Why do you ask? Do you know her?'

'Vaguely,' said Erlendur. 'Not well. But I happened to be chatting to her recently and your name came up.'

'Oh, I see. What's she up to these days?'

'Not much,' said Erlendur. 'She mentioned you used to work out at Keflavík years ago.'

The pump clicked. The tank was full. Mensalder added a few more drops, his eye on the price. Erlendur thought he was trying to finish on a round number.

'Yes, that's right, I used to work on the base,' he said. 'Why . . . were you talking about me specially? Why did she mention me?'

'Oh, we were just talking about the base and she said she had a cousin who used to work there and supplied her and her friends with goods he acquired from the Yanks. That he was very obliging like that.'

'Ah, I see,' said Mensalder. 'It was a long time ago, but it's true, you could get hold of this and that, stuff you couldn't find in town. Everything was in short supply in those days, but not for the GIs. Their stores were overflowing with goods. They had all the newest and best of everything.'

'I bet.'

'Saw my first fast-food joint there and that sort of thing.'

'Wasn't it tricky smuggling goods out of the area?'

'Not for me,' said Mensalder. 'But then I didn't operate on any big scale. Others might have done but I was never that greedy. I was employed directly by the army, so I was paid in dollars which was a real bonus. Until they put an end to that.'

'Did you live on the base?'

'Yes, quite a few of us did,' said Mensalder, beginning to clean the windscreen with a scraper. 'We were put up in army huts. A lot of the GIs lived in and around Keflavík. Rented basements or small flats. There was more mixing back then. Later they got worried about fraternisation and built accommodation for the soldiers on the base, and after that it all changed and . . . you know how it is – we've always avoided close contact with them.'

'True. It must have been child's play getting your hands on sought-after items if you actually lived on site. And could pay in dollars.'

'Yes, that's right. They had amazing shops and you could buy vodka and beer and cigarettes and all kinds of clothes that were almost impossible to find here in town. Things have changed a lot since then, you know. These days the shops are crammed with new stuff but it wasn't like that back then.'

'Records too?' said Erlendur.

He could still only see part of the man's face between his cap and jacket collar; the dull, weary expression of someone who had known little else in life but monotonous hard grind. Mensalder went about his work methodically, heavy on his feet and slow in his movements. He struck Erlendur as a pleasant man who seemed to enjoy reminiscing about the old days, even when talking to a stranger. Perhaps it was rare for people to show any interest in him, hence his willingness to talk when someone actually bothered to give him the time of day. Then again, maybe he was simply obeying orders in being polite to the customer. He spoke without emphasis, without varying his intonation, as if little took him by surprise these days and he had nothing exciting to tell.

'Yes, of course,' he said. 'The Americans had all the latest records. You could buy them in the shops but the GIs used to bring them out from home too. That's where I first heard Elvis. Sinatra was very popular there too.'

'Did you have a big collection yourself?'

'Pretty big, yes.'

Mensalder gave Erlendur a puzzled look, as if he felt that this encounter was becoming oddly drawn out and circumstantial for a casual chat with a stranger on a garage forecourt. Perhaps he would have commented on the fact, but two cars drove up to the pumps. One stopped behind Erlendur, so he climbed into his car, moved off and parked round the corner. Then he went inside, paid for the petrol, made a minor purchase as an excuse to loiter, and picked up a newspaper and started reading about the hostage taking at the American Embassy in Teheran. Mensalder dealt with the two cars, then a third arrived, followed by several more. The man on the till went outside to help. After about quarter of an hour the flow of traffic relented and Mensalder was able to return to his game of patience.

'Thank you,' said Erlendur, finally preparing to leave.

'Right,' said Mensalder, looking up from his cards. 'Was there anything else?'

'No, that's all. I'm sorry if I annoyed you by asking about the base.'

'Seems to me like you're mighty curious.'

'It's a bit of a hobby of mine at the moment,' said Erlendur. 'Anything to do with Keflavík and the soldiers, the Icelandic civilians who work there and their coexistence with the army. Of course, you've first-hand knowledge of all that.'

'Yes, I suppose so.'

'Did you have a car in those days? Car ownership wasn't that common back then.'

'When I worked at Keflavík? Yes, I had an old Morris. What did Rósanna say?'

'Well, she mostly talked about how good you were at getting hold of the latest records for her.'

'Really?'

'Yes, it stuck in her memory,' said Erlendur. 'How you supplied them for her and her friends. Especially the records you sorted out for her when she was at the Women's College and went to one of those girls' parties. I don't suppose you'd remember.'

'No,' said Mensalder.

'But she did – she remembered you getting her a Doris Day record and another by Kay Starr.'

Mensalder bent over his game without replying. Despite being indoors, he was still wearing his coat and baseball cap, though he had taken off his gloves and laid them beside him on the table. Erlendur thought the man was beginning to suspect that he was no ordinary customer and their meeting was not a chance one after all.

'Does that ring any bells?'

'No, I can't say it does.'

'The party was held at the house of a girl called Dagbjört,' said Erlendur. 'Remember her?'

'No, I can't say I do.'

A lorry drew up at the pumps and Mensalder glanced over, then rose to his feet and put on his gloves.

'Look, I haven't got time for this,' he said and, slipping past Erlendur, hurried outside, a stooping, work-worn figure, clearly shaken by this odd encounter.

42

Caroline sat thinking in silence for a while. Things had quietened down again outside the cinema. The last screening of the evening had begun and the audience had settled down with their popcorn, soft drinks and sweets to carefree enjoyment of the film.

'Is there any way you can prove that?' asked Marion at last.

'Short of finding the bombs, no,' said Caroline. 'I don't have any proof, it's just something my friend put to me, half joking. All he knows is that NCT's been employed for that kind of transport before and Cain's name has come up in connection with that sort of operation. But he wouldn't vouch for it. Just told me to draw my own conclusions.'

'Do you think they could be stored in the hangar? If it's true?'

'I doubt it. There's a whole lot of traffic passing through the hangar and if they want to hush up the presence of nuclear weapons on Icelandic soil, they'd put better precautions in place for hiding them. Or so I'd imagine.'

'Do you have access to the hangar?' asked Marion.

'I can get myself inside if that's what you mean,' said Caroline. 'I'm guessing you Icelandics haven't signed any agreement allowing nuclear weapons to be located here?'

'One of the conditions for the presence of the army is that they never store that type of weapon here without the permission of the Icelandic government,' said Marion.

'Do you think your government could have granted permission?'

'I very much doubt they'd even consider it. It would be impossible to justify the presence of the army if news leaked out that they were stockpiling nuclear weapons here. Even less so if it turned out there was a tacit agreement with the Americans that's been kept from the public.'

Marion looked at Caroline in the mirror.

'There would be a hell of a stink if the news got out.'

'So, in other words, it's a sensitive issue?'

'Extremely.'

'Enough that they'd need to silence a man who knew something?'

'Maybe,' said Marion. 'Kristvin was snooping around. He was in contact with a journalist in Reykjavík. He probably knew Wilbur Cain. I imagine this Cain must have tried to sound him out about what he'd uncovered. He may even have led Kristvin on, pretending to have information and fooling him into divulging how much he knew and what he meant to do with the knowledge. Cain would've had to decide how to proceed in light of that.'

'And?'

'Let's say he persuaded Kristvin to meet him in the hangar. Pushed him off the scaffolding. Then drove his body out to the lava field at Svartsengi.'

'That's one scenario.'

'What kind of bombs are we talking about?'

'There's a range of possibilities,' said Caroline. 'We have Lockheed P-3 Orions here. They can carry depth charges with nuclear warheads, designed to combat Soviet submarines. We also have F-4 Phantom fighter jets. They first arrived here six years ago. They can carry nuclear missiles designed for air-to-ground strikes.'

'So all the necessary equipment's available?'

'Yes.'

'We need to get inside that hangar,' said Marion. 'If Kristvin was killed in there, if he fell off the scaffolding, we have to examine the scene, even if all the evidence has been cleaned up. They may have started dismantling the work platforms, so we need to act fast.'

'What about Cain?'

'I reckon it would be best to smoke him out,' said Marion. 'I think we should force a face-to-face meeting as soon as possible, let him know what we suspect and that it's all on record. That way we can hopefully guarantee that you won't be in any danger from him. We need to make it clear to him that if anything happens to you, we know who's responsible. Where does he live?'

'No idea. Does that seem wise to you? To approach it like that? I don't think he or anyone else round here'll take the blindest bit of notice of the Icelandic police.'

'I don't know what else we can do. We've got to meet the man sooner or later and my instinct is that it'd be better to take him by surprise. He could go to ground or leave the country. You haven't told anyone what you know except me and Erlendur and your friend Brad, so Cain's presumably unaware of your enquiries.

You'd better keep it that way. You haven't told your superiors yet, have you?'

'The stuff I'm telling you now? No, no one but you. But I'm not sure that was very smart of me.'

'No, maybe not, but it's better to be cautious.'

'From what I hear Cain's an extremely dangerous guy,' said Caroline. 'If you're planning on paying him a visit, you'd better take precautions. Anyhow, we can't be sure he's in the country. He's a free agent and comes and goes as he likes. And he may well know what I'm up to. I've been asking a lot of questions today. That's why I wanted to know if my dorm was being watched.'

'I wonder if we could order his arrest in connection with the investigation into Kristvin's death.'

'On what grounds?' asked Caroline. 'You have nothing on him. All you have are vague suspicions. You'd need direct proof. The fact he may've been seen at a bar with Kristvin isn't enough. We don't even know if it was him.'

'Perhaps we could get permission to interview him.'

'You can put in a request,' said Caroline, 'but I'm guessing it'll be held up in the system and ultimately refused. On the grounds, of course, that the army has no record of any such person. You can be pretty confident that Wilbur Cain's an alias.'

'Where can we find evidence then?' asked Marion.

'In the hangar, maybe.'

'So shouldn't we head over there?'

'Right now?'

'Why not?'

Caroline sat up. 'Isn't that a bit . . .?'

'Do we have any alternative?' asked Marion.

'Well . . .'

'Not the way I see it.'

'Let's do it then,' said Caroline after a brief pause. 'Better get it over with before I'm arrested, dragged before a court martial and shot.'

Marion started the car, backed out of the parking space and drove over to military police headquarters, stopping a little way off. Caroline scanned the surroundings, checking out the traffic, any nearby cars and pedestrians. It was ten minutes before she summoned up the courage to dash over to the station and in through the door. Quarter of an hour later she emerged again, in uniform. She walked over to a row of squad cars, climbed into one and drove over to where Marion was waiting. She stopped and Marion got in beside her.

'How did it go?' asked Marion.

'Like a dream,' said Caroline, permitting herself a smile. 'I hear you were in earlier asking for me.'

She set off in the direction of Hangar 885. There were few cars on the roads and in no time she was approaching the gate by the hangar. Caroline slowed to a standstill.

'I know him!' she said with a sigh of relief, as a soldier came over. There were three guards on the gate. The other two remained at their post. 'Don't say a word,' she warned.

She wound down the window.

'Hi, Spence, how're you doing?' she said with a broad grin.

Spence, who was black like her, grinned in return. He shot a glance at the passenger seat where Marion had grabbed an instruction manual from the glove compartment and was poring over it, pretending not to pay any attention to what was happening.

'You on duty all night, poor soul?' asked Caroline.

'Oh, yeah,' said Spence. 'Do you need access to the hangar?'

'Aerospace engineer,' she said, nodding at her passenger. 'So I won't be seeing you at the Zoo later?'

'Maybe tomorrow,' said Spence and waved her through.

'See ya,' called Caroline and drove through the gate towards the hangar.

'Spence?' said Marion once they were through.

'Yeah, don't ask,' said Caroline.

She drove round the northern side of the vast building and parked out of sight of the guards. The hangar was situated on the edge of the airport; floodlights mounted on the roof illuminated the entire area. Further to the north, beyond the moors, they could see Keflavík and the lights of other settlements on the Reykjanes Peninsula. And there, far off in the distance, was Reykjavík. The glow from the city lit up the sky, revealing just how far the capital now sprawled to the east.

'Coming?' called Caroline in a low voice as Marion stood motionless, arrested by the view.

'Pretty, isn't it?'

'We're not here to admire the scenery,' snapped Caroline, visibly on edge. She was clearly having second thoughts. 'I don't know how you talked me into this,' she grumbled. 'I'm such a damn fool. Always the same damn fool.'

She ushered Marion to a door at the northern end of the building, which turned out to be locked. Caroline kept walking, rounded the western corner, then marched briskly alongside the hangar with Marion on her heels. Massive doors extended the length of this side, set into which were smaller doors for staff. Coming to one of these smaller entrances, Caroline tried the handle. It was locked as well. She was about to keep going when she heard a noise inside and shoved Marion back into a shallow recess formed where the full-size doors overlapped one another. Two soldiers emerged and marched off towards the other end of the building. The door swung to behind them but before it could click shut Caroline ran over and caught it. She peered inside to make sure no other personnel were near, then beckoned to Marion to follow.

43

Erlendur watched Mensalder attending to the lorry. He exchanged a few words with the driver, flicking the occasional surreptitious glance in Erlendur's direction. The young man on the till had nipped out to the gents. When he came back, Erlendur asked if Mensalder had been working there long.

'Mensi?' said the young man. 'About five years, I suppose. What . . . Do you know him?'

'No,' said Erlendur. 'Not really. Is he known as Mensi?'

'He's all right,' said the young man and picked up the phone that was ringing behind the counter. Erlendur went outside and crossed the forecourt towards Mensalder. On the way he passed the lorry driver who was heading for the shop.

'Bloody cold,' commented the driver and hurried into the warmth.

'I haven't been quite straight with you,' said Erlendur when he was within speaking distance of Mensalder. 'I'm trying to find out what happened to the girl I mentioned. Dagbjört. She went missing. I'm a detective, and I'm re-examining the case, talking to people, trying to come up with some answers. Your cousin Rósanna thinks you might have met Dagbjört. Talked to her. I wanted to know if you ever did. That's all.'

Mensalder was stooping over the fuel tank that was mounted on the side of the lorry. He held the nozzle in the tank, wiped the drip off his nose with the back of his hand and avoided looking at Erlendur. Acted as if he wasn't there. Erlendur thought perhaps the noise of the diesel pump had drowned out his words and stepped closer.

'Did you by any chance talk to Dagbjört shortly before she vanished?' he asked, raising his voice.

The man still didn't answer and kept his eyes averted.

'Mensalder? You're going to have to talk to me. You can't dodge the issue forever.'

'I have nothing to say to you,' he heard Mensalder mutter. 'You come here, pretending . . . come here and . . . I have nothing to say to you.'

Erlendur decided to back off for the moment. Before long the tank was full and Mensalder hung the hose up by the pump just as the driver returned. They spoke briefly. The driver, who apparently had an account at the garage, was on his way north and intended to drive all night. He said goodbye and the lorry pulled away amid roars and a cloud of exhaust fumes.

The two of them were left standing there in the cold.

'What are you frightened of?' asked Erlendur.

'Frightened?' said Mensalder. 'I'm not frightened.'

'Did you speak to Dagbjört?'

'I didn't do anything to her,' said Mensalder, hunching his back against the wind.

'Did you speak to her?'

'Why are you asking me this? Do you think I harmed the girl? That's crazy. Completely crazy! I don't know what Rósanna's been telling you but if she claims . . . if she claims . . . I don't believe it. Just don't believe it . . .'

'Do you remember when Dagbjört went missing? Do you remember the search for her?'

'Yes, I do. I knew she was at school with Rósanna.'

'But you don't know what happened to her?'

'Me? No. I don't know why you think I should. I don't under-stand all these questions.'

'You went to her house.'

'I went to fetch the records from her,' said Mensalder. 'I'd lent some to Rósanna because she was going to see her friends. Some of the girls at her school were having a get-together. But . . .'

'What?'

'I'd already sold them, you see. They weren't mine to lend. I'd promised them to a girl I knew. Doris Day, Dean Martin, that sort of thing.'

While they were talking they moved back towards the shop and took shelter in the lee of the building. Mensalder proceeded to tell Erlendur about the extra cash he used to make from smug-gling sought-after items off the base. He had used his old Morris to transport the goods, being careful to shift only small quantities at a time. If he was caught by the customs officials on the gate, which sometimes happened, he could claim they were his. He bought a wide range of clothing – jeans, even suits – direct from the GIs and acquired most of his records that way too. With the dollars he earned he was able to purchase household appliances from the shops on the base. Toasters were particularly popular.

And by having a word with the cooks at the servicemen's clubs he managed to get hold of beef which he sold on to Reykjavík restaurants or members of his own family. He made quite a tidy sum on the black market until in the end his luck deserted him; he was picked up two or three times in a row and lost his job.

One day, back when business was still thriving, Rósanna had come to see him and asked if he had any new records for her. She had asked him this before, as had other members of his family; he had even taken orders for specific records, just as he had once succeeded in procuring a three-piece suit for a friend, in the correct size, and a pair of leather shoes. The biggest demand was for the latest releases from America, and it so happened that he had four records in the Morris that he had yet to deliver. He let Rósanna borrow these. But she forgot to bring them home from the party and, because he was in a hurry to retrieve them and she herself was popping out of town, she gave him Dagbjört's address so he could go round and fetch them himself.

'She was very sweet and handed over the records, then I said goodbye.'

'Was she alone at home?'

'I assume so. At least I only spoke to her.'

'And that was all?' asked Erlendur.

'Yes. That was all. Next thing I heard there was a big search on for her and Rósanna told me she'd gone missing. Vanished into thin air on her way to school.'

'Did you tell Rósanna you'd spoken to Dagbjört?'

'I don't think so,' said Mensalder. 'I don't remember. Surely she'd have told you?'

'Yes,' said Erlendur.

'It just gave me a bit of a turn – sorry about that – when I worked out the real purpose of your visit here, what you wanted from me . . . it just gave me a bit of a turn, as you saw. No doubt that makes you think I've got something to hide but I can assure you that . . . It's just . . . when you act in an underhand way like that, it's a bit unnerving.'

'I don't see why it's such an awkward subject for you if you only met her once when you went round to pick up the records.'

'No, of course, but I was shaken. I've thought about her from time to time because she disappeared so suddenly shortly after I met her and I never told the police because I didn't see how it was relevant – still don't. Then you show up . . . like you're a ghost from the past and start grilling me about her.'

'No wonder you were taken aback,' said Erlendur, making an effort to appear understanding. 'Is there nothing you want to add to your account?'

'I don't think so,' said Mensalder. 'I don't know what else there could be.'

'Are you sure about that?'

'Yes. That was all. I fetched the records and took them round to my friend's house. End of story.'

Erlendur studied Mensalder: the dull eyes under the peaked cap with the petrol station logo, the thick jacket; the shoulders that seemed to sag ever lower as the conversation went on; the reek of diesel and lubricating oil that clung to his clothes.

'I get the feeling you're lying to me.'

'No, I'm not,' said Mensalder. 'I swear I'm not. Why –?'

'Because of how you reacted,' said Erlendur.

'But I'm trying to tell you why I . . . that it gave me a turn when you started going on about it.'

'That's not all. Just before she vanished Dagbjört told somebody that she wanted to know if you could get hold of some records for her. I'm willing to bet she raised the subject when you went round. She'd mentioned you specifically. I expect you were happy to oblige. You were used to fixing things for people. Enjoyed it, by the sound of it. Made a nice little profit too. So I can't think why Dagbjört wouldn't have asked you about it when you were standing on her doorstep. And I can't imagine why you'd have refused her.'

'She didn't mention anything like that,' insisted Mensalder.

'Are you sure you two didn't arrange another meeting?'

'Yes, quite sure. Positive. We did nothing of the sort.'

'So she didn't ask you to buy her any records?'

'No, she didn't, or . . . maybe I've forgotten. You're muddling me. But we definitely never arranged to meet like you're implying. I never saw her again after that. Never. Only saw her that one time and that's the truth. The absolute truth!'

'So you didn't meet up with Dagbjört?'

'No.'

'She didn't get into your car the day she vanished?'

'No, I swear.'

'All right,' said Erlendur. 'I don't suppose we'll get anywhere like this. We'll see what you say when the police come to take you in. You realise I'll have to notify them. You realise that, don't you, Mensalder?'

'I can't see why you have to take it any further. Why you won't believe me. I didn't touch her. I don't understand why you're acting like this. I just don't get it.'

'No, well, we'll see. Maybe my colleagues will make more progress with you.'

Erlendur crossed the forecourt towards his car. The instant he left shelter the wind latched its claws into him, sending an icy chill through his body. He found his keys and was opening the car door when he heard a voice calling. He couldn't make out the words and no longer cared anyway. He had leaned on Mensalder as hard as he dared and had got precious little out of him. The threat of going to the police was an empty one: he had no real evidence against the man. He started thinking instead about driving straight out to the base to try and track down Marion and Caroline and find out how they were getting on. He hoped to God that Caroline was all right and hadn't put herself at risk by colluding with them.

Again he thought he heard a voice.

'. . . never showed up,' he caught before the wind snatched the rest away.

Erlendur turned. 'What did you say?'

'She never showed up,' called Mensalder, looking around nervously as if he didn't want anyone else to hear.

Erlendur shut the car door and walked back towards him.

'What are you saying?'

'I waited for her with the records for more than half an hour but then I had to drive out to Keflavík,' said Mensalder. 'She never came to meet me. She said she would but she never came.'

'Dagbjört, you mean?'

'Yes, Dagbjört. Then I heard she'd gone missing and I never told anyone because I didn't see what it had to do with me.' Mensalder dropped his gaze. 'I didn't see what it had to do with me.'

44

Quickly adjusting to the gloom in the hangar, Marion followed Caroline in the direction of the giant work platform that towered up to the rafters. There was no one else around and the only illumination came from the dim fluorescent lights along the side walls. No work seemed to be in progress at present. Marion made out what looked like two fighter aircraft at the other end of the hangar. There were various aeroplane parts lying on the floor along the walls to the right. A jet engine was suspended from a pulley.

Marion's eyes travelled up the scaffolding, tall as a block of flats. It consisted of countless steel platforms slotted together, with a ladder in the middle providing access to the top level. The plumbers' paraphernalia had been removed as their job here was finished. Marion calculated that if Kristvin had fallen from the scaffolding there would be evidence on the floor below, but the concrete was so filthy and stained with oil and years' of other accumulated grime that without proper forensic analysis it would be impossible to determine if any of it was Kristvin's blood. There was certainly no way of telling in the present circumstances.

All was quiet in the hangar. Caroline stood stock-still, listening and peering around in the semi-darkness, alert as a wild animal. Only when she was absolutely sure they were alone did she gesture to Marion to follow her up the ladder. She felt her way slowly, rung by rung.

'Hope you don't get vertigo,' whispered Marion.

'I've always been shit-scared of heights – flying too – but right now I'm just shit-scared,' Caroline whispered back.

She reached the top surprisingly quickly, nevertheless, with Marion close behind. They stood on the platform, their legs trembling and jelly-like with the effort. It gave a good view of the hangar.

'Isn't the place guarded?' asked Marion in a low voice.

'I'd have thought so.'

'Haven't you ever been in here before?'

'No, never had any reason to. I had no idea how vast it was.'

'It's mind-boggling.'

Marion surveyed the platform. It was fenced in on all sides by a handrail a metre or so high. The new fire-extinguisher system was right in front of them. From the pipes, which ran along the steel girders, gold-coloured sprinklers hung like colossal Christmas decorations. There were two smaller wheeled platforms that reached right up under the roof. Marion assumed the plumbers must have stood on these while fixing the water pipes to the girders.

'Do you think they store bombs in here?' asked Marion.

'I wouldn't know where,' said Caroline, surveying the largely empty space. 'Maybe they keep them in different hangars, or underground.'

'Shouldn't they be stored within easy reach for loading? Isn't speed the main object?'

'Sure. Maybe Kristvin saw them in here and they've been moved since then. They might not even be in the country any longer.'

'True.'

'Could Kristvin have fallen off here?' asked Caroline, peeping gingerly over the edge. 'It's a hell of a drop. It's making me giddy.'

'He'd have died instantly,' said Marion. 'That's clear. No one could survive a drop like that, straight down onto a concrete floor. It would go a long way to explaining his injuries. We've been working on the assumption all along that they were the result of a major fall.'

'What can he have been doing all the way up here?' whispered Caroline. 'It's only been used for installing the fire extinguishers and I'm guessing that all the people who worked up here were Icelandics. Surely it's just as likely that it was a quarrel between locals that went badly wrong?'

'But the men working up here claim they didn't know Kristvin,' said Marion, 'though naturally there's a chance they were lying. But we couldn't find any obvious links. No, I'm thinking he may have fled up here. To hide.'

'This is the last place I'd hide,' said Caroline, snatching another nervous glance over the rail.

'I don't suppose he had much choice. If he was trying to escape.'

'Maybe someone thought this would be a good place to meet,' said Caroline, 'especially if he was planning to push Kristvin off.'

'I'm guessing it would've been from this side then,' said Marion, walking to the edge of the platform where there was a narrow gap, no more than a couple of metres wide, separating it from the northern wall of the hangar. It was also furthest from the lights. Marion peered down at the floor.

Caroline was far from happy up here and the feeling only intensified as the minutes passed. She had not been lying when she said she hated heights and it was obvious she could hardly bring herself to look down. She ran a hand along the rail.

'It would be no problem to push a man over this. It wouldn't even require a struggle. Just a good shove.'

'The pathologist said he'd almost certainly received a blow to the head before he fell,' said Marion.

'OK,' said Caroline. 'So it goes something like this: Kristvin's poking around in the hangar, maybe searching for missiles from Thule. Or he's come to meet a man who's promised him information, maybe even to show them to him. If he had any other reason for being in here, we don't know what it was. Then either something happens that forces Kristvin to seek refuge up here, or they meet up here to talk. I'd never agree to that but then I'm not Kristvin. They quarrel. Kristvin's hit on the head and falls off the platform.'

'Who's up here with him?'

'Wilbur Cain?'

'So it all comes down to the presence of nuclear weapons from Thule?'

'Looks like it,' said Caroline.

'We'd better get out of here,' said Marion, testing the rail in several places to check if it was loose. 'There's nothing to see up here. I'll try and take some samples from the floor over by the wall, then we'd better beat it.'

'Jesus, I'll be glad to get down from here,' said Caroline.

281

'Getting to you, is it?' said Marion, bending over the rail.

'I can't stand it. In my worst nightmares I'm falling off a cliff and there's no one to save me.'

'You should find yourself a man,' said Marion, in an attempt to lighten the mood.

'Yeah, right,' said Caroline.

She inched her way down the ladder with Marion just behind. Before long, weak with relief, she had her feet planted on terra firma again. Marion went round the corner of the scaffolding tower to the north wall and craned upwards, still marvelling at the height of the roof. Then Caroline called in a low voice and Marion saw she was pointing at some stains spattered up the foot of the wall. Moving closer, Marion crouched down, discerned four dark spots and tested one with a finger.

'Is it paint?' asked Caroline.

'Not sure.'

'You should take a sample.'

'It may have nothing to do with Kristvin,' said Marion. 'We're probably too late to collect any evidence in here.'

Nevertheless, Marion scraped at the marks with a knife and wrapped the scrapings in a handkerchief. Then straightened up again, gauged the position of the stains in relation to the scaffolding, and walked over to examine the floor for any signs of the blood that might have splashed from there onto the wall. But it was impossible to tell if any of the accumulated grime was blood.

'We should get out of here,' muttered Caroline.

'Martinez made a comment about Joan and her husband, Earl, when we were talking in the bar,' said Marion distractedly. 'I forgot to mention it. By the way, I think you've got a better friend in Martinez than you realise.'

'What are you implying?'

'Haven't you . . . hasn't it struck you?'

'What exactly did he say? And stop trying to meddle in my private life.'

'He reckoned Earl was supplying drugs to Icelanders,' said Marion. 'What if Kristvin bought the marijuana from him?'

'And slept with his wife?'

'Hadn't we better have another word with her?'

'Yes. Bitch though she is.'

'What about the weapons? Ought we to take a quick look round while we're here? See if we can find anything from Greenland? From Thule?'

'I very much doubt they'd be stored in here if they're trying to cover up their presence,' whispered Caroline, starting to move towards the door. 'Far too many people coming and going. They could be anywhere on the base. Come on, we need to get the hell out of here.'

45

Mensalder stood in the lee of the garage shop and stole a nervous look at Erlendur. He had finally revealed the secret he had not dared to breathe a word about for more than a quarter of a century.

'She never showed up,' he repeated, as if it was vital to make this understood. The most vital aspect of the whole story.

Erlendur could see how difficult this was for him, how he stood, shoulders bowed, by the wall, hardly daring to raise his eyes from the tarmac. The other attendant appeared round the corner.

'Mensi!' he called in a hectoring tone. 'Hurry up and serve these customers. I can't do everything.' He glared at them both, then disappeared back into the shop.

'Coming,' said Mensalder wearily, eyes flickering to Erlendur's face, then away again. 'You've got to believe me. She never showed up.'

'When do you knock off?' asked Erlendur.

'In an hour or so.'

'I'll stick around,' said Erlendur. 'I need you to show me where you waited for her. Will you do that?'

Mensalder nodded and looked over at the pumps. Three cars were waiting to be served.

'I didn't touch her,' he said. 'You mustn't think I did.'

'I'll talk to you in an hour.'

Erlendur got back in his car to wait for the garage to close up. He switched on the heater, chilled to the bone from running about after Mensalder in the icy northern blast, and listened to the radio news. The search for the missing men up north continued. A spokesman for the rescue team was quoted as saying that conditions on the Eyvindarstadir Moors were much improved. The snow had drifted over any tracks so it was difficult to guess where the two friends had gone, but now at least the wind had dropped and there was a bright moon.

Erlendur watched Mensalder dealing with the cars. His movements seemed even more ponderous than before, he no longer exchanged pleasantries with the drivers, and carefully avoided looking in Erlendur's direction. As closing time approached, the traffic thinned out and eventually the lights by the pumps went out and Erlendur saw Mensalder's colleague shutting up for the night. The two men emerged from the garage shop together and said goodnight, and after a brief hesitation Mensalder headed over to where Erlendur was sitting in the car. Erlendur wound down the window.

'Ready?' he asked.

'Do we have to do this?' said Mensalder. 'Haven't I told you enough?'

'You haven't told me anything,' said Erlendur. 'Let's get this over with. The sooner the better.'

'But nothing happened and . . . I don't know what it is you want,' whimpered Mensalder. 'She never came and I don't know –'

'Have you got a car?'

'Yes.'

'Leave it here. Come on, hurry up. You're not getting out of this, Mensalder. You've done that for far too long.'

Mensalder still hung back. But when it finally came home to him that Erlendur was not planning to give up, he walked round the front of the car and got into the passenger seat. Erlendur set off, heading for the west of town. They drove in silence the whole way, except when Mensalder gave directions, and in no time they had reached the place where he claimed to have waited in his car for Dagbjört that fateful morning. It wasn't far from the Vesturbær swimming pool, where Camp Knox had once stood. The wind had dropped and hot veils of steam rose from the open-air pool, reminding Erlendur of the time he had stood beside the milky-blue lagoon on Reykjanes, watching the clouds of vapour dispersing above the power station.

'Stop,' said Mensalder. 'It was around about here. All these houses have been built since then, and the pool too, of course, but this is where I parked and waited for her.'

'Why didn't you just go round to her house?' asked Erlendur, turning off the engine. 'Why all the secrecy?'

'She didn't want me to. She didn't want her parents to know – that she was wasting money on records. She was going to say she'd borrowed them. Anyway, what I was doing was black-marketeering and I wasn't keen to draw attention to the fact. I'd spent the night in town and was on my way back to Keflavík that morning, so it suited me fine.'

'Did she suggest this spot?'

'Yes, I think . . . from what I can remember.'

'Tell me what happened.'

Mensalder was still wearing his petrol-station jacket but had taken down the hood and removed his baseball cap, and Erlendur now saw that he looked much older than his years. It was the drooping cheeks and greying hair but most of all the deep creases around his mouth and eyes that created this impression. Mensalder lowered his gaze and rubbed his hands as he told again how he had needed the records back urgently because he had promised them to someone else, and that Rósanna had suggested he fetch them himself from her friend Dagbjört; she was sure it would be OK. So he had gone to her house and picked them up and had a quick chat with Dagbjört. She was alone at home and asked if he would be able to get her some records. She wanted American jeans too, if he came across any. She told him her size. But mainly it was the latest hits she was after. He remembered well the artists she mentioned: Billie Holiday, Nat King Cole, Frankie Laine.

Not long afterwards he had acquired two Billie Holiday records from a corporal he sometimes did business with, and a Frankie Laine from one of the army stores. He'd had less success with the jeans. He had taken his dollars to the shops on the base and found a pair that were slightly larger than Dagbjört wanted. Although the size was wrong, he had taken them anyway as he knew he could easily find another buyer in town. At the same time he had bought a nice coat as a birthday present for his mother.

Dagbjört had given him her number and answered the phone herself when he rang. He said he could drop by her house that evening but it turned out she was busy, and besides, would prefer to keep their dealings away from home. When he said he had to return to the base early next morning, she asked if she could meet him outside the Women's College. He felt this would be a bit too conspicuous, so they agreed to meet closer to her house, near Camp Knox, and that he would give her a lift the rest of the way to school.

He had arrived earlier than intended and parked the Morris as arranged, in a spot which at the time had been slightly off the beaten track. Nowadays, of course, it was surrounded by houses. He had the records with him, and the jeans as well, even though they were the wrong size. He meant to offer them to Rósanna if Dagbjört rejected them.

Time passed and there was no sign of Dagbjört. He thought back over their conversation in case he had misunderstood her or was waiting in the wrong place. He didn't know the area very well as he had grown up in the east of town, but her directions had been so straightforward and clear that he was sure this was the spot. Fifteen minutes after the appointed time, he started the Morris and drove away.

'I swear to you,' said Mensalder, 'she never showed up.'

'Do you expect me to believe this story?' said Erlendur, who had remained silent while the other man was speaking.

'Yes, of course,' said Mensalder. 'Because that's how it was; there's nothing more to tell. I just did as she asked and waited for her, but when she didn't turn up, I drove out to the base. Next thing I heard they'd launched a massive search for her all over Reykjavík.'

'And you did nothing to help?'

'No, I –'

'Didn't let on to anyone that you'd spoken to her. That you'd waited for her that morning. Didn't try to help her family. Or any of those who were devastated by the incident. Something about this doesn't add up, Mensalder. You're lying to me. Or not telling me the whole truth. I don't know how but I believe you played a part in her disappearance. Come on, admit it.'

Mensalder didn't answer.

'Don't you think it's time, after all these years?' said Erlendur. 'Time you stopped trying to hide?'

46

Joan made to slam the door in their faces the instant she saw who her visitors were but Caroline shoved hard in the opposite direction and the woman stumbled backwards. Caroline barged in, and Marion, following on her heels, closed the door. A pungent reek of cannabis filled the flat and there was soothing, hypnotic music playing on the hi-fi. The kitchen light was on, dimly illuminating the hall. Candles were burning in the sitting room.

'Cosy,' said Caroline.

'Get the fuck out of here!' shouted Joan. 'You have no right to come in here. And who's that freak with you?'

'Keep a civil tongue in your head,' snapped Caroline.

'Get out, you bitch!'

'I thought dope was supposed to make you nice and mellow,' said Caroline, surveying the flat. 'Doesn't seem to work on you. Where's your husband? Is he back yet?'

'I have nothing to say to you,' said Joan. 'I'm going to call the police. They'll throw you in jail. You can't just force your way in here like this.'

'Aren't you afraid we'll confiscate your dope?'

Joan paused, muddled. She had forgotten Caroline was in the police and gaped at her armband in bemusement.

'What would Earl say?' asked Caroline. 'If the cops took all his shit away?'

'I don't know what you're talking about,' said Joan. 'What shit?'

'The stuff Kristvin bought off him,' put in Marion.

'Kris?'

'Isn't it correct that Earl supplied him with marijuana?' said Marion, speaking as clearly as possible so that Joan would grasp what was going on.

'Are you using his drugs?' asked Caroline.

'No, I –'

'You admitted to sleeping with Kristvin,' said Caroline. 'You admitted to cheating on Earl with Kristvin. We need to know if Earl found out. We also need to know if Kristvin owed Earl money and had trouble paying him back. Can you tell us anything about that?'

Joan listened dully. Her gaze swivelled back and forth between Caroline and Marion as if she was trying to figure out what had led to this violent invasion of her apartment and how it was connected to her affair with Kristvin and his death.

'Earl didn't touch him,' she said at last, believing she had hit upon the nub of the matter.

'Did Kristvin buy his dope from him?' asked Marion.

'What dope?'

'The stuff you're smoking now, girl,' said Caroline.

'Is your husband a dealer?' asked Marion.

'I . . . I don't know what you're talking about,' said Joan.

'All right,' said Caroline. 'Then you'd better come with me and we'll have another chat down at the police station.'

'Police station . . .? No, it . . . I . . . can't say . . . I mustn't . . . mustn't talk about that. You'll have to ask him. I don't know nothing. Nothing at all.'

'You'd better come with me,' repeated Caroline.

'How's his sister?' asked Joan suddenly.

'Kristvin's sister?'

Joan nodded.

'What do you know about her? Did he tell you about her?'

'I know she's sick. That's why he needed the grass.'

'She wants to know what happened to her brother,' said Marion. 'She believes he died because he was trying to score drugs for her. She feels guilty. We know Kristvin bought marijuana from somebody here on the base. Was it Earl?'

'Wait a minute,' said Caroline. 'You told me you didn't know Kristvin used marijuana. Now suddenly you know all about his sister and why he needed the drugs. What else have you lied about? Is everything you say a lie?'

'You shut your mouth. I'm not lying.'

'Was Earl in the country when Kristvin died?' asked Caroline.

Joan didn't answer.

'I haven't had time to check,' Caroline said to Marion. 'Joan claimed he wasn't on the base the day Kristvin was killed. But I still haven't verified that. You can't trust a word this woman says.'

'Sure you can,' protested Joan.

'Was your husband in the country?' asked Marion, moving closer to Joan.

'He flew out that evening or night. He wasn't in the country. I'm one hundred per cent sure of that.'

'Evening or night? Which night?'

'The night Kris was here.'

'You swore Kristvin left you before midnight, around eleven o'clock. Had Earl left the country by then or not?'

'Earl left here about 6 p.m. I called Kris once he'd gone and he . . . I don't remember exactly . . . it was the same day. Earl was gone.'

Joan wandered into the sitting room. She seemed to have given up complaining about the intrusion and snapping at Caroline. She sat down in the soft glow of the candles. A look of weariness crossed her face and she stared silently, blankly at the flames, the Dolly Parton wig a little askew on her head.

'Where did he fly to?' asked Caroline. 'Do you know?'

'He went to Greenland. I'm sure he'd left by the time Kris came to see me. Earl didn't know about us. He knew nothing. He was gone.'

'Where in Greenland?'

'I don't remember what it's called. I always forget.'

'Thule?'

'Yes, Thule, that's it,' said Joan, giving Caroline a wondering look. 'How did you know? Did I tell you?'

'We have a big airbase at Thule,' said Caroline. 'Any idea what he's doing over there?'

'No. Earl doesn't talk much about that kind of thing. Doesn't talk much to me at all. You know, doesn't tell me anything. He doesn't treat me good. Not like Kris. He was different. He was . . .'

Her words petered out and Caroline sat down beside her. There was a TV in one corner and a small bookcase containing paperback romances and thrillers by big-name writers. A couple of Danielle Steels on the coffee table. But almost no ornaments. Only a large framed AC/DC poster on one wall and a wedding photo of Joan and Earl on a table. Marion noticed a collection of hunting knives in a glass cabinet and assumed they were Earl's. Perhaps he liked to hunt back home. The knives looked extremely sharp, sharp enough to skin big game. Marion wondered if Earl was capable of that. Through a doorway they could see into the bedroom where there was an empty wig stand on the dressing table.

'What do you think happened to Kris?' asked Caroline.

'I don't know. He was OK when he left here. That's all I know. There's no point asking me. I don't know what happened. He often used to drop by the Zoo and he loved the States; he loved living there, and he was . . . he was kind, you know what I mean? He was a nice boy, you know? We got talking and it was fun and one time when Earl was away I . . . I just invited him home. I just did. And we . . . I don't know why it had to turn out like that. I don't know. I know nothing about what happened. Nothing. He just left and never came back.'

Joan looked up.

'How's his sister?' she asked again. 'Kris told me she was real sick.'

'Tell us a bit more about Earl. What exactly does he do here on the base?'

'Do? What do you mean? He's in the marines.'

'What does he do in the marines?'

'This and that. Security at the moment. I believe. I don't

know what he does. He never tells me about his assignments. I think . . . I don't think he's allowed to. That must be the reason. He's so quiet. Never speaks to me. Not a word. I gave up asking a long time ago.'

'Where does he work?' asked Caroline.

'Earl works in the hangar.'

'The hangar?'

'Yeah, the big one.'

'Hangar 885?'

'He's there all day and all night and never tells me a thing about what he does.'

'Are you saying he's a security guard in the big hangar?' asked Caroline, her eyes on Marion.

'Last I heard. I don't know. I don't care what he does.'

'Where is he now?' asked Caroline. 'Greenland?'

'He was in Greenland but I thought he was coming home this evening.'

'What's he doing there?'

'He wants a transfer. To the base whose name I always forget. I think he's going to drag me there next.'

'Has he been planning this for a while?'

'No idea.'

'Was it him who slashed Kris's tyres?' asked Marion.

'Why won't you leave me alone?'

'Did he lie in wait for Kris outside the building?' asked Caroline.

'Why are you asking me? Why don't you ask him?'

'Oh, I intend to,' said Caroline, 'but first I want to hear it from you.'

'I can't talk to you.'

'Why not? What are you afraid of?'

Without warning Joan leapt to her feet, as if to rush out of the flat and escape all this, but Caroline was too quick and caught her before she could reach the door. Joan tore herself loose and Caroline grabbed hold of her again, trying to restrain her. Joan struggled, screaming at her to leave her alone, trying to twist out of her arms. Marion, watching the scuffle, saw that Caroline suddenly had Joan's wig in her hands. It had come off in the fracas, and when Joan realised, she ceased her flailing about, clasped her hands over her shaven head and collapsed weeping to the floor in the corner by the door. Her scalp was covered in plasters and bandages which Marion initially took to be fastenings for the wig but then realised were stained with blood.

'What's this?' asked Caroline, stunned, as she stood with Joan's hair in her hands, gaping at her head. 'What . . .? What . . . what in hell happened to you?'

'Don't look at me,' whimpered Joan and snatched the wig back from her. 'Leave me alone. Go away and leave me alone . . . don't look at me . . .'

Caroline caught Marion's eye, then knelt down beside Joan on the floor and put her arms round her.

'What happened?' she asked gently. 'Was it Earl? What did he do to you?'

'Isn't it hideous?'

'It's . . .' Caroline didn't know what to say.

'It was . . . he used one of his horrible hunting knives. Isn't it . . . isn't it hideous?' said Joan, weeping from a combination of anguish, fury and humiliation. 'Then he took his razor to me and . . . I couldn't do anything, he's so strong, so terribly strong . . . and he threatened me . . . threatened to . . . threatened to kill me . . .'

The dressings on her head formed an irregular pattern and Marion and Caroline stared at them uncomprehendingly until Joan began to tear them off, revealing the letter 'K' gouged into her scalp with a sharp knife, from her forehead to the nape of her neck.

'"K"?' said Caroline. 'Is that . . .?'

'Kris. Earl went for me when he came home from the Animal Locker one evening. He'd heard . . . heard about me and Kris. He went crazy.'

'How did he hear about you and Kris?' asked Caroline.

Joan didn't answer. She sat, her eyes lowered, her shoulders shaking with sobs. Caroline let her be for the moment. Marion held out a handkerchief and Joan took it gratefully. All resistance was at an end and she sat there on the floor, frightened and vulnerable, sniffing into the hanky.

How did Earl find out about your affair?' asked Caroline again.

'Somebody must . . . must have told him,' whispered Joan. 'I don't know. We tried to be careful. Somebody at the Animal Locker. All of a sudden he knew and . . .'

'And what?'

'He couldn't stand it,' said Joan. 'He threatened to kill me, and I know he's capable of it, the fucking sadist. He threatened to kill me if I went to the police after he . . . after he cut me. Like he's any better, screwing around over there in . . . in Greenland.'

Joan raised tear-filled eyes to Caroline's face.

'He couldn't stand that it was an Icelandic,' she said. 'I reckon that was the worst part for him. To be cuckolded by an Icelandic. He couldn't give a shit about the money – Kris owed him for the grass. Earl was pissed about it but that was all. Though when he heard we were . . .'

'Yes?'

'He swore he was going to kill him. God, I can't . . .'

Joan started crying again and Caroline waited patiently for her to recover.

'What happened?' she asked eventually.

'I don't want . . . it wasn't my fault how . . .'

'How what?'

'Earl made . . . Earl made me call him and invite him over. He stood over me with the knife. God, I . . . I didn't dare not to. I tried to warn Kris when he came here and he left almost at once but they were waiting for him –'

Joan broke off.

'I don't know why I'm protecting Earl. I don't know why I should. The fucking jerk.'

'Did he attack Kris? He and his friends?'

'I don't know . . . I don't know how he found out,' said Joan, weeping silently. Then suddenly she seemed to wake out of her daze and stared at Caroline in terror.

'You can't tell him I told you this!'

'It'll –'

'You can't! No way! He'll kill me. He . . . Look what he did to me.'

'It'll be OK,' said Caroline, hugging her tight. 'It'll be OK.'

'Earl says it's all my fault,' said Joan, wringing the blonde wig in her hands as if it were her only fixed point in life. 'He keeps saying that. He made me call Kris . . . said he just wanted to talk to him. Said he wasn't going to hurt him. He promised. He promised me. I regret it so much but what was I . . . what was I supposed to do? I didn't know what Earl was planning. He wasn't here when Kris arrived. I thought he was planning to be here but he didn't show up. I told Kris to go right on home, that Earl was after him. I told you he was with me for two hours – that wasn't how it was at all. He left at once. I told him it was over between us and that he might be in danger . . . the poor boy ran out and . . . by then they'd slashed his tyres . . .'

47

Caroline and Joan walked out of the building ahead of Marion, intending to go to the squad car that Caroline had parked a little way off, when they saw three men coming towards them.

'Who's this?' whispered Marion, stopping behind the two women.

'Christ knows,' said Caroline with a groan, looking for an escape route between the barracks buildings, but immediately giving it up as a bad idea. 'I've never seen them before.'

'What's happening?' asked Joan, petrified.

The men were wearing air-force uniforms and from his insignia Marion guessed the leader was some sort of officer. He was short and powerfully built, with a crew cut and a stern expression. The other two looked equally stern but stayed in the background; Marion assumed these two were ordinary airmen. All three were armed with revolvers at their belts. The airmen were also carrying automatic rifles.

'May I ask what you were doing in the barracks?' said the officer.

Caroline bit back her initial impulse to ask what business it was of his. Instead she gave her name and rank. She also explained who Marion and Joan were, and said that the military police were helping Icelandic CID with their inquiry into a death on the base.

'We had a meeting with a witness, Joan here,' said Marion, 'who we fear may be at risk. She knows who was responsible and –'

'Joan has to file charges for aggravated domestic assault,' chipped in Caroline. 'I'm taking her to the hospital. She needs medical attention.'

'Are you conducting this inquiry with full authorisation from Fleet Air Command, Sergeant?' asked the officer, his face still expressionless.

'There hasn't been time for permission to come through yet,' said Caroline. 'May I ask who you are?'

'Master Sergeant Roberts,' said the officer. 'Do you have the required authorisation to interview base personnel?' he asked them again, glancing at Joan.

'No, like I said, it hasn't come through yet, sir,' said Caroline. 'What's your unit, if I may –?'

'I'm with 57th Fighter Squadron,' said Roberts, and stepped up to Marion. 'You're from the Icelandic police?'

'Yes.'

'If I'm correctly informed, your request to conduct an inquiry on the base was refused, so authorisation is not in the pipeline, as your lady friend here seems to think. That's bullshit. What are you two playing at?'

'Playing at?' said Marion.

'Yes, Detective. What are you playing at?'

'We tried to get the Defense Force to work with us,' said Marion. 'But you people refused all cooperation.'

'Would you follow me, please?' said Roberts. 'I'll have to ask you to surrender your weapon, Sergeant,' he added to Caroline, then turned back to Marion. 'I gather the Icelandic police don't carry firearms.'

Caroline looked at Marion, who shrugged.

'What about Joan?' said Caroline. 'She needs to see a doctor. She also needs protection from her husband. I can't leave her.'

'You have no say in the matter, Sergeant. My men will escort her to the hospital,' said Roberts, indicating the two airmen accompanying him. 'They'll protect her.'

'Protect her?'

'Yes. You can rely on us.'

'I want to go with her, sir,' insisted Caroline. 'To see everything's OK.'

'You're coming with me, Sergeant,' said Roberts. 'You have no choice. She'll be fine. She has no reason to be afraid.'

'Where are you taking us?' asked Caroline. 'I don't see why we need to go anywhere at all with you.'

'You're coming with me, Sergeant,' repeated the officer, holding out his hand for Caroline's gun.

She hesitated.

'Your weapon!' ordered Roberts.

Caroline made eye contact with Marion, who nodded. She took the pistol out of its holster and handed it over. Then she turned to Joan and told her to go with the men to the hospital. Joan protested but Caroline assured her she would be safe. The men escorted Joan to a military jeep parked a stone's throw from the barracks, and Caroline walked along with her, reassuring her, telling her everything would be all right, nothing would happen to her and they would see each other again very soon.

'There's nothing we can do,' said Caroline. 'We simply have to trust these men.'

'What'll happen to you?' asked Joan.

'I'll be OK,' said Caroline. 'I'll see you later. I promise.'

She watched the jeep drive off down the street.

'Follow me,' ordered Roberts, leading the way to another jeep.

'Where are you taking us, sir?' asked Caroline as they headed in a westerly direction towards the airport runways.

'You'll see,' replied Roberts.

'If anything happens to Joan –'

'Nothing's going to happen to her. What do you think we are?'

'How did you know where we were?'

'It wasn't hard to track you down. This isn't a big area.'

'Were you watching Joan's apartment?'

Roberts didn't answer.

'Why? Because of Earl Jones?'

Still no response.

'Do you know what happened in the hangar?'

'You'd better be quiet, Sergeant.'

Caroline lost her temper. 'Maybe you were with Jones?'

Roberts turned to her. 'Do you think it was right to go behind the backs of your colleagues and friends in the military? To collaborate with these people' – he jerked his head at Marion – 'without reporting the fact? Doesn't your part in all this seem rather irregular? What is it you want, Sergeant? You can hardly expect to continue your career in the military. In fact, you can forget all about that. And I advise you to keep your mouth shut from now on.'

Seeing that Caroline was poised to fly off the handle, Marion unobtrusively grabbed her hand, silently warning her to let it drop; there was no point quarrelling with this man. Hurt and angry, Caroline kept her eyes on the road ahead.

'Where are you taking us?' It was Marion's turn to ask.

'Here,' said Roberts.

In front of them were two hangars currently under construction for the accommodation of F-16 fighters. They consisted of steel-frame skeletons with walls, roof and vast doors attached, but as yet no fittings, insulation or equipment inside. Roberts parked by one of the hangars and Marion and Caroline climbed out. He ordered them to follow him. Two guards were standing there, armed with rifles. Roberts opened a door in the side wall, ushered Marion and Caroline through, then closed the door behind them, remaining outside himself.

Inside it was cold and bare. Two powerful lamps hanging from the ceiling cast a harsh glare into every corner of the empty building. In the middle stood a tall, lean man, aged about fifty, dressed in khaki trousers and shirt, with a square jaw and a thick, greying crew cut. He had the air of a man who let little disturb his composure, and regarded them with small, weary eyes, as if he had far more pressing and important business to deal with. He neither greeted them nor introduced himself but came straight to the point.

'What were you two doing in Hangar 885?'

'Who are you?' retorted Caroline, as she had to Roberts earlier.

'I am in charge of security on the base.'

'Are you in Military Intelligence?'

'I repeat: what were you doing in Hangar 885?'

'As a military police officer I can go where I like,' said Caroline.

'What do you mean by bringing us here? Who are you? And who's Master Sergeant Roberts?'

'A delegation will be sent to the base to look for me if I don't report back soon,' said Marion, which was not a complete lie. 'I'm a detective with the Icelandic Criminal Investigation Department. My colleagues are aware I had business in the hangar. I don't know if you're Wilbur Cain or if you're working for him, but the Icelandic police have his name. We gather he was acquainted with an Icelander called Kristvin. They were spotted together at a bar here called the Animal Locker, also known as the Zoo. We have reason to believe that Kristvin was pushed off the scaffolding in Hangar 885. And we are now reasonably confident that a marine called Earl Jones was involved, so we would request that you deliver him into our custody. Caroline has been assisting us. That seems to be public knowledge now. We owe her a great debt of gratitude. If anything were to happen to the two of us – if our bodies were found smashed up in the lava field outside the base, for example – you should be aware that the information about Kristvin, Wilbur Cain, Earl Jones and Hangar 885 is on record.'

'Why are you telling me this?' asked the man.

'I thought you ought to know,' said Marion.

'Do you think I give a damn what you have to say? How would you react if the FBI flew into Reykjavík and started interrogating people all over the place without obtaining permission? Would you welcome them with open arms? Would you think it was all fine and dandy if the FBI were running their own police investigation in Reykjavík? Wouldn't you want to prevent it? Ask what was going on?'

'But you people refused to cooperate!'

'Do you think we give a shit if a cop like you starts threatening us? You're on US territory. Your threats have no substance here.' He turned to Caroline. 'What I don't understand is why you got involved in all this, Sergeant.'

'The Icelandic police came to me for help, after all cooperation had been refused. I wanted . . . to find out what happened. I'm a police officer. That's my job.'

'Is it also your job to disobey your superior officers? The military police received orders, along with everyone else, that all inquiries about this particular case should be referred to the base authorities. I know for a fact that you received those orders. Why did you choose to ignore them?'

'What are you hiding in the hangar?' countered Caroline. 'Why wouldn't you just cooperate with the Icelandic police? What do you have to hide?'

'What were you doing in Hangar 885?' repeated the man. 'What do you think we're hiding? What exactly were you looking for?'

'I've just told you,' said Marion. 'We believe that an Icelandic civilian employed by Icelandair was killed in there. And we now believe we know who was responsible.'

'Earl Jones?'

'Yes. The Icelander was on the base that night and we've established that he fell from a great height. The only place this could realistically have happened is in the hangar. He used to work there from time to time. Earl Jones is a security guard in the hangar, as we've learned.'

'Why was this man killed?'

'Jealousy. Revenge. A moment of insanity. Jones found out his wife had been cheating on him with Kristvin. Are you Wilbur Cain?'

'Cain?'

'Yes.'

'I'm not familiar with that name. My name's Gates and I'm in Military Intelligence. Is that the only reason you entered the hangar?'

'The only reason?' said Caroline. 'What do you mean? Isn't that enough?'

'Why don't you just answer the question?' said the man.

'Do you really want to know?' asked Marion.

'I wasn't talking to you.'

'Do you want to know what we were looking for?' Marion asked again, unabashed.

'Marion . . .' Caroline was afraid Marion was going to say too much.

The man studied Marion in silence. From his weary expression it was evident that he considered Marion a particularly tedious nuisance. At that moment the door opened and Master Sergeant Roberts appeared in the gap and gave the man a sign.

48

Billows of steam danced over the outdoor swimming pool before vanishing into the darkness. A bus drove down the street, a few passengers huddled by its windows. Three girls walked past, shrieking with laughter, but paid them no attention. Mensalder sat quietly in the car, rubbing his hands. Erlendur avoided putting any more pressure on him. He didn't know what sort of mental struggle Mensalder was engaged in, but sensed it was far from easy for him to talk about Dagbjört. The minutes passed. Finally Mensalder seemed to pull himself together. With a heavy sigh he straightened up in his seat and met Erlendur's eye.

'I suppose this is what I've been dreading all along,' he said. 'This moment. When suspicion falls on me. I've always dreaded that. That it would happen one day and I'd be in deep trouble, with nothing to plead in my defence.'

'I'm not with you.'

'No, why should you be? I can hardly understand it myself. I never married, you know. Did Rósanna tell you that? I wanted to but I've never been very confident where women are concerned. I . . . then you get older and you've either wasted or messed up the few chances you had and find yourself on your own. And it had an effect on me, you know. What happened. She was so . . . lovely. So genuine. I sensed that as soon as I got talking to her. She showed an interest in me, thought it was exciting that I knew how to get my hands on all kinds of goods that were unobtainable, different, exotic and . . .'

Mensalder paused.

'The thing is, I'd met someone else and that's why I kept quiet about Dagbjört and never dared tell. I thought she'd come forward and point the finger at me if I owned up . . . And then there was the bloody smuggling. I was operating on a pretty big scale by then. It would all have been exposed and I'd have got into deep water for that too.'

'Who's "she"? What do you mean you'd met someone else? You'll have to be clearer.'

'A girl from Keflavík,' said Mensalder. 'I went out with her for a bit and she stole some dollars from me. I . . . she was a real bitch. This was a few months earlier. She worked on the base and used to go with the GIs. She was a real handful, kept getting into screaming matches with me and once it actually came to blows. After that she threatened to go to the police and say I'd attacked her – that I'd beaten her up and raped her. I was afraid she'd come forward if my name was linked to Dagbjört. So . . .'

'What happened that morning?' asked Erlendur. 'What really happened?'

'It was my idea to give her a lift to school,' said Mensalder. 'We were figuring out how and where to meet and I suggested I pick her up and drive her to school so she could collect the records and pay me at the same time. I was on my way out to Keflavík anyway. I could have let Rósanna take care of it and I've often thought since how much easier things would have been if only I'd done that. How my life might have turned out. But I . . . wanted to get to know Dagbjört. She was so . . . there was something so beautiful about her. So lovely. She was warm. A warm person. And I sensed she was interested in me too. There was . . . it was what she said, the way she said it. The way she smiled at me. I only met her that one time when I fetched the records from her house, and spoke to her once after that on the phone, but I immediately sensed there was some spark between us. Some connection. She was like that. She was giving. Kind. Took an interest in you.'

'But you couldn't just pick her up at her house?'

'No, she was quite willing to accept a lift to school but insisted I meet her here. Perhaps she didn't want to be seen with a black marketeer. I could understand that. And she'd have had a lot of explaining to do to her parents about who that man was waiting for her in the car outside her house first thing in the morning. We laughed about that.'

'So it was all your idea from the beginning?' said Erlendur. 'To get in touch with her? To persuade her to meet you in secret? You prepared it well. You pretended you were going to drive her to school but took her somewhere else instead. Where? What happened? For God's sake, what did you do to her?'

'But that's the whole point, I didn't do anything!' exclaimed Mensalder. 'Not a thing! Haven't you been listening to a word I said? The reason why I've never come clean about it?'

'You said it was your idea to give her a lift. I assume you lured her into your car.'

'This is just what I was afraid of,' said Mensalder, extremely worked up by now. 'Nobody'll believe me. That's why I've never dared tell. Because everyone would instantly come to the same conclusion as you. That I'd seduced her. That she owed me money for the goods and I wanted payment in kind. That I hit her, like that bitch in Keflavík accused me of. That I raped her. And killed her. All that rubbish.'

'Didn't you?'

'What?'

'Attack her?'

'I didn't touch her! I'm trying to explain. The only thing I did wrong was not coming clean. Not telling people that we'd been planning to meet but she never showed up.'

'Because you were afraid you'd be blamed for her disappearance?'

'Yes, that they'd pin it on me. Can't you understand that?'

'You didn't dare take the risk?'

'No, I didn't want to take the rap. It was nothing to do with me. I wasn't involved. All I regret is that I didn't speak up when she went missing. I deeply regret that. Regret it every day.'

'You've had plenty of opportunity over the years.'

'I know,' whispered Mensalder, his voice cracking. 'Do you think I'm not aware of that? That I haven't thought about it? I justified it to myself that it didn't make any difference that I'd arranged to meet her. It didn't change anything. I had no more idea than anyone else about where she'd gone.'

'Why should the police believe you now? You've made your behaviour appear ten times more suspicious by your silence. Your long silence.'

'I know! None of this is new to me. It was a vicious circle I could see no way out of. I was desperate. Didn't know what to do. People would have pointed the finger at me for the rest of my life. I'd always be the murder suspect. What do you think that would've been like? I couldn't bear the stigma. Couldn't bear it. You may think I was a gutless coward but that's how I felt.'

'But if you weren't responsible for her disappearance and she never came to meet you, something must have happened to her before she got here.'

'It just doesn't make sense,' said Mensalder. 'At one point I thought she must have done it deliberately. Taken her own life for some inexplicable reason. It was . . . I . . .'

Mensalder's brow furrowed.

'Or someone stopped us from meeting,' he said at last.

'Did anyone else know about it?'

'No. No one. As far as I'm aware. *I* didn't tell anyone.'

'Are you sure about that?'

'Yes.'

'Not even Rósanna?'

'No.'

'You definitely didn't tell anyone you were planning to meet?'

'No. Or it would have come out during the search.'

'Yes, I suppose it would,' said Erlendur thoughtfully. 'So if you're not lying and she didn't change her plans, something must have happened to her in the short distance between her house and here.'

'Yes, I suppose so. It must have done.'

'It's not . . .'

'What?'

'No, it's not far,' said Erlendur, preoccupied, watching the steam brushing along the surface of the water, then mounting into the air and assuming a variety of strange shapes before dispersing and fading from view. And suddenly an image flashed into his mind, as it had so often during the last few days, of a garden suffering from years of neglect and a pair of furtive, protuberant eyes, peering from the shadows at the girl next door.

49

Marion had no idea what was happening. Roberts went outside again and the man who appeared to be in charge moved closer to them.

'Don't you feel you're betraying your country?' he asked Caroline.

'We'll just have to see about that, won't we, Gates?' she said. 'If that's your real name.'

'My name is Oliver Gates, I'm a colonel in the 57th Fighter Squadron,' the man said, smiling. 'It's my real name. I take care of security on the base.'

The door opened again and Roberts reappeared, this time pushing a soldier ahead of him, so roughly that the man fell on the floor. He got up slowly, a lanky young man with long arms and the regulation crew cut, nervously taking in his surroundings.

'Come here, Private. No need to be afraid,' said Colonel Gates. He turned to Caroline. 'This is Private Matthew Pratt, a security guard on Hangar 885. I hear you've been asking questions about him. Private Pratt has confessed to his part in the affair. Two of his buddies, also guards on the hangar, were involved as well. We've already arrested one of them here on the base and have him in custody: Private Thomas Le Roy, twenty-five years old. We're expecting the third man to enter the country shortly. He was responsible for killing the Icelander, according to his accomplices. It was his idea to abduct and murder the victim. We see no reason to doubt their testimony. They confirm what you already seem to know.'

The soldier stood awkwardly in the middle of the hangar floor.

'Tell us who it was,' ordered Colonel Gates, rounding on the soldier, who flinched. 'Tell them what you told us, Private.'

The young man's gaze flickered from Colonel Gates to Marion. Then he looked behind him to where Roberts was blocking the exit. Finally he fixed his eyes on Caroline and mumbled something, so indistinctly they couldn't hear. Then he coughed and said loudly and clearly:

'It was Jones, sir. Earl Jones.'

'Go on,' said Gates.

Coughing again, the soldier began to tell them about his friend, Earl Jones, who had been supplying the Icelander with drugs. The Icelander owed him big time and it didn't help that Joan, Earl's wife, turned out to be screwing him. Earl had heard rumours that she was receiving visits while he was away and that the man in question was an Icelander. He confronted his wife and forced her to confess to cheating on him, then ordered her to call the guy and get him to come round to see her the evening Earl was due to fly out to Greenland. The Icelander had turned up at her place but only stayed a short time, like he suspected something was up. Earl and Pratt were lying in wait. They had slashed the tyres of his car and caught up with him in a quiet spot as he was running for the gate. Then they drove him to the hangar. The third man, Le Roy, let them in. They thought Earl was just going to knock the guy around a bit to give him a fright. The Icelander broke free but they cornered him by the scaffolding. Then he fled up the ladder to the top with them hot on his heels, and realised he was trapped. They grabbed him and a scuffle ensued which ended when Earl struck the Icelander on the head with a metal pipe he had found. The man was knocked out cold and there was an odd hush for a moment, then Earl dropped the piping and before Pratt and Le Roy knew what was happening he had heaved the man over the rail and thrown him off the platform.

Pratt paused. He showed no sign of having been subjected to violence. He was wearing his uniform and black, lace-up army boots, but rubbed his wrists as he spoke, as if he had been tightly handcuffed.

'We didn't know what to do and after panicking a bit we decided to cover our tracks, clean the floor where the guy fell and smuggle his body off base in Earl's pickup. We didn't want him found in the area. Earl made me and Tommy dispose of the body. He had to catch a flight to Greenland. We saw all this steam coming from the lava field and that's when we hit on the idea of sinking the body in the hot pool nearby. We didn't expect it to be found. We thought . . . we thought it was a good place for . . .'

'Do you have anything to add?' asked Colonel Gates, after a moment's silence.

Pratt shook his head.

'I can't hear you, Private.'

'No, sir, I have nothing to add,' replied Pratt, his eyes on the floor.

'What put you on their trail, sir?' Caroline asked Gates.

'We launched our own inquiry,' he said. 'The base is a very small community. Kind of like Iceland, I guess,' he said to Marion. 'We heard you were interested in the hangar and checked the duty roster for that week. One of the guards was Jones. We learned that his wife had been friendly with an Icelander. We called one of Jones's comrades in for questioning and he quickly broke down. That was our friend Pratt here. Jones was in Greenland at the time, but we arrested the other guard. Their statements are quite convincing and consistent as regards the main details. I'm inclined to accept them. The three men all work in Hangar 885 and I have a hard time believing they'd be stupid enough to deliberately murder this Icelander in their workplace. They're dumb, but not that dumb. They must have intended to shake him up a bit but Jones lost control of the situation and went berserk, according to his comrades. Apparently he's a mean customer.'

Caroline walked up to Pratt who was still staring at the ground, put her hand under his chin and raised his head so he met her eye.

'Is this correct, Private?'

'Earl threw him off the platform, ma'am,' said Pratt. 'I . . . I thought we were just going to scare him a little but Earl . . . he went crazy. He wanted . . . he wanted him to suffer for . . . because of Joan. He didn't give a damn about the money the guy owed him. Earl just couldn't stand that she'd been with . . . with that guy.'

'With an Icelandic, you mean?' prompted Caroline.

Pratt didn't answer. He shot a nervous glance at Gates.

'Answer her!' barked the colonel.

'Yes, ma'am,' said Pratt. 'With an Icelandic. Earl couldn't stand that. He hated it.'

'Who told Earl about Joan and Kris?'

'I don't know.'

'Was it Wilbur Cain?'

'I don't know.'

'Are you familiar with the name?'

'No, ma'am.'

'Sure?'

'Yes, ma'am.'

Colonel Gates made a sign and Private Pratt was escorted out of the hangar.

'Where is Jones?' asked Marion. 'Where is he now? Have you got him in custody?'

Gates nodded.

'We'd like him handed over,' said Marion. 'We'd like all three of them handed over.'

Gates consulted his watch. 'The plane's due to land in an hour,' he said. 'Earl Jones was arrested in Greenland this morning. There's no question of handing him over. We don't extradite our military personnel. You are now in possession of all the relevant information and can be sure the inquiry is safe in our hands. Your part in this is over.'

'But they murdered an Icelandic citizen,' said Marion. 'Earl Jones assaulted his wife.'

'We'll deal with that.'

Gates turned on his heel to march out of the hangar.

'You asked what we were looking for in Hangar 885,' Marion called at his retreating back. 'Don't you want to know what it was?'

Gates didn't react.

'Isn't that where you keep the nuclear warheads?' Marion asked.

Gates opened the door.

'We know about Northern Cargo Transport,' Marion added.

Gates turned back and rested his gaze on Marion. Then he pushed the door to again.

'What do you mean by Northern Cargo Transport? What are you talking about?'

'We know you use fake airlines to ferry weapons between countries,' Marion said, improvising frantically.

'And?'

'We know about the flights to Thule.'

Gates studied Marion and Caroline in turn, as if weighing up what to believe. Marion tried to keep a poker face, praying the bluff would work.

'I don't believe you know anything,' Gates said.

'Where's Wilbur Cain? Why was he in contact with Kristvin?'

'I told you we are not aware of the existence of anyone by the name of Wilbur Cain.'

'He's –'

'Why do you keep asking about this man? We're not aware of his existence.'

'You're disowning him, you mean?'

'I mean we don't know who he is.'

'What was Cain doing with Kristvin at the Animal Locker?'

Slowly Gates retraced his steps towards them.

'All I know is that we heard there was an Icelandic employee snooping around our aircraft, asking questions about matters that didn't concern him. When the case was looked into it turned out that he had a head full of half-baked conspiracy theories that were laughable at best.'

'That's not what we heard.'

'You're getting mixed up in things that are no concern of yours,' said Gates.

'We want the men. We want to take over the investigation. We want to question them and try them in an Icelandic court,' said Marion.

'Out of the question.'

'All right,' said Marion. 'Then you can expect a visit from a delegation to inspect your activities here on the base. To open up the hangars. Look inside the planes. Examine the contents of your storage facilities. I reckon we have enough information about Northern Cargo Transport, Thule and the planes carrying nuclear weapons landing here to have the whole nation up in arms against you.'

There was a pregnant pause.

'You won't find anything,' said Gates.

'I'm not sure we need to,' retorted Marion.

Gates shook his head. 'I don't advise you to try.'

'We just need to make enough noise,' said Marion. 'You must realise it's not in your interests for this situation to last much longer. To have us nosing around up here and persuading people like Caroline to assist us. Talking to military personnel without permission. Entering controlled areas you'd prefer to keep closed. It can't be convenient for you to have us disrupting your activities here with all kinds of inquiries and other aggravation. I assume you'd prefer it to stop sooner rather than later.'

Gates still wavered.

'We want those men,' repeated Marion.

Gates looked at Caroline standing quietly beside the Icelandic police officer, contributing nothing to the conversation.

'OK,' he said at last. 'I'm prepared to help you with the investigation into the death of this Icelander. Would that be sufficient to create trust?'

'I don't know,' said Marion. 'Help us how?'

'If we come to an agreement, I must stress that it would not in any way constitute recognition of the validity of your insinuations regarding nuclear weapons.'

'Meaning . . .?'

'You can arrest the men. Conduct the interrogations and complete the inquiry. But they'll be tried by us.'

Marion turned to Caroline.

'Would you like the honour of locking Jones up?'

Three-quarters of an hour later an inbound military transport from Greenland taxied up to one of the hangars. Marion and Caroline watched the huge beast approach with a thunderous roar that gradually died away once the engines had been turned off. Colonel Gates and his men were nowhere to be seen. Caroline had called for backup from military police and several other officers were standing behind her as the ramp was driven up to the plane. The door in the fuselage opened and after a brief interval a man appeared accompanied by two military policemen, a short figure, in handcuffs, dressed in green combat trousers and jacket. He had seen what was happening from the window of the plane as it taxied to a halt by the hangar, and stood looking down apprehensively at the reception committee on the tarmac.

Reluctantly, he descended the steps until he came face to face with Caroline.

'Private Earl Jones?' she said.

'Yes, ma'am,' said the man. He had a narrow face with dark stubble and black eyebrows that almost met in the middle. Despite his muscular build his shoulders were a little rounded and he had an obtuse look in his eyes.

Caroline slapped his face so hard that her palm stung afterwards.

'Joan says hello.'

50

Erlendur parked in front of the house, marvelling yet again at how it had been allowed to go to rack and ruin. Neither the building nor the surrounding plot showed the slightest evidence of care. Instead, the whole place bore witness to a paralysing apathy, to long years of neglect and decay, as if blighted by death itself. He lit a cigarette. Mensalder was no longer with him. He had dropped him back at the petrol station where his car was parked. Mensalder had been so depressed and subdued that Erlendur hardly heard his goodbye. They had spoken little on the return journey. Having told him everything that mattered, Mensalder had retreated into his own thoughts, doubts and regrets – old enemies that Erlendur suspected would weigh on him more heavily than ever before in the coming days.

Erlendur sat for a considerable time outside the house. A newsflash on the radio announced that the two men lost on the Eyvindarstadir Moors had been found dead. It appeared that one had fallen into a hole in the ice and been unable to climb out again. The other man had tried in vain to help. When the rescue team found him he was lying frozen to death a few feet from the hole, as if he would not for the world have abandoned his friend.

Erlendur cursed the cruelty of fate, the pitiless elements and the men's cold demise. Then, lighting another cigarette, he turned his attention to what Mensalder had told him about his arrangement to meet Dagbjört and her failure to appear. He could see no movement in the house. No sign of light. The curtains were drawn across the windows. Dagbjört's house also stood dark, silent and empty, with the 'For Sale' notice still in the kitchen window, waiting to be brought back to life. Two houses side by side and a girl on her way to school. Was that as far as Dagbjört had got? To the house next door?

Stubbing out his cigarette, Erlendur stepped out of the car and surveyed the building, then went up to the front door. He knocked, then after a pause knocked again, louder this time. When nobody answered, he turned away and walked into the garden. The illumination from the street light barely reached this far and it took a while for Erlendur's eyes to adjust. He stood amid the long, withered grass, straining to discern any movement indoors and wondering if Rasmus had gone to bed.

Going over to the back door, he discovered that it was locked but that the lock was old and rotten, like everything else in the house. All it required was a hard jerk to open it. He called Rasmus's name, and although he received no answer, decided to go in anyway.

His eyes now accustomed to the gloom, he entered what he took to be the dining room. From his previous visit, he remembered that this had faced the garden. Again he called Rasmus's

name, raising his voice this time. He stood still for minute or
two, listening, but the only answer was the profound hush inside
the house. He groped his way as far as the hall and staircase, with
the idea of trying upstairs, then heard a door shutting quietly
somewhere off to his left where the garage adjoined the house.
All at once another door opened and Rasmus appeared. He
seemed preoccupied and didn't notice Erlendur. Switching on
the light, he closed the door carefully behind him and headed
for the stairs. Erlendur could hear him muttering under his breath
but couldn't make out the words.

'Rasmus,' he said, and although he spoke softly in an attempt
not to startle the man too much, Rasmus was so shocked that he
emitted a piercing shriek and crashed back into the wall.

'You didn't answer the door,' said Erlendur.

'Who . . . who's there? What . . .? Thief! Are you a thief?'

'It's me – Erlendur.'

'Oh . . . is it you . . . you . . .?' Rasmus had been winded by
the shock and was so badly shaken that he couldn't get his bear-
ings. 'What . . . what do you mean by giving me such a fright?
Why are you persecuting me like this?'

'I'm sorry, the back door was open,' said Erlendur. 'I didn't
mean to frighten you.'

'Frighten me?' echoed Rasmus, recovering slightly. 'The door
open – what nonsense. It's never open. Do you mean to say you
broke in? Get out of my house this minute. I don't want you here.
How many times do I have to tell you? How could you do this to
me? I've never . . . I've never been so shocked in all my life. You
have no right to let yourself in here. I want you out. Get out!'

'Where were you? In the garage? You can't have heard when I
knocked.'

'I didn't hear a thing,' said Rasmus, trying to adopt a more confident manner, running a hand over his greasy mat of hair and standing taller, though his shoulders were still hunched and stooping. 'Why don't you do as I ask? Will you please leave?!'

His voice broke as he tried to give force to this order, ending in another high-pitched shriek. Erlendur studied him, this pathetic human being, isolated, imprisoned, afraid, and experienced an odd sense of sympathy.

'I'd like a proper chat with you about Dagbjört,' he said. 'We now know where she was going the morning she vanished and –'

'Well, I have no interest in discussing that any further with you,' said Rasmus. 'You can just get out of here right now.'

'– and we know the route she took,' Erlendur continued stubbornly. 'It wasn't far and there weren't many obstacles on the way and there's every likelihood that she passed your house.'

'I'm not listening to this,' said Rasmus. 'Please leave; I'm going upstairs and I hope I never have to see you again.'

He went to the stairs and had mounted two steps when Erlendur seized his arm and yanked him down again.

'Stop it,' said Erlendur sharply. 'Wake up. It's over. Finished. Tell me where she is.'

'No,' screamed Rasmus. 'You're using violence! I have nothing whatever to say to you. Nothing!'

'Did she want you to stop spying on her? Was that why she came round? Did she threaten to report you? She saw you outside your house, didn't she? What did you do? Wave to her? Call her over? Invite her in? Lure her inside?'

Erlendur still had hold of his arm but Rasmus had his head averted as if he couldn't bear the relentless questioning or didn't dare meet his eye. His body writhed as he tried to tear himself loose, break Erlendur's grip, evade the merciless interrogation. Erlendur hung on tight, then realised that Rasmus had begun to cry. His body shook with silent sobs and he covered his face with his free hand, overcome with humiliation. Eventually he seemed to grow calmer and even rallied a little. He looked down at Erlendur's hand which was still gripping his arm.

'No one's touched me in all the years since Mama died,' he whispered.

'What did you say?'

'No one,' breathed Rasmus. 'No one's touched me.'

'I'm sorry,' said Erlendur. 'I didn't mean to hurt you.'

'No, it's fine,' said Rasmus. 'You didn't.'

'Are you all right?'

'Yes, I'm all right,' said Rasmus. 'I'm all right now. Thank you for coming by. It's a pity I wasn't expecting guests. I don't have anything to offer you.'

'That doesn't matter,' said Erlendur, 'really, don't worry about it.' As on the last occasion, Rasmus seemed to have reverted, with disorientating suddenness, to the role of embarrassed host. He kept making excuses about having no refreshment to offer.

'I ought to put on some coffee. It's the very least I could do.'

'Please don't –'

'No, hold me,' said Rasmus urgently, sensing that Erlendur was about to release his arm. 'Don't let go of me. I . . . I want you to hold me.'

'Is there somewhere we could sit down?' asked Erlendur. 'Do you want a glass of water? Can I get you some water?'

'No, thank you,' said Rasmus. 'I want you to know I'm not a monster. I know that's what you think, but I'm not. You must never talk to me like that. I'm a person like anyone else. Do you understand? Do you understand what I'm saying? I haven't always been like –'

'Of course,' said Erlendur. 'I know you've had a tough time. You don't have to tell me. All you need do is tell me about Dagbjört, then it'll be over. I know you'll feel better if you own up. I know that deep down that's what you've been wanting all these years. For someone to come here and listen to you and understand what you did.'

'Nobody understands me. Nobody. No one'll ever be able to understand. Who I am. What kind of person I am. Nobody understands. Nobody.'

Rasmus ran two fingers over the back of Erlendur's hand. They were almost fleshless, with long, yellow nails. They caressed his hand, then felt their way up his arm to his cheek. Erlendur didn't dare move as Rasmus softly stroked his face with his bony fingers, his eyes brimming with tears.

'I loved her,' he whispered gently, then laid his own cheek on Erlendur's chest. 'I loved her so much. She was my girl. She's always been my girl. You're not taking her away from me. You can't. No one can take her away from me.'

Erlendur stood dumbstruck, not daring to move, with Rasmus pressed to his chest, and listened to him rambling about the girl he loved. He was so thrown that he didn't see as Rasmus's fingers reached out to a large pair of scissors that lay on a shelf beside them, grasped them cautiously, then raised them and plunged them deep into Erlendur's body.

51

Dagbjört hastily finished dressing, put her school books and pencils in her satchel, checked her pocket to make sure she had the money for Rósanna's cousin with the funny name, then bounded downstairs. She grabbed a slice of toast in the kitchen, pulled on her coat, called goodbye to her mother who was engrossed in the newspaper, and flew out of the door. She didn't want to be late for her meeting with Rósanna's cousin. He wasn't only going to sell her some records but give her a lift to school as well.

As she passed Rasmus's house, she saw him standing at the front door, waving to her. It looked as if he needed help.

She couldn't pretend she hadn't seen him, so she went over and asked if everything was all right. She didn't like Rasmus. On the rare occasions she had bumped into him in the street or the corner shop and stopped for a brief chat, his manner had struck her as oddly smarmy. And after this latest business she was going to give him an earful. His behaviour had upset and angered her, but she knew he had recently lost his mother, had few friends and was probably lonely, so she felt a little sorry for him. He and his mother had been very close. Perhaps that was why she hadn't told anyone yet about him spying on her.

'Could you help me a moment?' asked Rasmus. 'I'm in a spot of bother.'

He quickly closed the door behind her, then dithered, unsure how to begin, as they stood there in the hall, so she asked what the matter was and how she could help. She couldn't stay long; she was in a hurry to get to school.

'I wanted to talk to you about what you saw,' he said, leading her along the hall towards the stairs. 'When you . . . when I was in the window. It may not have been quite what you . . . you might have thought.'

'Oh?'

'No, I'm . . . it was a coincidence, I assure you. A complete coincidence.'

'Why did you spy on me like that?' asked Dagbjört.

'It wasn't really spying,' said Rasmus apologetically. 'I just want us to be friends. Good friends. I wasn't doing anything nasty. I wouldn't dream of it. Of doing anything nasty to you. Please believe me. It's important you don't think I'm . . . it's important you . . .'

'I have to get to school,' said Dagbjört when it became evident that Rasmus didn't know what he wanted to say or how to phrase it. 'Did you want help or not?'

'Yes, no, I . . . I thought . . . perhaps . . . you'd be my friend. I've been a bit lonely since Mother died and I was hoping we could . . . because we're next-door neighbours and so on, and

330

you're so pretty, such a lovely person, I thought maybe we could be friends.'

'I've got to go.'

'Oh, but –'

'And I want you to stop spying on me,' Dagbjört said in a harsh voice. 'It's disgusting. I've seen the curtain moving. And if you don't stop, if I catch you doing it again, I'll tell my dad and then you'll have him to deal with.'

'Your dad? You mean you haven't told him . . . haven't told anyone?'

'No. But I will. If I see you there again I'm telling my dad.'

'Dagbjört, dear,' said Rasmus. 'I don't want you to leave while you're angry. I don't want you to be angry with me.'

'I've got to go,' repeated Dagbjört. 'I've got to get out of here!'

'Don't be angry, darling. My love. I can't bear it.'

'I'm not your love! I'm going to tell Dad . . . I'm going to tell him. How you –'

Dagbjört tried to return to the front door but Rasmus blocked her way.

'You mustn't.'

'Get away from me!' shouted Dagbjört.

'You mustn't leave here angry,' said Rasmus, regarding her gravely. 'You mustn't tell anyone. You mustn't . . .'

She tried to push him away but he resisted and shoved at her. Dagbjört lost her balance, fell backwards and as she landed her head hit the bottom stair. She was dazed by the blow. Rasmus seized her as she lay there on the floor and started banging her head again and again against the step.

'You mustn't leave . . . mustn't . . . mustn't leave . . .'

* * *

331

'I thought surely someone must have seen me when I called her over so I waited in a panic for the police, but nothing happened. Nobody had noticed her come in here. I was asked lots of questions like everyone else in the street but said I didn't know anything and unfortunately couldn't help; I'd slept in that morning until lunchtime. When I told the police that they left me alone. I even took part in the search. Nothing happened. Nothing at all. Right up until you came to the door and started pestering me with your questions and I couldn't get rid of you. Came here uninvited, banging on all the doors and windows and insulting me. There's no other word for it. You insulted me, like those hooligans who cornered me that time.'

Erlendur had been taken by complete surprise when Rasmus stabbed him with the scissors. Unable to defend himself, he had clutched at his belly and sunk to his knees, then toppled to the floor unconscious. When he came to, Rasmus was sitting on the floor beside him, telling him how he had called out to Dagbjört and how their subsequent conversation had led to her death. The scissors had penetrated Erlendur's abdomen on the right-hand side and he could feel the blood seeping from the wound into his clothes. A searing pain ran up the whole of his side, accompanied by a paralysing weakness. He heard Rasmus talking to him in a soothing voice about his love for the girl and how it had never been his intention to hurt her.

'Something came over me,' he heard Rasmus say. 'Something horrible. I don't know what it was. Something came over me and I shoved her. Pushed her much too hard. Much too hard, you see. I completely lost control of myself and started banging her head on the stairs. I didn't want her telling tales about me to her father or those friends of hers. Those sluts. I don't know what came over me . . . but . . . but all of a sudden she was dead . . . when I came to my senses she was dead in my hands. So I picked her up and took her . . . I don't know . . . I don't know what to do with you.'

'You've got to help me,' said Erlendur, feeling his strength waning. 'I'm bleeding to death. You can help me, Rasmus. And I'll help you. You're sick. You need help. Let me –'

'I don't need any help,' said Rasmus. 'That's absurd. As if I needed any help. All I need is to be left in peace. That's all I ask. Is it too much to ask, to be left in peace?'

'Rasmus . . .' Erlendur felt himself losing consciousness again.

'I'd better check on her. Nothing stays the same. Everything changes. Except here with us. Here with us everything's just the way it always was. With us nothing's changed.'

'Rasmus . . .'

Erlendur blacked out and Rasmus stroked his head.

'Wait here, my friend, I need to check on her a moment,' he said and rose to his feet.

Erlendur didn't know how much time had passed when he surfaced again, opened his eyes and looked around. It took him a while to work out where he was but finally it came back to him that he was lying wounded on the floor of Rasmus's house; that he had been stabbed. He had been pressing his hand against the wound, trying as hard as he could to staunch the bleeding, and he kept up the pressure now that he had regained consciousness, clutching his hand to his aching side. Rasmus was nowhere to be seen but he couldn't be far away. With a great effort Erlendur managed to raise his head, then sit up and prop himself against the wall while he mustered his strength. The bloodstained scissors lay on the floor and he reached out for them, then braced himself against the wall and somehow succeeded in levering himself to his feet.

He listened out for Rasmus but couldn't hear so much as a cough or a groan anywhere in the house, only his own laboured breathing. He had to get out of here as soon as possible and call for help, but then he remembered that Rasmus had entered the hall from a door that presumably led to the garage. Erlendur wavered until curiosity overcame common sense. Taking a deep breath and clutching the scissors tight, he set off in the direction from which Rasmus had come.

Slowly he hobbled to the door. It was closed but not locked and he opened it cautiously. Inside was a laundry room. There was an old washing machine against one wall. A musty stench of dirty clothes. When he stepped inside, his hair brushed against washing lines fixed to the ceiling. There was a fuse box on one wall, with meters next to it. On the other side of the laundry was another door which stood a little ajar, admitting a strip of light from the garage.

Erlendur limped warily over and peered inside. A dim bulb hung from the ceiling. The floor space was almost entirely occupied by something covered in a thick, white tarpaulin. Erlendur went over and tugged clumsily at the cover, hampered by the scissors, until he managed to pull it off to reveal a classic American automobile that had once, long ago, been reversed into the garage. It was a two-door Chevrolet Deluxe, a 1948 model, bright green, and so lovingly cared for that it looked almost like new. The paintwork was polished, the windows shone, the chrome fittings gleamed and you could see your reflection in the hubcaps. On second glance, there was no air in the tyres and the rubber was cracked and perished, but in all other respects the car was a vision and one would have thought, from its appearance, that it was still in use.

Although gleaming and beautiful on the outside, inside the car was full of dust and dirt that hadn't been disturbed for many years. Erlendur's attention was drawn to a shapeless mass on the back seat. It was leaning against the window, covered in a yellowed blanket. He needed two hands to open the door as it was stiff and heavy and the hinges creaked as if it hadn't been moved for a long time. He tipped the driver's seat forward and reached into the back. Blood from his wound dripped into the interior as he stretched out his arm, grasped the blanket and jerked at it. He had to tug three times before it came away and fell to the floor of the car, stirring up a cloud of dust. He was confronted by a skeleton in old, rotten clothes. The skull, which was leaning towards him, had dead, dusty tufts of hair down to the shoulders, empty eye sockets and a jaw gaping in silent anguish.

Filled with sadness and horror at the sight, Erlendur failed to notice Rasmus materialise in the doorway behind him. But he heard him – as the other man emitted a screech and pounced on him, gripping him round the neck and trying to tear him out of the car. Finding the scissors still in his hand, Erlendur jabbed them into Rasmus's thigh. He was rewarded with a cry of pain. Then Rasmus leapt onto his back and tightened his throttling grip until finally Erlendur managed to turn and, with the last of his strength, batter Rasmus against the door frame. He stabbed behind him with the scissors, heard Rasmus scream, and felt the grip on his throat slacken. Rasmus fell off his back, landing half inside the car. Erlendur grabbed his legs, pushed him into the front seat and slammed the door. Rasmus started frantically hammering and kicking at it and Erlendur, exhausted from the struggle, wondered how long he could hold the door against him. Casting round desperately for an implement, he seized a shovel and wedged it firmly between the car door and the wall. Rasmus tried to wind down the window but the handle broke off. He threw himself over at the passenger door but could only open it a crack because the car was parked close to the wall on that side. He rattled it madly like an animal in a cage, then, panicking, banged at the window on the driver's side with his bare fists, weeping and shouting and hammering until his delicate fingers were bloody, and the realisation finally sank in that he was trapped.

52

The funeral, which was held at the Fríkirkja church, was a simple affair, attended only by Dagbjört's friends and remaining relatives. The unexpected revelation of her fate had, unsurprisingly, caused a sensation in the press but the reporters mostly stayed away from the church. The vicar spoke of being robbed of a young life in an incomprehensible manner, but avoided any other reference to the horrific crime and the ghastly scene that had confronted the police in Rasmus's garage. A small female choir sang the funeral hymn 'Just as the Flower Fades'. Dagbjört's old school friends carried her coffin and weeping was heard from all sides over the tragic waste and loss.

Svava had invited Erlendur to attend. He had managed to crawl to the nearest house to raise the alarm before fainting again from loss of blood. He hadn't woken up until noon next day. Marion told him they had found Rasmus locked in the car just as Erlendur had left him. He had put up no resistance and even asked if

Erlendur was all right. The car turned out to have belonged to Rasmus's mother; he didn't have a licence so had never driven it himself. It had been taken off the register shortly after Mrs Kruse's death and had remained in the garage ever since. Forensics had established that the body had in all probability been kept in the back seat from the beginning.

One of Erlendur's first actions once he was feeling a little better, though still stuck in hospital, swathed in bandages, with an ache in his side, was to send someone round to see Svava and fill her in on the events of the last few days. He had needed an operation to repair the damage caused by the scissors but Erlendur was quick to recover and his strength was improving by the day. He was still in charge of the Dagbjört inquiry. Rasmus had been remanded in custody at Sídumúli Prison where he was undergoing psychiatric tests.

Once he was out of hospital, Erlendur went round to see Svava himself to tell her the whole story, explaining how he had picked up the trail as a result of exhaustive interviews with a number of people. He reported his encounter with Mensalder who had kept quiet all this time about his planned meeting with Dagbjört for fear of being implicated in her disappearance. It was unlikely that he could have saved the girl's life by coming forward at once, but she would almost certainly have been found much earlier. Suspicion would immediately have fallen on Dagbjört's nearest neighbours, including Rasmus. The man hadn't attracted any attention at the time since there had been no reason to suppose that Dagbjört had died so close to home. He had been regarded as an eccentric recluse but not dangerous. He had nothing to do with his neighbours and they had nothing to do with him and so it remained.

'What kind of person is he?' asked Svava.

'I don't know,' said Erlendur. 'Disturbed, obviously, but pathetic too. He said he wasn't always like that. Perhaps the secret in the garage gradually warped him into what he's become today.'

'How's it possible? How could he have kept it secret? Their next-door neighbour!'

'I don't kn—'

'Why wasn't the man ever investigated?'

'It's not a crime to live alone and shut yourself off from the world.'

'Perhaps he lived too close to her,' said Svava. 'It didn't occur to anybody that she could be in the house next door. Nobody dreamt of such a thing. That she could have vanished only a few yards from home.'

'Yes, of course, it was highly improbable. He . . . he says he loved her and I think there's a grain of truth in that. In his own peculiar way he did love her.'

'I don't believe that for a minute,' said Svava. 'As for that business with the car . . . Who would do such a thing? Why did he keep . . .?'

'Obviously Rasmus is very ill,' said Erlendur, 'and I don't know how far to trust what he says, but he claims it was all he could think of. He couldn't bear to bury her in the garden. And he was proud of how well he'd looked after the car. Says he polished it lovingly at least once a month.'

'Dagbjört's coffin.'

'He says he did it for her. But he never went inside the car. In all those years. He drew the line at that.'

'The poor, darling girl,' sighed Svava. 'I've been trying to come to terms with what happened, what became of her, but I . . . I just can't.'

'No, I can well understand that.'

'What about the boy from Camp Knox? Didn't he exist after all?'

'We still haven't found him,' said Erlendur, 'and I don't suppose we ever will now. No one's come forward and they're hardly likely to after this. The case has received a lot of publicity following Rasmus's arrest, just as it did when Dagbjört originally vanished, and that's one of the details that has been disclosed on the news, but nobody's . . . I'm not saying Silja was lying. Perhaps Dagbjört did know a boy from Camp Knox.'

'So you're not ruling it out?'

'No, there's no call to do that.'

'I'm so glad,' said Svava. 'I've always . . . I've always indulged myself in a little fantasy that she'd met some nice boy. 'That's what I like to think. That she had a chance to discover what it is to . . . that Dagbjört had a chance to experience love. To know what it's like to be in love. Even if only for a short time.'

'Perhaps he was only passing through and never looked back. There are some places in their past that people don't like to acknowledge. They don't want to look back. I get the feeling Camp Knox was one of those. You wouldn't want it to dog you through life but it would be hard to shake off.'

Svava looked curiously at Erlendur.

'It sounds as if you're talking from experience.'

'I think we all have places like that,' Erlendur said. 'Our own private Camp Knox.'

'But what about . . .?'

She kept up a relentless flow of questions and Erlendur tried to field them as best he could but knew he had no real answers, only reassuring platitudes. And with these he tried to comprehend and to provide comfort, for himself as much as her.

Nanna listened as Marion Briem described her brother's fate, his affair with Joan and how Earl had taken revenge on him as a result. Marion attributed the success of the case above all to Caroline. Without her the Icelandic police would probably never have laid hands on the three men currently sitting in custody at Sídumúli Prison where they were undergoing interviews. The Icelandic and American authorities had come to an agreement about the handling of the case. Caroline had escaped with no more than a reprimand for disobeying orders. She kept her job with the military police and was part of the team questioning the three men along with the Icelandic police. She told Marion she had been in touch with Joan and was trying to support her through the investigation. She was an important witness and had stuck to her testimony against Earl and his friends. Earl claimed not to remember how he found out about her affair with Kristvin. Caroline was convinced he was lying. Wilbur Cain must have been involved and perhaps even egged Earl on as a way of putting an end to Kristvin's snooping.

'My brother never mentioned her – this Joan,' said Nanna. 'I didn't even know she existed. I'd have thought he'd have told me –'

'They hadn't known each other long,' said Marion. 'I'm sure he'd have told you sooner or later.'

Erlendur was there too but took little part in the conversation. He stood by the window, gazing out at the playground. They had found a quiet room in Nanna's nursery school where they could talk in private.

'I'm really surprised he got involved with a married woman.'

'She didn't tell him at first. She was scared of her husband. But it's possible she was trying to make Earl jealous too. She's a bit vague on that point. Earl had been in trouble with the police back home in America before he joined the army. He was accused of assault on two occasions but never charged. He carried out a brutal attack on Joan when he heard she'd been cheating on him, then forced her to call your brother and ask him round. She'd never have done it if Earl hadn't used violence against her.'

'And they were lying in wait for him?'

'Yes.'

'I can't stop thinking about him in the hands of those men. Alone and helpless, one against three.'

'I know.'

'He didn't deserve what they did to him. Not him of all people.'

'No, of course not,' said Erlendur. 'No one would deserve that.'

'I thought it was my fault,' said Nanna. 'What happened to him. That he'd got into trouble because of me. Because he put himself in danger buying drugs for me.'

'It wasn't like that.'

'And this Joan, who is she, what kind of person is she?' Nanna asked after a lengthy pause.

'To be honest I don't know,' said Marion. 'I can put you in touch with her, if you like. Kristvin told her about you. She knew about your illness. Asked after you.'

'Maybe,' said Nanna. 'We'll see.'

The sound of the children's voices carried in to them. Nanna went to the window where Erlendur was standing watching them. His thoughts were with another little girl in a different playground, in red waterproof trousers and a woolly hat, playing alone in the sand.

'I miss him,' said Nanna. 'I keep expecting him to ring . . . It . . . losing him hurts so much.'

'How are you otherwise?' asked Marion. 'How's your treatment going?'

'They think I'll live,' she said, 'but what do they know?'

53

One evening several weeks later Erlendur took a last stroll down the street where Dagbjört had lived and died, then kept on walking until he reached the site where Camp Knox had once stood as a memorial to military occupation and Icelandic poverty. For many years he had been haunted by Dagbjört's story, by her inexplicable disappearance, the mystery shrouding her fate. He had immersed himself in the details of her life, followed in her footsteps time and again, stood brooding in front of her house and now, at last, discovered what had befallen her so heart-rendingly close to home.

It was a cold day and a biting northerly whipped up the loose snow and blew it along the street. He dug his hands deeper into his pockets and headed into the wind, conscious that the Dagbjört affair had only intensified his fascination with those who never came back. Solving the case had given him no more than a temporary respite. Lately the old pop song 'Dagný' had been running through his mind, conjuring up an image of the school-girls who once came together to sing about joy and delight, that poignant melody that would always remind him of Dagbjört. It was a relief to have found answers to the questions about her fate that had preyed on him so long, but he knew that for him there would be no closure. Her song would continue to haunt him for the rest of his days.

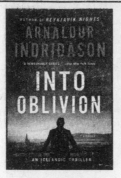

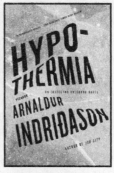

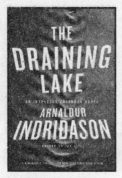
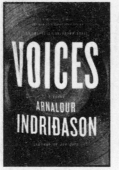
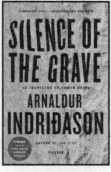
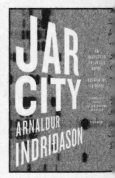